COLLATERAL DAMAGE

LIMELIGHT #3

ELISABETH
GRACE

Cover Design by: Regina Wamba of *www.MaeIDesign.com*
Photo Credit: Sara Eirew Photographer
Developmental Edits: Angela Smith
Line Editor: Sheri Thomas
Interior Design and Formatting: Perfectly Publishable

COLLATERAL DAMAGE

LIMELIGHT #3

Collateral Damage

Now trending.
Hollywood It Girl, Francesca Leon, has just landed the biggest
role of her career . . . one that could clinch an Oscar nomination
and open doors. If she's going to move her career to the next
level and work with top directors, she has to nail this part—and
keep her sexy, but unreliable leading man from screwing everything up.

Team Calder
Bad boy Calder Fox is the son of Hollywood royalty and fresh
out of rehab after his best friend's death sent him on a downward spiral of drugs and alcohol. While his fans still love him
and the paparazzi stalk him, he's never taken life, or anything
about his career, seriously. He may be charming and drop-dead
gorgeous, but if he doesn't stay sober, he could ruin Frankie's
future and expose her long-hidden family secret to the vora-
cious media.

Behind the scenes.
Things heat up during filming and have the potential to become hotter, deeper, and much more real. But can Frankie
trust Calder with her secret? Or is he doomed to sabotage his
own happiness yet again?

For the readers . . . for every encouraging word, social media share, and the connection you've forged with my characters. For giving my work a chance. If you feel like you need one, I hope you find your own second chance. My belief is that it's *never* too late.

prologue

More Than A Year Ago . . .

Calder

Gasoline and smoke burn my lungs as I inhale a sharp, painful breath. The pounding in my head is unrelenting and my ears ring with a dull buzz. I manage to pry open my eyes, only to find that darkness consumes my surroundings. Not that it matters since my lids are so heavy that I have to close them again.

When I'm able to open them, I realize there's a small amount of light permeating the darkness from the flickering clock on the mangled dash.

1:38 A.M.

I try to remember where I am. Bit by bit I become aware of the crushing pain in my arm—it feels as if it's on fire. I draw a deep breath, singeing my throat, and look down to see my right arm bent at a funny angle. The constant ringing in my ears and the throbbing of my head have my thoughts moving like sand through an hourglass.

My thoughts are sluggish, but I'm cognizant enough to recognize the all-consuming ache throughout my body. I consider closing my eyes again—all I want to do is forget the pain I'm in, but somewhere in the back of my head it registers that the thick smoke has become suffocating. I cough and bring the arm that isn't broken up to cover my face.

A strangled breath sounds from my right and I turn inside the crushed metal can I'm in, immediately wishing I hadn't. Bile rises up in the back of my throat and my breathing becomes even more ragged and shallow than before.

My best friend, Akoni, lies unconscious in the driver's seat, blood trailing down his face. The steering wheel presses further into his belly than nature should allow.

Guilt consumes me like a tidal wave and I'm flailing on the inside. This is all my fault.

I attempt looking out the front window, but it's almost impossible to see through the shattered glass. I'm just able to make out the buckled hood of the car and the smoke pouring out from underneath.

I cough again, trying as best I can to get some clean air, but there is none to be had. I need to get out of here.

With my good arm, I release my seat belt and lean over with my left hand to open my door, ignoring the stabbing pain in both my arm and abdomen as I do. After a bit of fumbling, I'm finally able to pry it open enough to squeeze myself out, just in time to see flames rising up from under the car's hood. I flop out onto the ground clumsily, landing with my broken arm underneath me, my feet still pinned between the dash and the seat.

I cry out from the pain of having my weight resting on my broken arm, and I'm unable to control my body's reaction. I vomit as I lie there on the grass, a mixture of the evening's earlier festivities spewing out onto the ground.

Recovering enough from the pain, I pull my legs out. Before I know what's happening, there's commotion around me. People are shouting but I can't make out what they're saying. Someone pries my legs out of the car and a pair of hands pulls me up, helping me to stand upright.

The image in front of me becomes hazy, black spots edging

the corner of my vision. I drop my head down, trying not to puke again, while people on either side hold me steady and help me hobble away from the wreckage.

As they sit me on the curb a ways down from the carnage, my vision and thoughts come back to me more clearly.

Horror twists my insides as I set my sights on the piece of twisted metal. The front of the car is bashed in, the driver's side almost wrapped around a tree trunk. Flames shoot skyward and lick some low-hanging branches while black smoke illuminated by a nearby streetlight continues to pour out from under the hood.

"Akoni!" I scream, my voice hoarse, my throat raw and swollen from the smoke. I push away from the helping hands and turn to race back to the car as fast as my broken body will let me.

"You can't go over there! You're hurt!" a faceless person in front of me screams. With my good hand, I push them to the side, adrenaline and maybe the cocktail of other narcotics from earlier in the night surging through my veins, releasing me from most of the pain. I have to get Akoni out before the flames reach him.

"I'm not leaving my friend," I shout at no one in particular.

Sirens sound in the distance, drawing nearer. Thank God. The fire department will be here any minute. They'll put the flames out and get my friend—

The sound of an explosion rips through the night. It's reminiscent of some of the on-set blasts I've heard, only this one is so much worse. So much more terrifying. Because it's real.

An unseen force pummels me backward until I crash to the ground, hitting the pavement below. Complete and utter terror grips me as I watch the flames engulf the wreckage, the lifeless body of my friend lying motionless in the middle of it.

I scream . . . and scream . . . and scream—unable to stop until mercifully everything goes black.

chapter one

Calder

"Remember, they're not to ask anything about the accident," my manager, Chelsea, said to the production assistant of *The Diane Gayle Show*.

"Diane is aware of the parameters of the interview," he assured her.

"Yeah, well make sure it stays that way during filming," Chelsea said, flicking her blond hair behind her shoulder. You'd never know looking at what I was sure was a heavily Botoxed face, but she'd been in the biz long enough to know that interviewers sometimes "forgot" which topics were off-limits when the cameras started rolling. They didn't refer to her around town as 'The Barracuda' for nothing.

I sat in the make-up chair, sipping on water, while a bunch of other people primped me before I'd head out for my interview. In truth, I would've loved to have a beer, or hell, a whole bottle of Jack in my hand, but managing the cravings was what I was supposed to be able to deal with now.

My nerves were frayed at the edges. This was it. This was my one and only chance to redeem myself in the eyes of the public and filmmakers alike, to convince them I'd changed my ways. After all my fuck-ups, no one wanted to hire me for their movies anymore. If I wanted to change that, the world needed to believe that I was a different man. And make no mistake—the world was watching.

No pressure, right?

"And she can only discuss Calder's life since being out of rehab. Let's not dwell too long on why he was there in the first place," Landon added from behind me. Landon Steele was the owner of my new PR firm I'd recently signed with, and they were the ones that had landed me the interview. Every penny I paid them was worth it for that reason alone, since *The Diane Gayle Show* was one of the most watched primetime interview programs. However, the way the press spun my appearance today would make all the difference.

I inhaled a deep breath, trying to steady myself. "You alright?" Landon asked, clamping a hand on my shoulder from behind.

"I'm good, man." If we were defining 'good' as being scared shitless.

"Just remember how we talked about handling her questions. You're going to do great," Landon said.

"Five minutes until showtime," someone yelled from the hallway.

The production assistant with the receding hairline turned to face me. "You're the first guest up. If you want to follow me, I'll take you to the set. Wait until Diane introduces you and then you can head out."

I nodded, took another sip of water, and stood to follow behind, giving Chelsea and Landon a weak smile before I left.

Standing there in the darkness at the side of the stage, I felt every ounce of the weight on my shoulders. After everything I'd been through, all the ways I'd screwed myself and so many others over, this could very well be the defining moment in my life.

I was determined that all the pain I'd caused others wouldn't be in vain. I'd do something good with my life, achieve something, give something back. Even if I didn't know what that something might be, it was the least I could do.

chapter two

Frankie

Unbelievable. I stared at the screen in front of me displaying the taping going on at *The Diane Gayle Show* as Calder Fox sauntered onto the set. He was as attractive as ever—of course. He seemed to have lost some of his usual arrogance, but my guess was it was just a PR ploy. God, I couldn't believe I'd ever fawned over that guy when we'd worked together as teens.

I turned to my manager, Brock. "Did we ever find out how Calder got top billing on this instead of me?"

"He offered an exclusive to Diane—won't be taking any more interview requests after his appearance here."

I leaned back against the green room couch and crossed my arms like a petulant child. "Figures. What Calder wants, Calder gets. It doesn't hurt that he's the son of Hollywood royalty."

Brock shrugged. "Frankie, you know as well as I do that no one will turn down an exclusive, especially with someone like Calder Fox. Besides, if he doesn't get his shit together, it's not going to matter who his parents are—no one will work with him."

I didn't respond. I'd been taught by my mom and my PR camp that if I didn't have anything nice to say, to say nothing at all. Calder and I had only worked together once before—both having bit parts in a TV sitcom where we played brother and

7

sister. We'd only been seventeen at the time, but he'd consistently shown up late to the set and always hungover—hell, he had probably still been drunk most of that time. He'd acted like the pompous ass that he was, ordering people around and treating them like shit, like he was better than everyone there because his daddy happened to be a big-time director and his mother, a famous actress. I'd been like most of the other idiot girls in this town at the time, thinking his attitude was cool and wishing he'd pay attention to me. Now I was able to see him for what he really was—extremely entitled.

Today I was appearing on *The Diane Gayle Show* at the tail end of a press junket for my latest indie film. I supposed that wasn't as interesting as confessions of the rich and famous. Poor little Calder had issues. Boo-freaking-hoo . . . what else was new?

I let out a huff as I settled back in my seat to watch his interview until I had to head to the set.

Diane had on her sympathetic face—she must be getting ready to try and pull some heartstrings. "So Calder, you recently left rehab for substance and alcohol abuse. What was your experience there like?"

"It was eye opening, that's for sure," he responded with a nervous laugh. Diane gave him an encouraging nod and he continued. "I needed to be there. My life had spun out of control. It was difficult, but . . . it was healing at the same time."

I rolled my eyes as I watched Diane take his hand, fully buying into his apologetic act.

"I know this is difficult to talk about, Calder, but I have to ask . . . the public will want to know. What specifically were you addicted to?"

Calder ran his free hand through his shoulder-length, sunbleached locks. I ignored the way the dark roots peeked out here and there and just *how* hot it made him look. Hot guys in Hollywood were usually douchebags and Calder was no exception.

He sucked in a big breath before answering. "I've been drinking since I was about thirteen years old. When you grow up in show biz, there isn't much that isn't available to you. Looking back now, I can see that I'd been an alcoholic since the time I was sixteen or seventeen. Back in the day, I used to just drink when I was chillin' with my friends, but it developed into an everyday thing I needed to feel normal." Calder used air quotes around the word normal, while Diane nodded her head like she knew exactly what he was going through. "At some point in my early twenties, the booze wasn't enough and I started dabbling in cocaine and other recreational drugs. I've probably tried everything under the sun, but coke was my drug of choice."

Calder's neck flushed a bit and he played with the collar of his shirt, seemingly embarrassed by his confession. I hated to admit it, but I understood. The limelight was not an easy place to be, even when you were an up-and-coming media darling like myself. I couldn't imagine what it would feel like to have all your darkest secrets laid bare in front of the world, up for discussion and dissection for anyone with a Wi-Fi connection. I shivered, my hair standing on end as I considered for a moment what the press would say if they ever got hold of *my* secret.

"You cold? I can ask if there's a blanket or something you can use." Brock's voice brought me back from my reverie.

"No, I'm fine. Thanks." I gave him a weak smile and focused my attention back on the monitor.

"What's been the most difficult part about all of this for you?" Diane asked Calder.

He answered without hesitation. "Losing my friend in the accident. Being sober allowed me to see all the mistakes I'd made over the past several years with complete clarity . . . to recognize all the people I've hurt along the way." He swiped at the tears building in his eyes. "That's hard for me to accept and work through." Calder looked up to the ceiling and blinked back tears, blowing air from his mouth in a rough exhale.

He seemed sincere, I'd give him that. But with actors, you never really knew what was genuine and what was not. Diane gave his hand a squeeze and turned her attention to the camera.

"We're going to take a break. We'll be back in a minute to talk some more to Calder Fox and find out where it all went wrong."

Calder immediately sprang up from his seat and shoved a hand through his long hair, then paced around the set taking deep breaths with his hands on his hips. It genuinely appeared as if his conversation with Diane was affecting him. Could I have been wrong about him? Maybe he *had* grown up since the last time we worked together. It had been years, after all.

Brock rose from the couch and turned to face me. "I'll be right back. I'm gonna see when you're up."

I nodded absentmindedly, watching as everyone on set scattered to get out of the camera shot except for Diane and Calder, who had now taken his seat again.

Diane flashed her veneers at the camera and began. "We're back and still talking with Calder Fox, the reigning prince in Hollywood's royal family and everyone's favorite bad boy." She turned to face Calder once again. "Before the break, we were discussing what it was like for you in rehab. What are your plans moving forward now?"

He drew in a breath. "Well, I plan to make amends with all the people I've wronged in the past and I'm going to continue living the healthy lifestyle I am now. More than anything though, I want to get back to work." *I'll bet he did.* "I know I've burned a lot of bridges with my on-set behavior in the past, but I'm determined to show that I can act like the professional I am and get the job done."

"Anything in the works right now?" Diane looked like a pit bull, salivating to get the inside scoop and dig her teeth into him.

"Nothing I can talk about at this point." He flashed her a panty-melting smile that lit up his blue eyes and caused a shiver of need to run through me. I refused to even examine what the hell *that* was about. Sure, it was no mystery why A-list celebrities dropped their drawers for the 'Hollywood Fox,' but it pissed me off to know I could be affected by his charm. I didn't like the guy. Not even a little.

He'd basically been blacklisted for the past year so

whichever director and studio took him on next deserved whatever they got.

"You're up in six, Frankie." Brock strolled back into the room with a sheet of paper in his hand. "I've cleared the list of questions they're going to ask you. Take a look for yourself though."

I leaned forward and reached for the paper, giving it a quick once-over. Same shit, different day. That was the thing about doing a press junket. You were asked the same questions a hundred different times but only in ten different ways. By now I'd perfected all of my answers and could do these interviews as drunk and high as Calder on a Saturday night.

I mentally scolded myself . . . that was mean. I didn't know what it was, but something about Calder brought out my bitchy side.

Handing the paper back to Brock, I said, "Got it," and rose from the couch, smoothing my skirt over my thighs when I was upright.

He led me down the hallway until we stood at the side of the stage to wait for my turn. We didn't have long to wait. Calder came sauntering off stage, appearing completely relaxed and not at all like he'd just been forced to discuss what was supposedly one of the hardest times of his life.

His gaze inched slowly up the length of my body before he met my eyes, a small smirk forming on his lips. My traitorous nipples pebbled underneath my silk shirt, and I was sure he could tell given the fact that I wasn't wearing a bra. Note to self—avoid backless shirts around attractive men. I pressed my teeth together, more irritated than ever that I found him so physically appealing.

"Have we met?" Calder asked me with that stupid grin still on his face.

I'm sure I looked like I was trying to catch flies with my mouth. *Was he shitting me?* I schooled my reaction as best I could and responded through clenched teeth. "Francesca Leon."

"Oh, right. You're that chick that does all the indie films."

Seriously? He was going to act like we'd never met be-fore—like we'd never worked together? Why did that grate on me so much? It's not like I should care one way or the other what *he* thought. I gave him a quick nod, not saying anything.

He put his hands in his pockets and rocked back on his heels. "Well, good luck out there," he said before walking past me. His cologne wafted by as he passed, a mix of the outdoors and the ocean. I resisted the urge to close my eyes and breathe in deeply. I would not let that idiot's charm affect me like it did so many other women. I was smarter than that.

A production assistant walked up, a frantic expression on his face. "You're due on set."

"Coming," I said. I swept all thoughts of Calder from my mind, remembering why I was here. This was the final push for my film that would be releasing next week, after which I'd be starting production on my first mainstream, big-budget studio film. This was is it . . . the one I was determined would launch my career and make Francesca Leon a household name.

chapter three

Calder

I looked out toward the angry ocean, more than happy to be staring at the grey sky and the wind-tossed waves with their whitecaps standing out against the darkness of the water. The sea today matched my mood. Admitting to the world what a complete and utter fuck-up I was wasn't an easy thing. It was even harder to do sober. Add that to the fact that I was still holding something back, something that had the guilt eating away at me piece by piece, day after day, and it became almost too much to bear.

I'd wanted nothing more than to leave that studio this morning and go on a bender. After spilling my guts to the world and then not recognizing Francesca right away—as if I needed any more proof of what an asshole I could be—I'd reached my limit. I wasn't sure if I was to blame for the latter though, because she sure as hell hadn't looked like *that* when I'd worked with her all those years ago. Was it my fault it took a minute for her name to click?

For a bit I'd imagined heading over to my favorite liquor store and buying out the place, calling up a few of my so-called 'friends' and telling them to round up the troops for a party at my place. I'd get shit-faced, maybe snort a line or two, and then bang whatever stupid female with zero respect for herself was available.

But I couldn't do it. They'd warned me in rehab that emotional turmoil would make me want to fall back into old habits. I was told to find something to clear my mind, a healthy way to deal with all the self-loathing.

And so I found myself standing in front of the turbulent ocean, surfboard in hand, fine crystals of sand whipping me in the face from the wind. It was a nasty day and the whitecaps were out in full force. I wasn't worried. I was a California boy, born and bred. I'd practically been surfing since I could walk. There was nowhere I was more at home or comfortable in my own skin than riding a wave.

"Thought I'd see you here." I diverted my attention from the waves crashing against the shore and looked to my left. Hendrix had just come from the ocean, water dripping from his wetsuit, dark hair slicked back, surfboard in hand.

"Hey, man," I called out as he jogged toward me.

"Couldn't resist these waves either?" Hendrix asked.

I nodded. "Needed to clear my head."

"No better place to do it than inside the green room." So true. I sure as hell preferred this kind of green room over the one I was in earlier today.

Hendrix was a cool guy I'd met through Akoni back in high school. A bit of an adrenaline junkie, not unlike myself, only he directed his efforts in a more positive way. The reigning X Games motocross champion, Hendrix was as badass as they come.

"How are you doing?" Hendrix asked.

I shrugged. "Some good days. Some bad."

He nodded in understanding. "What's today?"

I moved my gaze from the unsettled ocean to look him in the eyes. "Bad."

About the time I'd decided to get my fix partying and doing equally reckless—though undoubtedly more illegal—things, Hendrix and Akoni had grown closer. At the time I'd resented him, thinking he was taking my lifelong friend away. Now I knew it was me who'd been pushing Akoni away with my wild behavior.

We stood there for a few minutes, neither of us speaking, though it was obvious Hendrix had something on his mind.

"Just say it, man. Whatever it is you want to say," I finally said.

He chuckled to himself. "That obvious, eh?" Did I mention Hendrix was Canadian by birth? "I wanted to let you know that if you ever need to talk, or if you want to just hang or something . . . I'm game." He shrugged, playing it off like it wasn't a big deal—like he wasn't throwing me a lifeline. "I know we weren't that close when Akoni was alive, but maybe we can change that."

That was surprising. "I would've thought you'd hate me." Hendrix and I hadn't discussed the accident much after it happened.

"It's not your fault, Calder. You didn't force him to get behind that wheel."

Pain lanced through my chest as if he'd ripped my skin open with a blade. If he only knew. "Akoni didn't deserve to die in that car crash." *It should have been me.*

Hendrix stayed quiet for a moment. "You're right. He didn't. But we can't change what's already happened. All we can do is move forward and not take our own lives for granted."

My substance abuse counselor had told me I needed to start surrounding myself with healthy people and Hendrix fit the bill. I decided to push away the guilt and force it to the back of my mind. For now.

"Well then . . . I guess I'll take you up on your offer. Let's hang sometime."

"Cool."

"You been here long?" I asked him, going with my natural inclination to get past all this deep shit and move on to lighter topics.

"Nah, probably about twenty minutes or so. You headin' in?"

"Yeah. Give me a minute and I'll be there."

Hendrix jogged off toward the raging sea. "Try not to eat it when you get in there, bro."

"You might own the track, but I'm still better than you in a barrel." The wind carried the sound of Hendrix's laugh back to me.

I pushed my surfboard down into the sand until it stood on its own. Now that I had two free hands, I pulled my wetsuit up my abdomen and grabbed the zipper at the back, yanking it all the way to the top before depositing my sandals in the wet sand. Then I took the elastic from around my wrist and used it to tie my hair back.

I drew a deep breath through my nose, held it for seven seconds and then slowly exhaled through my mouth. It was a relaxation technique I'd learned in rehab—one I hoped would help bring me back to a place where the guilt and shame seemed somehow bearable.

Picking up the surfboard, I made my way to the ocean just as Hendrix caught a wave. That right there was exactly what I needed—to be on top of the water, in the moment, all my fuck-ups far from my mind.

By the time I tossed my surfboard into the back of my Jeep, I was feeling much more centered—like I could actually deal with all the shit that was about to come my way. Namely the backlash I was going to get when *The Diane Gayle Show* aired in a couple of days.

I decided to head out to Malibu since I didn't have any business in L.A. this week. My dad had rented me a beach house, figuring I could use time outside of the celebrity cesspool to ease myself back into society. In reality, I don't think he believed I could handle being around temptation and all the enablers my life there held. He'd never said so, but I had no doubt I was a disappointment and an embarrassment to him.

I was an only child whose parents divorced when I was ten. My mom ended up moving to Europe a couple years after the divorce and only came back to town when she was filming. I'd begged to stay in L.A. so I could pursue my acting dream.

I shook my head. Look how that had turned out.

As I drove down the Pacific Coast Highway, Sublime

blasted through the speakers, taking my mind away from everything for a few precious minutes. Hunger pangs pierced my stomach so I decided to stop for some chow at my favorite Mexican restaurant, not too far from the beach house.

I hadn't been paying much attention to whether I was being followed or not, so when I got out of my Jeep and walked across the parking lot to the restaurant, I startled when some stalkarazzi surrounded me and started snapping off shots. I wasn't sure if they'd been tailing me the entire time or were camped out here expecting a big name to come out and got lucky that Hollywood's notorious bad boy had made an appearance.

"Calder, we heard you were taping with Diane Gayle today. Did you guys discuss the accident?" one of them yelled.

"Think you'll be able to stay sober?" another piece of shit photographer threw out.

I ignored them and walked into the joint to order my food, knowing full well they had to stay out of the place if they didn't want to be arrested. After placing my order, I stood at the takeout counter to wait and checked my phone. My sponsor, Alisha, had called. I knew she was worried about how things went today and whether it'd sent me straight for the bottom of a bottle, so I made a mental note to call her back later.

"Hey, you're Calder Fox, right?"

I turned to see a teenage busboy standing behind me, wide-eyed, as if he almost couldn't believe I was real.

"Hey, man. Yeah, I'm Calder." I held my hand out to shake his and he took it, practically pulling my arm from the socket in his excitement. My arm had recovered fully from the accident, but on days like today when I'd done a lot of physical activity, it still ached afterward.

"Holy shit. I can hardly believe you're in here."

Though it was the last thing I felt like doing, I smiled at him, hoping I didn't seem too impatient for him to leave me alone. I knew better than anyone that it went with the job description. "What can I say, I got hungry."

The kid with acne-prone skin laughed like I'd just told the

funniest joke in the history of the world. "I saw you in the news a while back with that chick from that singing group. What's her name . . . the blond one? Shit." He scratched his head.

I knew exactly who he was talking about, but I wasn't gonna give him what he was looking for. "Anyway, you know the one I mean. She's one fine piece of ass. What was it like hitting that?"

This was the thing about meeting fans when you're a celebrity. People were one of two ways. They're either overwhelmed and barely able to utter a word, or they think they know you and they're your best friend, telling you *way* more than you ever wanted to know about them and asking you *way* more than you'd ever tell them.

"Listen, man. I'm just here—"

"Calder," the guy behind the takeout counter yelled. Saved by the overweight, hairy guy with a goatee that hung down to his collarbone.

"Well, I gotta run. Good to meet you."

"Same here," he said, smiling, and I turned around to collect my food.

As predicted, the maggots with cameras attached to their faces were still outside when I left, barking more of their idiotic and intrusive questions at me. I ignored them again, though it was all I could do to keep it together when one of them asked what porn star I planned on spending the night with. It was one fucking party, douchebags. One party—get over it.

I put my Styrofoam box containing the world's best enchiladas down on the passenger side floor, started the engine, and backed out. Since all the paps were busy getting into their cars to tail me, I didn't have to worry about hitting them.

I sped down the P.C.H. as the sun was setting, painting everything with an orange glow. The wind whipped my hair all around and Zeppelin now blared from the speakers. I almost felt . . . normal. I laughed to myself at how foreign normal actually felt.

When I reached the gates to the beach house, I punched in the code to open the gates and then glanced behind me. The jerk-offs had actually followed me. A picture of me fucking up in some way must be paying a hefty price.

They were going to be disappointed, I thought, as the gates shut behind me. I had no plans to offer them anything news-worthy.

chapter four

Frankie

The hair and make-up people deserved an award. I stood in front of the floor-length mirror taking in the image of myself. My long, dark hair was pinned on top of my head in a loose bun, stray hairs strategically falling down to give the impression I hadn't spent too much time on it when, in fact, the hairdresser had taken more than an hour to get it perfect.

The smoky eye make-up she'd applied made my green and hazel eyes pop, accenting the hints of hazel flecks inside them. The bright red lipstick perfectly matched my long sleeve red lace evening gown. I wasn't well endowed in the front so the lace went all the way up to my neck. The surprise was when I turned around. The fabric dropped below the thin silver belt wrapped around my tiny waste, showing off my slender back. I'd wanted to look my age—I was only twenty-three and didn't want to dress like I was forty—but I also wanted to keep it classy. This dress perfectly straddled the line between chic and sexy.

"You look amazing."

I turned to see that my assistant, Angela, had come into the room.

"I completely agree." My mom, Gianna, dressed in a floor-length, strapless black gown, came in behind her. She'd been getting ready in another room of the suite.

"Mom, you look so beautiful." She walked toward me, spinning on the way so I got the entire effect of her gown.

"Thanks, sweetie. But I have to say . . . if one of us is going to be in the best-dressed spread, it's going to be you. You look wonderful." She placed a hand on my cheek and smiled. I treasured these rare moments when she was truly happy.

Tonight I was walking the red carpet for my latest release. It was an indie project but had garnered a lot of buzz, so the event felt more like a big-budget film premiere than those I usually attended. If I didn't have a date, which was almost always the case, my mom normally accompanied me if she felt up to it.

"I think you both look great. And good thing . . . you need to be leaving. The limo is downstairs waiting," Angela said.

"Thanks. Will you be sure that all our personal items make it back to my place?" I asked. "Leave it all in the foyer, just inside the door."

"Of course." She smiled and chuckled a bit. "I still don't understand why you don't just have the hair and make-up crew do all this at your place. I've told you I can make them sign an ironclad non-disclosure agreement."

When she first started working for me, I'd told Angela that I preferred getting ready in hotel rooms because I was concerned about my privacy. Lame, but she'd accepted it.

I put on my best fake smile, which was pretty damn good at this point. "I know, but that's just a piece of paper. Besides, it's fun to get ready in these nice suites. It feels so much more . . . Hollywood." It sounded stupid even to my own ears, but Angela seemed to buy it. She shrugged and grabbed my evening bag off a nearby dresser and brought it over to me.

"Everything you need is in here. Brock said he'll see you on the red carpet."

I took the black satin purse from her. "Perfect. Thanks so much. When you get to my place, leave my mom's stuff with mine please."

Angela gave me a quizzical look but didn't question me. My mom lived with me, albeit in a completely separate area of the house. It worked for the two of us given the circumstances. I could keep an eye on her and alleviate some of my worries, and she was left to her own devices to . . . well, to do what she did.

We made our way from the hotel room and as the elevator doors closed in front of us, my mom took my hand and squeezed it. I took in her reflection on the back of the polished elevator door and smiled. I wish it could always be like this between us.

"Are you nervous?" she asked.

"I'll never get used to these things. Hundreds of camera flashes blinding you, everyone yelling your name and wanting a piece of you. It's overwhelming." I got a tingling feeling in my stomach just talking about it.

"You're a pro by now. You can handle it."

That much was true. I could. I always worried about my mom, though.

The elevator dinged and the doors opened in front of us, giving a clear view through the lobby to the outside world. The limo sat waiting for us and a few paparazzi were hanging around. Most of them were probably already perched somewhere along the red carpet, but no doubt some had hoped to get lucky and catch me leaving my hotel with someone on my arm so they could be the first to break the news. I was only too happy to disappoint them.

Pushing my chin up, I sucked in my stomach and flashed a smile as we drew closer to the doors. Time to push Frankie into the shadows and become Francesca Leon—movie star.

chapter five

Frankie

I stepped out onto the red carpet and it didn't take a second before every camera within a hundred feet was flashing in my face. If you ever wondered why there's always a hulking security guard with dark sunglasses standing in the background on the red carpet, I could tell you—because you couldn't see shit.

Despite the fact that the blinding lights and my name being yelled over and over again were an assault on the senses, I smiled and struck a pose so the photographers on this end could get a shot. The fashion critics all needed a good picture if they were going to work you over the next night on an entertainment show. I was pretty sure my stylist had struck gold with this dress, so I wasn't too concerned about ending up on the worst-dressed list. When I turned and smiled over my shoulder to give the crowd a view of the back of my dress, they went crazy, yelling my name even louder. There were even some catcalls and whistles to be heard over all the commotion. I was sure I came off more confident than I really was.

My mom stood off to the side, knowing the drill. The press would want pictures of me on my own before getting some of us together. When I was sure they'd gotten what they needed, I turned back around to motion to my mom to come stand beside me and noticed Brock making his way over from the theater. He stood to the side until my mom and I were finished, then came up and gave us both kisses on the cheek.

"You two look fabulous," he said.

"Thank you," my mom responded with a big smile.

Brock leaned into me and spoke directly in my ear. "We need to talk."

He had a smile plastered on his face when he pulled away, but there was worry in his eyes. Which, in turn, made me concerned. Very concerned. Brock had an even temperament, regardless if the situation was ideal or not. It was clear to me that whatever he wanted to talk about wasn't going to make me happy.

I darted my gaze to my mom. Had someone found out? "What's going on?" I asked, my heart rate kicking up a bit.

He shook his head. "Not now. Later. After the screening."

Terrific. Not only did I have to sit through a screening of my film anxious about what everyone would think of it, but I had to wonder what the hell he needed to talk to me about.

I pursed my lips and nodded before sticking the smile back on my face. The last thing I needed was for someone in the media to pick up on the fact that there was something wrong.

We made our way down the red carpet, my mom and Brock hanging back again so this end of the press line could get their pictures of me. Meanwhile, the press continued yelling questions at me—as if I could decipher what they were saying. Even so, I was sure I heard Calder Fox's name a few times. What was that about? Maybe they wanted a sound bite from me after Calder's big exposé with Diane the week prior? Screw that, he'd gotten more than his fair share of attention in the press this week.

One of the red carpet handlers approached me and asked me to head over to the press line so I could give some interviews. I walked up to Missy, one of the entertainment reporters I'd enjoyed speaking with in the past, figuring I'd start off on an easy note.

"Francesca, you look amazing tonight. Who are you wearing?" she asked, smiling wide to showcase her perfectly white teeth.

"This is Valentino." I kept my focus on her so I wouldn't find myself squinting at all the flash bulbs or blinking rapidly like I had something in my eye.

"Absolutely stunning."

"Thank you." I smiled at her.

"So before I ask you any questions about the film we're all here for tonight, I need to know how you feel about Calder Fox taking over Jake Radley's role in your next project, *Collateral Damage?*"

My smile faltered for a second. I know it did. I recovered quickly but seriously though—what the hell? *Collateral Damage* was supposed to be my big break into the mainstream and solidify my position as a serious actress. And I was starring in it with Jake—a reliable, likable, seasoned co-star. Not an unreliable screw-up like Calder.

"P-pardon?" was all I could manage.

"Now that Jake's father is sick and he's removed himself from the project . . . how do you feel about working with Calder given his recent troubles?" Missy pushed the microphone in front of me, waiting for her sound bite.

I opened my mouth to answer—to say what, I wasn't sure, because my mind was still reeling with the news. But before I could say anything, a warm hand wrapped around my waist, pulling me back into a hard body.

"Oh, come on, Missy. You know you can't believe everything you read in the press." Calder's warm laugh reverberated through me, sending tingles cascading throughout my body.

I looked up at him in confusion and he answered me with a smile, that practiced Hollywood grin that made all the ladies swoon. All the ladies but me.

No, I wasn't swooning. At all. I was pissed. Pissed that I'd been blindsided by this question while on a press line. Pissed that Calder was going to undoubtedly ruin the project that was supposed to be huge for me. And pissed that on some basic level, I was enjoying being pressed up against this man, even though I didn't even *like* him.

Missy's giggle cut through my inner turmoil. She was

looking at Calder like he was the most charming man in the world before she responded. Somehow I was able to suppress an eye roll. "True, Calder. Though after seeing your interview on *The Diane Gayle Show* last week, I'm sure you'd be the first to admit that you've had your share of struggles."

Calder's jovial tone from a moment ago turned serious. "I won't deny that. But I'm ready to put that part of my life behind me and move forward in a more positive direction. This project with Francesca is the first step. One I'm excited to take with this beautiful woman." He squeezed me into his side a bit and the smell of him almost made my knees go weak.

Missy moved her microphone into my face, which was now frozen in that same fake smile that had formed when she'd first mentioned Calder's name. "What about you, Francesca? Do you feel the same?"

I inhaled a deep breath and took a lesson straight out of PR 101: the non-committal answer. "I'm so excited about this project and I'm sure Calder is going to do everything in his power to make it a great experience for us both."

"Now you two have worked together before, haven't you?" Missy's toothy grin and her annoying questions were beginning to grate on me.

I smiled anyway and responded, "We have. It was a long time ago though."

"When we were both teenagers. You could tell even then that this girl had special talent," Calder interjected.

I was going to chop his nuts off and feed them to him. He was so full of shit. Last week he couldn't even remember working with me and now he recalls how talented I was? I wanted to scream, but I refused to let my own reputation suffer at the hands of Calder fucking Fox. So instead, I turned to him with as genuine a smile as I could muster. "Thank you for the compliment. I'm embarrassed to say I don't recall too much of our time working together, but I'm sure that if I could I'd feel same."

Calder's gaze flicked down to me and he smirked. Judging by his expression he knew I was full of shit, but I didn't care.

Before Missy could interrogate us any further, the handler came over and told us it was time to move on. I thanked Missy for the interview and wished her well, then turned toward Calder so I could speak to him without the whole world knowing what was said. He wore his shoulder-length hair down tonight and I had no choice but to lean into it to reach his ear. I didn't know if it was his cologne or his shampoo, but I pretended to ignore how good he smelled.

"Get your hands off of me," I hissed. He dropped his hands immediately and pulled back, giving me a searching look.

"Relax." The self-proclaimed 'Prince of Hollywood' did *not* just tell me to relax. I inhaled a deep breath again, desperate to maintain my composure.

"This is my red carpet tonight. Stay out of my way." I smiled while I said it so any pictures taken wouldn't give away the rage I felt burning a hole in my stomach. However, there was no mistaking the venom in my voice that a snake like Calder would undoubtedly recognize.

I walked around him, giving a sidelong look to Brock to let him know that I was not happy and we would most definitely be having a not-so-pleasant conversation later.

"What the hell, Brock?" I ground out through clenched teeth. I wasn't able to get a moment alone with my manager until we'd arrived at the after-party.

He held his hands up in front of him in defense. "I didn't know anything about it until right before you hit the carpet."

"I cannot work with Calder fucking Fox. He's going to tank this production—you and I both know it."

Now his hands were in front of him in a placating gesture. "Come on now, Frankie, calm down a bit. He needs this film to be a success just as much as you do."

"That might be the case, but that doesn't mean he's going to be able to stay clean long enough to make that happen."

"Look, production is all set to start next week. The studio needed someone to fill in that had heartthrob potential and was available on short notice so they wouldn't lose all the money they've already put in."

I clenched my fists until my nails were digging into my palms. "I hate that my future is riding on this guy."

Brock pressed his lips together. "I know it's less than ideal. But what choice do we have but to make it work?"

He was right and that's what really pissed me off. I was going to have to do whatever was necessary to make sure Calder got through this shoot, clean and sober. I closed my eyes and let out a long exhale, then grabbed my drink off a nearby table, slamming the remainder back in one big gulp. "I need another one. I'll be back." I didn't wait for a response, instead stomping off toward the bar, hoping to lose myself in the blissful oblivion of an alcohol-induced buzz.

The irony of the situation wasn't lost on me.

chapter six

Calder

The film premiere's after-party was at the Roosevelt Hotel's Tropicana Bar and Pool. How very Hollywood. The Roosevelt was one of my typical haunts back in my party days.

As I walked into the space that held so many temptations and so many memories—most of them a little foggy, to be sure—I put my hand in my pocket to finger my silver sobriety chip. It helped to calm me and keep my priorities clear. This would be my first time in a party atmosphere since getting sober. I was only here to make an appearance because the studio heads for *Collateral Damage* wanted some pictures of Francesca and me to show up in the press. It was good buzz for the film.

I glanced around and realized it was almost like seeing the place for the first time. Which was sad, really. In all the times I'd been here—and there had to have been hundreds—I don't think I'd every actually seen the place sober. The pool was in the center and lit up, though no one was in it. Lights strung around the surrounding palm trees twinkled in the water's reflection. Wood couches with black cushions and bulky wood coffee tables sat atop the polished black concrete, dotted with all of L.A.'s movers and shakers. A lot of people had come out for the event and after seeing the movie, it was clear why.

Francesca had owned that fucking movie. I was looking forward to working with her.

It seemed though my new co-star was not looking forward to working with me. I couldn't really blame her—I was Hollywood's poster boy for overindulged 'fuck-up' at the moment. Even still, a small part of me was irked at the way she'd acted toward me. She'd been at the taping of *The Diane Gayle Show* last week so she must've seen my interview and therefore knew I was trying to be a better person and focus on figuring out who I was without the drugs and booze.

The list of people I'd screwed over or treated with no respect was a long one, but she wasn't on it. What did she have to be pissed about? Rehearsals started next week. It'd be best to address her animosity toward me now, before we officially started working together. Better to get all the bullshit out of the way early.

I chatted with a few industry folks, content to nurse my water and watch as Francesca worked the room, mingling with everyone who was anyone at the party. It wasn't long before she made her way to the bar for only the second time that night. No dependency issues there.

It was hard not to watch her glide across the room in that skintight lace number. When I first saw her on the red carpet, I'd had to curb my natural instincts to try and use the Fox charm to get her into my bed. Sometimes I still needed a reminder that I wasn't that guy anymore. Besides, my sponsor had told me to stay away from women until I'd been sober for at least a year. My right hand was getting a lot of action lately. Which proved how serious I was about getting my shit together.

I made my way over and stood beside her as she waited for the bartender to make her drink. When she looked over and saw me, she rolled her eyes and turned her attention back to the bar.

We weren't off to a great start. "Can we talk?" I asked her.

She ignored me, ordering a shot of Patrón to go with her drink instead. I sighed. Clearing the air between us was going to be harder than I'd thought. I watched as the bartender finished her drink, setting it in front of her, and poured her shot.

The smell of tequila that wafted my way made my mouth water. It had me instantly digging into my pocket and rubbing my sobriety chip, hoping to draw strength from it. I could almost feel the cool glass in my hand as I imagined bending my elbow and tilting the glass into my mouth. Muscle memory was a bitch sometimes. I was rubbing that damn chip so hard I'd be surprised if the wording didn't rub off.

Without even glancing over to me, she picked up the salt shaker from the bar top, licked her wrist, poured salt on it, and lifted the shot glass to her lips, swallowing it in one gulp. The bartender held a lime out to her. She smiled, taking it from him and bringing it to her mouth, then wrapped her plump lips around it and sucking all the juices out.

Something about that whole display had my dick twitching in my pants. Man, it really had been too long since I'd been laid if watching an attractive woman lick her wrist and suck on a lime gave me a semi. I decided I'd try and focus on that feeling, rather than the desperate need to drink that was currently clawing at my stomach.

She tossed the lime on the bar and turned to me. "Okay, I'm ready. Let's do this." She took a long pull from her cocktail then looked up at me with determination in her eyes.

Huh. I found it somewhat ironic that I was the sober one and in order for her to be able to have a conversation with me, she needed to be buzzed.

"Are you sure you should be drinking that much?" I asked, unable to rein in my concern.

Francesca rolled her eyes. "Did *you* of all people seriously just ask me that?"

I pushed aside my irritation. "You're so tiny. I'd think a drink or two and you'd be shitfaced, that's all."

She narrowed her eyes. "You worry about yourself, okay?"

She sure was a prickly little thing. "Fine. I was hoping we could have a conversation."

"I gathered that much when you came over and wouldn't

take the hint that I wanted you to leave."

I was beginning to lose patience with her attitude toward me. She may have thought that made me more likely to leave, when, in fact, all it did was make me that much more determined to resolve whatever her issues were with me. "Can we sit over here for a minute?" I motioned with my hands to an empty seating area.

She sighed but made her way over to one of the couches set back into the corner. It afforded us a small amount of privacy at this busy party. When we were both seated, she set her drink on the wood table and turned her attention to me, a let's-get-this-over-with expression on her face.

"I've obviously done something to piss you off. I don't know what that is, but if I saw you out somewhere when I was still using and I did or said something stupid—"

"I never saw you out anywhere," she said quickly. "I'm not a fan of the whole club scene." She wrinkled her nose like she smelled something bad.

"What is it then? Is it because I put my arm around you on the red carpet? I'm sorry. The producers of *Collateral Damage* wanted me here tonight. They said we should act friendly and excited to work together. I assumed they'd given you the same speech. I didn't mean anything by it."

She pursed her lips for a moment before speaking. "I'm just not into fake people. God knows there are enough of them in this town. I try to steer clear. And you," she shoved her index finger into my chest, "are most definitely one hundred percent—fake." Francesca crossed her arms in front of her and arched a brow.

I sat there in stunned silence for a beat, trying for the life of me to come up with any goddamn reason why she would've said that. "What the hell are you talking about?"

"On the red carpet . . . you went on about how you knew when we worked together the first time, that I was talented, blah, blah. That's complete crap. I ran into you last week and you had no idea who I was." She pinned me with a glare that had half of me wanting to run the other way and the other half wanting to push her down onto the couch and have my way with her.

My mom always told me that no woman wanted to be forgettable—damn, she wasn't kidding. "Look, when I saw you backstage at Diane's show, I'll admit . . . I didn't recognize you at first. Only because five years ago you were a skinny, awkward teenager, and now . . ." she narrowed her eyes, "now you're a stunning, flawless, sensual woman." Those narrow eyes went wide and I was pretty sure I saw a slight blush creep across her cheeks. "I didn't put two and two together until I'd already walked away and your name finally registered. Everything I said on the red carpet was true. That's exactly what I thought of you back then. Even half-corked most of the time, I knew talent when I saw it."

Francesca parted her lips and closed them a few times like she was going to say something but didn't know what. I hoped that was a good thing so I kept my mouth shut, content to wait for her response. It finally came a minute later.

"Skinny and awkward, huh?" She half-smirked, giving me hope that the ice between us was thawing, and then let out a resigned sigh. "I don't know what to say to that. You must think I'm a complete bitch." Her stiff posture relaxed.

"Not a complete bitch, just a partial one," I said with a straight face.

She just stared for a minute, then laughed. "I deserve that, I suppose." Francesca looked down at her hands in her lap as if embarrassed.

Now I was the speechless one. Her laugh, the way her face lit up and her mouth opened a bit, how it emphasized the apples of her cheeks—it left me staring at her openly, appreciating how uninhibited and beautiful she looked when she let herself go like that.

She glanced up and gave me a peculiar look. "What? Is something wrong?" A crease formed in between her brows. This was closer to the expression I was used to seeing on her face—both times we'd met and in all the images Google had supplied me with when I'd looked her up earlier.

"Sorry, yeah. Everything's fine. It's just . . . you should smile more often. It does nice things to your face."

She gave me a shy smile and reached for her drink on the table.

It does nice things to your face? What the hell? Apparently, sober me had way less game than the using me did. I couldn't imagine how I'd ever gotten laid with lame lines like that one.

Not that I was trying to get laid. I wasn't. I couldn't help it if the sight of Francesca Leon letting go for a minute turned me into a tongue-tied idiot. I was still human. And male.

"What I meant to say is that you don't seem to smile very often. You're always so serious."

She took another sip of her drink and set it back on the table, pinning me with a—wait for it—*serious* stare. "Can I be honest with you?"

This was bound to hurt my ego. Good thing there was an abundance for her to chip away at. "Please."

She inhaled deeply before speaking. "I knew nothing about Jake being replaced when I was questioned about it on the red carpet. I was taken aback. *Collateral Damage* is my big break into doing mainstream blockbuster films so I have a lot riding on this movie doing well. If it doesn't, well . . . you know how it goes. Studios don't sign actors that don't put butts in the seats or awards on the mantels."

I nodded. "I get it, believe me. This is my one shot at proving I'm not a complete asshat to work with. I can't afford to screw it up either or it'll be the last time I work in this town. I'll be reduced to doing infomercials, regardless of who my parents are."

I thought that would make her feel a bit better, but she pursed her bright red lips—that didn't seem like a good thing. "Since you mentioned it . . . when I heard I was going to be doing the film with you, I'll admit . . . I was not pleased." She cringed a little after she said it, which I would've thought was cute if I wasn't busy trying not to let her comment sting. "Don't get me wrong, I think it's great that you're trying to get the help you need . . . very admirable. But with your track record, it's just hard to not assume that there are going to be problems on set, that's all." She shrugged. "I can't afford for this movie to be anything other than Oscar worthy." She sucked in her bottom lip and waited for my reaction.

This wasn't the first time I'd had my past thrown in my face, and it wouldn't be the last. It used to be that if I was confronted like this and uncomfortable, I'd toss a few shots back to numb myself from having to feel—anything.

I brought my hands up and gripped her upper arms, looking right into her piercing eyes, willing her to believe me. "I can't argue with anything you just said, so I won't bother. But I can assure you that I have every intention of taking this job seriously. I'm not going to fuck it up."

"I take my career *very* seriously, Calder." I was pretty sure it was the first time she'd said my name. I like how it rolled off her tongue—with a combination of authority and pleading.

I chuckled. "I think we've established that you're serious." I brought my drink to my lips and took a sip of water. "I promise I'm not going to screw this up for either of us."

After a moment, she nodded and smiled. "Okay. I believe you. Please don't make me regret it."

"I won't," I said in a determined tone, removing my hands from her and immediately wishing I didn't have to. I'd examine what the hell that was about later.

"Sorry I was so nasty to you earlier," she said, looking chagrined. "Can we start over?"

She'd said the magic words and had no idea how badly I needed to hear them. Starting over was exactly what I was trying to do. "Of course we can." I stuck my hand out in front of me. "Hi, Francesca, it's good to see you again after all this time. It's been what. . . . five years since we worked together?"

She grinned and took my hand in hers, shaking it. "At least five, I'd say. And please, call me Frankie. All my friends do."

chapter seven

ℱrankie

Later that week I sat in my trailer on set after spending the day with wardrobe to get the final fittings done on the outfits I'd be wearing throughout production. I figured Calder would be on set today too, since he was having to play catch-up—fast.

Because I really needed to make this situation with Calder work, I asked Brock to arrange for us to run lines together this afternoon. He was due to be here any minute.

I was nervous. Although I wanted to believe an addict fresh out of rehab could handle all the pressure associated with a movie of this caliber, I wasn't sure it was possible. There was also a part of me that was uncomfortable about my reaction every time he was around. I mean, yeah, Calder was attractive if you liked blue eyes, a hard body with tanned skin, and a head full of shoulder-length hair with dark roots and sun-bleached blond at the end.

Ugh. I sounded like every other girl on the Internet and social media who fawned over him. Maybe I'd been single too long because this wasn't me. I was responsible and made decisions only after weighing all the pros and cons, always choosing what made sense and what was best for me and my mom.

A knock sounded on the trailer door, startling me from my thoughts. "Come in."

Calder popped his head in the trailer, his panty-dropping

smile in full effect. "You okay to start running lines?"

"Yep, I'm done with my fittings for the day. How did yours go?"

He made his way over, script in hand, and sat across the small kitchen table from me. "Most of the stuff doesn't fit. It seems I'm a little broader in the chest than Jack was." He chuckled.

It took all of my self-control not to shift my gaze down to the blue t-shirt stretched across his pecs. "Oh yeah?" I played with the corner of the table, keeping my eyes there, trying to appear nonchalant. I wasn't sure I succeeded.

"Thanks again for offering to run lines with me. If I'm being honest, I'm kinda nervous about the table read tomorrow. I haven't had a lot of time to prepare."

I looked up at him and his expression reminded me of something you'd see on an unsure young child, sending a twinge of guilt through me. I hadn't been completely upfront with him at the after-party that night. I'd played nice, figuring the best way to try and make a success out of the less-than-deal situation was to align myself with him, to work with him rather than against him. But I still wasn't happy about the turn of events and I wouldn't be taking any of his shit. The minute any of the old Calder reared its ugly head, he and I would be having words.

"I thought it would help you out and let us develop a bit of chemistry together before the cameras start rolling."

"Well, whatever the reason, I appreciate it." The sincerity in his eyes brought the guilt back into the forefront of my mind. Who knew—maybe we really could work well together.

I cleared my throat. "So, is there a specific part where you want to start?" I asked as I pulled my script in front of me and began thumbing through it.

"I thought maybe we could try the 'first kiss' scene."

My eyes darted up to see an amused grin spreading across his face. He shrugged. "You said you were concerned with our chemistry. Seems like the best way to test the waters."

Good Lord, he was cute when he was joking around and

flirting. If that was even flirting. I could barely remember since I'd been so focused on work for the past couple of years.

I chastised myself mentally. I was not going to swoon over this guy. I wouldn't let myself be lured into the Fox trap. "I think it might be better to start with something else. What about the scene where they meet?" I kept my tone neutral.

He chuckled. "That's as good as any."

Collateral Damage was a drama about a man who falls in love with a mentally ill woman. They met in college, fell for one another, and were supposed to live happily ever after, but it became apparent to Calder's character after they married that my character had been hiding her issues. The screenplay was brilliantly written, but it was up to Calder and me to deliver the emotional punch needed to make it a hit.

I found the part in my script and nodded over at Calder to start.

An hour later, we'd been through the scene more than a few times and I had to say—I was impressed. For a guy that'd only been given the script a week ago, he'd done really well. He seemed to know the material and had obviously been working hard to learn it, though I got the sense that he was still holding back and not quite giving it everything he could.

I was just about to say something to him about it when my phone started buzzing on the table. I picked it up and saw that it was Beatrice, my housekeeper, calling. Panic made my stomach churn before I'd even accepted the call. "Hi Beatrice, is everything okay?"

"Not really, Miss Leon. I'm at your place to clean like I always am on Thursdays, and your mom . . ." She trailed off like she wasn't sure what to say, or whether she should say anything at all.

"Go ahead. Tell me what's going on," I said in my most reassuring voice.

"Well, I was in the kitchen cleaning and your mom came in. She was looking for something. I'm not even really sure what. She was going on and on about having put it down in the kitchen but said that she couldn't find it. I offered to help her look—"

My earlier panic turned to fear and fisted my heart in a stranglehold. "You didn't—"

"No. I didn't go check in her part of the house. You told me to never do that, so I wouldn't." She sounded affronted.

"Sorry. Then what happened?"

"Well, I offered to help her look and she freaked out and accused me of throwing it out. Whatever it is. I told her that I'd just arrived and hadn't thrown anything out, but she began ripping the place apart looking for it. She was really upset and it scared me. I didn't know what to do so I called you."

Tears pricked behind my eyes and I blinked to try and clear them, then turned around so Calder wouldn't notice. "You did the right thing. Where is she now?"

"I think she went back to her place. Do you want me to go check on her?"

"No!" I responded a little too quickly. "I'm leaving the studio now. You go home for the day and we'll see you next Thursday."

"I'm really sorry, Ms. Leon. I swear I didn't throw anything out."

"I'm not angry at you. Don't worry about it."

I heard her sigh into the phone. "Okay. I'm going to gather my things and go then. See you next week."

"Thanks for calling." I ended the call and squeezed my eyes shut, trying to take in some deep breaths to calm myself. Tonight was going to be a long night—they always were when my mom had one of her episodes. We were doing the first table read with the director and producers tomorrow, but hopefully I'd be able to get some sleep.

"Are you okay?"

Shit. I'd totally forgotten Calder was here for a second. I opened my eyes, then turned to face him with my best fake smile. Good thing I was an actress. "Yeah, but I gotta run. Something's come up." I stood to grab my purse off the trailer's couch, threw my phone inside, and slung my purse over my shoulder.

"You sure? Because you're looking kinda upset right now."

"I'm fine. Nothing for you to worry about." With that, I spun on my heel and headed out of the trailer, my two feet carrying me as fast as possible to the car that would take me to the trainwreck waiting for me at home.

I threw my car in park in my driveway, happy to see that Beatrice's car was no longer here. Without even grabbing my purse from the passenger seat, I raced into the house. "Mom! Mom!"

No answer.

Not good.

I checked all the rooms on the main level of my side of the house. Nothing. Still calling her name, I ran up the stairs, but she wasn't there either. I headed back out the front door and sprinted around the house until I reached the door on the far side that was the entrance to her living area. I braced myself for what I knew was hidden behind the expensive wrought iron and frosted glass door and then entered without knocking.

"Mom! Where are you?" She didn't answer, but I could hear her sniffing and I mentally prepared myself for her tears.

The overwhelming smell of the place was the first thing to assault my senses. It wasn't the smell of decay but dust and stale air with nowhere to move. I squeezed in past the plastic containers and stepped over a pile of books and a mass of various types of paper. When I reached the living room, it wasn't until I got past a five-foot pile of clothing that I saw her, sitting on the one tiny corner of her sofa not covered in *something*. Her hands were wrapped around her waist and she was rocking back and forth as tears streamed down her face.

My chest constricted, stealing my breath. I'd never get used to seeing her like this. I made my way to her and pushed some stacked papers over onto the coffee table, managing to make a small space to perch myself on. "Mom," I almost whispered. She didn't react to my presence so I placed my hand on her cheek and brushed away the streak of saltwater left behind from her tears. Moments like this I felt more like a mother to her than the other way around.

My mom was a hoarder.

Among other things.

Obsessive Compulsive Disorder being one of those other things. This was the secret I could never let get out. Not because it might hurt my career or send unwanted press *my* way—I wasn't concerned about that—but because the media attention would destroy my mother. She was embarrassed and ashamed of something she had no control over, something she never asked for.

She eventually stopped rocking and looked up at me with such a weary and pained expression that guilt and frustration had my throat clogging with emotion because I couldn't snap my fingers and make it all go away for her.

"What happened?" I asked, taking her hand in mine.

"I bought a magazine at the store and I know I put it on your kitchen counter." She straightened up and wiped the remaining tears from under her eyes. "I wanted to make tea and I knew I was out of milk, so when I got home I went to your place first to borrow some." She looked at me like I might get angry with her, but it's never bothered me when she's ventured over to my place. In fact, I preferred it rather than knowing she was sitting here in this environment, which had to be unhealthy.

I gave her hand a squeeze. "It's fine, mom."

She inhaled a deep breath before she continued. "After I made my tea, I realized I'd forgotten the magazine. I went to get it, but it was gone. Obviously that damn housekeeper moved it or threw it out or something."

"I asked Beatrice and she said she didn't see it," I responded.

Her eyes widened and she started shaking her head back and forth. "She's lying. She has to be. I know I left it there."

I knew where this was going. There were times when my mom did really well and could cope with things, and there were other times when she'd focus on what—to me—seemed like something completely inconsequential. When this happened, the best option was to appease her. I'd learned over the years that trying to talk sense into her was not going to work. My energy was better spent helping her bring to fruition whatever she was currently fixating on. Today, that meant finding a magazine.

"Alright, what does the magazine look like?" I asked.

"It's the latest issue of *In The Know*. I got it because I thought there might be pictures of you from the premiere last week. You looked so pretty and I wanted to cut them out and scrapbook them so your kids can see you years from now."

I sighed. My mom was forever scrapbooking. At this rate, if I ever did have kids, they'd have a hundred different books to look at. "Okay, why don't you go look around my place again and see if you can find it? I'll start looking over here."

My mom placed her hand on my cheek, pressing her lips together. "Thank you, sweetie. I know it's silly, that it's just a magazine and we could go get another—"

"You don't need to explain," I assured her, placing my hand over the top of hers.

She nodded and stood before making her way over to my place.

I stood there, hands on my hips, surveying her house for a few moments. No matter how many times I'd been over here, it was still hard for me to bear seeing her live in this squalor. But I had to accept it. I'd seen the distress I caused when I tried to force her to give up things she wasn't ready for.

I sighed and began picking through the piles on the couch and the coffee table. This job would be a lot easier if my mom didn't have such an affinity for paper.

About an hour later, I finally located the magazine on a pile near the kitchen. I figured she must have set it down there at some point and forgotten about it. I pushed past the heaps upon heaps of stuff until I made it to the front door, happy to take in a lungful of fresh air. I wasn't claustrophobic, but whenever I was in my mom's place, the weight I carried around like a sack of sand on my back seemed to gain a few pounds, making it harder to breathe.

I soaked in the California sunshine as I walked along the stonework leading to my front entrance, free—for the moment, anyway—of the gloom and oppressiveness that had become my mom's existence.

chapter eight

Calder

My nerves were getting to me, so I paced inside my trailer as I waited to head to the table read.

Me.

Pacing.

It wasn't so long ago that I'd be sitting in a trailer exactly like this with my lips wrapped around a bottle or eight inches deep in some random girl. Either way, back then I wasn't feeling anxious in the least. What I was feeling now was . . . foreign to me.

I stopped in the middle of the small living room, sick of passing by the same scenery over and over again. Running both hands through my hair, I inhaled a deep breath through my nose, blowing it out through my mouth. Then I did it again. And again.

That wasn't working so I shoved my hand in my pocket and fingered my twenty-four hour sobriety chip. That took the edge off a bit. A few minutes later, I glanced at my watch. Showtime.

I grabbed the script off the small kitchen counter and headed off to prove to everyone that I was the right person to star in this movie. I wanted them to know that I wasn't just the unreliable playboy whose face they'd seen splashed across the front page of every gossip rag for the past year. I was Calder

Fox, a professional actor who could bring it under pressure.

And then my subconscious with all its negative self-talk tried to kick in. I pushed those thoughts far back in my mind, willing them not to take root in my brain until they drained every positive emotion I was feeling like the succubus that they were.

I reached the room where we'd be doing the table read and it looked like almost everyone was already here, even though I was right on time. Damn, I hated to think of how long people used to sit around waiting for me to show up to these things.

The chair beside Frankie was empty so I sat there. It made sense because most of the scenes we were going through today involved the two of us.

"Hey," I said, "everything okay? You sort of tore out of here yesterday."

A pink tinge appeared on her cheeks, which was cute on her. "Yeah, sorry. There was something I had to deal with that was time sensitive."

"No worries." I shrugged. "Just wanted to make sure you were alright." Where had that come from? What was I, her friggin' big brother now?

Frankie just looked at me with wide eyes for a moment. "Oh, well thanks for that." She shifted in her chair, then leaned in closer so only I could hear her. She smelled like lavender. The urge to draw in a lungful of her soothing scent was overwhelming, but I resisted. "How are you feeling about the read-through today? You good?" She looked me straight in the eye like she was trying to read me. Her eyes were so unique with that hazel center surrounded by a striking green. "Calder?" She scrunched up her forehead.

"Oh, uh . . . sorry. I'm a little nervous, but nothing I can't handle." That was sure to inspire confidence. If I kept it up, she really was going to think I was still using.

"Well, if you need any reassurance at all, just look at me. Remember, we're in this together. We sink or swim as a team."

A team. I'd never really been part of a team. Oh sure, I'd had a whole entourage at one point, and yes, I had people that worked for me now. People I trusted. But that wasn't a team. That was everyone trying to get their own piece of me. Even the people who remained in my life to this day, the ones I trusted, were there because they benefited somehow. My manager was around because she got a percentage of my take, my PR guy, Landon, was there because I paid him to be. I had no doubt they wanted what was best for me, but we weren't a team. I'd always been on a solo mission.

So for Frankie to refer to us as a team meant something to me, even if she didn't realize it. Her words struck a chord that reverberated though my chest, warming me from the inside out. "Thanks," I said softly and with sincerity. "You have no idea what that means to me."

We held each other's gazes until the director, Niles, commanded our attention. "Listen up, everyone!" The chatter in the room died down until we all faced the middle-aged man, waiting for him to say something. "I want to welcome everyone to set. This is our first go-round with everyone in the room and with our new leading man." He motioned over to me from the head of the table and all eyes turned in my direction. I gave a small smile and nodded at Niles in thanks. "I have no doubt we have the right crew assembled here to do this script justice, but it's going to be a lot of work and a long road to get there. I'm sure we're all aware that there's already been some Academy Award buzz about this film. That's not going to happen on its own so I expect every single person in this room to give it their all. Every day." He paused and swept his gaze around the large table. I'm pretty sure he made eye contact with all twenty-something people so we'd all know that no one was excluded from that statement. "Now, everyone's aware that Calder has only recently been brought in, but he assures me that he's been working hard to learn the script and get up to speed. Let's be sure to give him all the support he needs."

There were murmurs of agreement around the table. I couldn't help but wonder what everyone's *real* opinion of having me on the project was. I'd learned in rehab that we become what we think about most, so I tried again to push those thoughts away, reaching into my pocket to play with my sobriety chip.

Niles clapped his hands together to get everyone's attention back on him. "Why don't we get started? We can take it from the top and see how it's working, and from there we might jump around a bit so I can test out some of the scenes I'm unsure about."

I drew a deep breath in. Here goes everything . . .

I'd never worked with Niles before, but he had a reputation for being intuitive and a perfectionist. Two and a half hours later, I'd say I agreed with that assessment. He was able to pinpoint exactly what wasn't working in each scene, which we continued to do over and over again until they were to his liking.

"Let's run that scene one more time. Calder and Francesca . . . I need to feel the chemistry between you two. I know you don't really know each other, but loosen up. You're two college kids meeting at a party for the first time. You're attracted to each other. Francesca, your character is in a bit of a manic state right now. I want to feel how into each other you are when we run the scene this time. Got it?"

We both nodded at Niles in agreement. I looked down to the script in front of me, more out of habit than anything else. I didn't need it anymore. We'd done it enough times that I pretty much had it memorized. The same was probably true for Frankie, which gave me an idea.

"Frankie, why don't we try facing each other this time? It'll be easier to connect with you if I'm actually looking at you. I know it's a table read and all, but I'd rather look into your eyes than this script." I dropped the bundle of papers on the table. I'd spoken before really thinking better of it, though it was true. She had the most unique eyes.

She blushed and laughed, looking a bit uncomfortable, but turned her chair to face me, so I did the same. We were close enough that I had to put my knees on either side of hers. She wore a pair of shorts, as did I, and when our skin came in contact, her gaze flicked up to meet mine.

Oh, I'd felt it, too. That little spark of something, an ember in a slow burn waiting for a gust of wind or some kindling to set it aflame. A knowing smirk spread across my face before I could help myself, which Frankie promptly ignored, instead starting in on the script.

"So were you just going to stand across the room and watch me all night, or were you actually planning to come say something to me?" She giggled like she'd had a few too many and looked up at me with half-lidded eyes. If I didn't know any better, I'd think she actually wanted me. That's how good she was.

I gave her a cocky grin. "This is the age of women's lib—I thought you girls liked to take control nowadays."

"Pfft. That's only after we've hooked you."

I arched a brow. "Oh? And how exactly do you plan on *hooking* me?"

"For starters, I'd probably give you a big smile." She smiled and looked up at me from under her thick lashes. "Then I might touch you innocently a few times by accident, but of course it would be on purpose." She leaned forward a bit and pretended like someone had bumped her from behind, then placed her hand on my chest. Looking up at me while biting her bottom lip, she ran her hand lightly down the front of my chest before she removed it. My heart began beating faster and I hoped Frankie hadn't noticed. I swallowed hard, trying to remember my next line.

"Anything else you might do?" I asked, my voice husky.

"I'd probably tilt my head to the side like this, maybe twirl my finger around my hair like this, and wait for you to kiss me." She seemed to drink me in as she gazed up at me and licked her lips.

"This has been quite the education. I think you might have snagged one." I leaned in slowly, ready to feel her lips on mine and—

"Alright! Good job, you two." Niles broke my train of thought and reminded me that, not only were we in a room full of people, but more importantly, my character didn't actually

51

kiss Frankie's character in this particular scene. I cleared my throat and sat back in my chair. "That's what I'm talking about! You really had me believing you wanted each other. Let's break for lunch. Everyone take an hour and report back here."

I looked over at Frankie, who was doing her best to avoid making eye contact with me. "You were really good there. Almost had me believing you actually liked me."

Her head whipped over to look at me. "Well, that *is* my job, you know," she said with sarcasm.

I chuckled. "True enough. Want to grab something to eat?" Most everyone had left the room by that point. Only a few stragglers remained in the doorway, discussing blocking for the scene we'd just rehearsed.

"I'm not really that hungry," she responded. "I think I'm going to go back to my trailer and relax for a bit."

I nodded. "Alright, see you in an hour then." I pushed my chair out and stood.

"Can I ask you a question?" she asked.

I turned to face Frankie and because she was still sitting, it resulted in my junk being only a couple inches from her face. She looked from my crotch to my face and back to my crotch before hurriedly pushing her chair out to stand too. The pink in her cheeks was damn adorable and I couldn't help but laugh out loud. She did the same.

"Don't worry, we're not to that scene yet."

She continued to laugh and smacked me across the arm. "Whatever."

"Hey, you're the one checking out my junk," I said with a good-natured laugh.

Her eyes expanded and her mouth dropped open. "Excuse me, but you're the one who put your junk in my face, leaving me with nowhere else to look."

I chucked her on the chin. "Whatever you need to tell yourself is fine with me, darlin.'"

She crossed her arms over her chest and cocked a hip to the side. "You may be the one laughing now, but just wait until it's time to film *that* scene. You think I did a good job of sucking you in today? You won't even know what hit you."

I stared at her, unable to speak for a moment. The images of Frankie on her knees in front of me and the words she just spoke—specifically, the part about sucking me in—were bombarding my mind. I was now a little too eager for that day of filming to arrive.

"Cat got your tongue, Calder?" She laughed again, bringing me out of my R-rated reverie.

"You're good." I ran a hand through my hair. "Now, what was it you wanted to ask me before we got sidetracked?" I needed to get us back on topic before my mind really had a field day. I had to work with her for months and then there were all the press junkets we'd have together surrounding the movie release. The last thing I needed was a case of blue balls that whole time. No thanks.

"I noticed you fiddling with something in your pocket as we ran some of the lines . . . I was just wondering what you were doing."

This conversation had gone from easygoing sexual banter to serious territory—fast. "I was playing with my sobriety chip." I reached into my pocket, grabbed it and placed it into the palm of her hand.

She held it up and turned it over to inspect it. "It's a one-day chip." She looked up at me, frowning.

"I have my other ones at home." I reached out to take it from her and put it back in my pocket. "I'm more than one day sober, don't worry."

She blew out a relieved breath. "Why do you carry this one then?"

I ran a hand through my hair. "I use it as a reminder that every day is a fresh start, a choice to live my life the right way." I looked down at my feet and toed the ground. "I know it sounds stupid, but it helps me remember to take it one day at a time."

Frankie surprised me by taking my hand in hers and squeezing it. "I think that's a really smart thing to do. That's all any of us can do really is to take one day at a time."

Her sincerity and compassion were a welcome change

from the usual judgment or pity I received. The comfort I took from our physical contact should've been a clue to me that something was building between us.

We held each other's gazes for a few beats and when she dropped my hand, the moment—the connection—was gone. "I better get to my trailer or I'm going to have no down time at all."

I cleared my throat. "Right. Well, enjoy. I'll see you in a bit."

She gave me a small smile, grabbed her script off the table, and left.

I watched her small frame disappear through the doorway and realized that there was a good chance this job was going to be even more difficult and complicated than I'd originally thought. And not for any of the reasons I'd anticipated.

chapter nine

Frankie

I closed the trailer door behind me and made my way over to the couch, plopping down on it then lying back with one hand draped over my eyes.

What the hell was that? Picking up his hand and squeezing it? I was a total moron. He probably thought I was hitting on him or something.

I couldn't deny the connection I'd felt when we were rehearsing the scene *and* when I'd been holding his hand. There was something there. And when I'd rubbed his chest? Holy hell. It'd been all I could do to keep from panting in front of a room full of people.

I pushed it out of my mind though because I was pretty sure Calder had that effect on everyone. His string of dalliances had been well documented in the tabloids. Besides, I had more pressing things to worry about anyway.

I shifted onto my side, sliding my cell phone from my back pocket and then dialing my mom.

"Hello."

"Hey, mom. It's me."

"Oh, hi honey. How's it going on set today?"

She sounded like she was in decent spirits. This was good.

"It's going really well. How are you doing?"

"I'm okay. Just trying out some new make-up I got."

"Did you call and make an appointment with Dr. Barker?"

"I'm scheduled for tomorrow."

I blew out a relieved breath. She'd been seeing her therapist, Dr. Barker, on a weekly basis, but after yesterday's meltdown I suggested she make an appointment to get in and see him right away. My mom seemed to go through periods where she was able to manage her issues, and then there were other times where her anxiety got out of control and her hoarding would ramp up. I wanted to avoid that if at all possible, and if anyone could help it was Dr. Barker. He'd been seeing her for a couple of years now and had really made a difference in her life . . . and by default, in my life as well.

"I'm glad to hear it."

"Honey, don't worry about me." She paused for a moment and let out a deep breath. "I'm sorry if I scared you yesterday," she said a little softer.

"Mom, you know I'm gonna worry about you. I hate seeing you like that."

She paused again, not saying anything. "I realize that and I'm sorry. If I could do something to make sure I never had another episode again, I would."

"I know that, mom. And you don't have to apologize. I know you're doing the best you can."

"Don't worry, Dr. Barker is going to help me get all sorted out."

"Alright. Well, I gotta go. I'm about to have to get back to work, but I'll stop in when I get home later."

"Have a good rest of the day, honey."

"You, too."

I hit 'end' on the phone, optimistic yet still cautious. She didn't seem like she was headed in a downward spiral, which hopefully meant I'd get some decent sleep tonight. I'd been up most of the night before, stressed about what challenges the day might bring.

I shoved the phone into my front pocket and rolled back over so I lay on my back. I stared up at the ceiling of the trailer for a few minutes, willing myself to relax. Finally, I inhaled a deep breath and closed my eyes.

"Frankie, Frankie." Someone was shaking me.

My eyes flew open to see Calder's face inches from my own, causing my heart to beat quickly in my chest. "What are you doing in here?" I asked, my voice still groggy.

"Everyone's waiting for you."

Confusion swarmed my mind as I tried to remember what day it was and what I was supposed to be doing. The table read. *Shit.*

I shot up and just missed whacking Calder in the head by mere inches. "Oh my God. I'm late. I'm so sorry."

He was eye level to me now, hunched down beside the couch. "No worries," he said and laughed it off.

"You've got quick reflexes." If he didn't, I probably would have broken his nose with my skull. Yeah, the studio heads would have *loved* that.

He shrugged. "It's probably from surfing."

"You surf?" I asked, my interest piqued.

"For as long as I can remember." He smiled wide, his expression so open and blissful that I knew without asking that it brought him great joy.

"I've always wanted to surf," I commented, more to myself than anything.

"Yeah?" He raised a brow.

I nodded. "Since I came out to California years ago. I've never had the time to learn though."

He frowned at that. "Maybe I'll get you out and teach you sometime."

"Sounds like fun." We sat there for a moment—me smiling at him, him smiling at me, and that feeling washed over me again. The one that left me speechless because I was so drawn to him that whatever connected my brain and my mouth seemed to have been temporarily severed. I leaned forward a bit without really thinking about what I was doing, the air around us feeling weighted with possibilities.

Calder cleared his throat and stood up, breaking our connection. I was an idiot for falling under his spell. I had no doubt he was used to countless fangirls gazing up at him with stars in their eyes. When did I start to become one of those? Maybe the idea of the two of us being friendly wasn't a good one.

"We'd better get back. I told everyone you'd mentioned having a conference call and that it probably ran over."

Shit. I was late. No time to sit here gawking at my co-star. "I appreciate that. I can't believe I fell asleep."

"Late night?" he asked and reached out his hand to help me off the couch. I pretended not to see it and got up on my own. The less physical contact between the two of us the better.

"Something like that." I ran my hands through my hair in an effort to get rid of any bedhead I might I have. "Okay, I'm good to go."

We made our way out of the trailer to the room we were in earlier. Why had I allowed myself to fall asleep? I prided myself on my professionalism. Here I'd been judging Calder, and I was the one making a room full of people wait for me. Talk about amateur hour.

chapter ten

Calder

It'd been a little more than a week since I'd been on set and things had been going pretty well. Today was my first day filming though, and that was worlds away from a table read.

We were filming the frat party scene where Frankie and my character meet. We'd nailed it during the table read so I didn't know why I was so friggin' nervous. Must be a side effect of sobriety—second-guessing everything you do.

Frankie had turned out to be the consummate professional. It was like she could snap her fingers and transform into her character at any given moment. It was no secret that she hadn't wanted to work with me so I wanted nothing more than to prove her wrong. Not because of some ego trip or anything, but because, in some strange way, I looked up to her. She was what I should have been.

I'd been born into the perfect family if you were someone who wanted to make movies for a living. And yet I'd managed to screw it up. My dad was a big-time movie director. He loved me. I know he did—he'd put up with all my antics for years. But he'd always been the kind of parent who was more comfortable throwing money at a problem, as opposed to dealing with feelings and shit. My mom and I got along just fine, but she was a continent away most of the time so there was only so much say she could have in my life.

I wanted Frankie to see that I could do this. Her opinion of me mattered, and I wanted to demonstrate to her that I wasn't who she'd first assumed me to be. I wanted her to like me, though I refused to examine the why of that statement too closely.

Speak of the devil. Or angel as it were.

Frankie walked on set, talking to one of the producers. Wearing a low-cut, skin-tight white tank top and short, hip-hugging jean skirt, she looked . . . well, she looked fucking hot as hell, to be perfectly blunt.

I hadn't seen any of her wardrobe for the production yet so this caught me by surprise, though I probably should have expected it given that she was playing a hard-partying college girl. I'm sure that's all it was. Frankie had always looked striking—at least every time I'd seen her. But she normally veered more toward the classy side so I'd never seen her dressed quite so . . . revealing.

Not that I was complaining. She wasn't particularly well endowed, but I still found the small swell of her breasts difficult to take my eyes off of.

Fuck. I glanced up to her eyes and realized she'd caught me looking. I sheepishly smiled at her as she made her way over to me.

"Hey," I said, sounding like the slack-jawed Neanderthal my ogling had implied I was.

"Hey yourself." She gave me a small smile.

"You look . . ." I trailed off, unsure what to say without putting my foot in my mouth.

She put a hand up, motioning for me to stop. "Yeah, I know. I had to squeeze myself into this outfit. I didn't even know I had these." She pointed to her chest and giggled.

I laughed, thankful she was making light of my blatant perusal of her assets.

Niles approached us and saved me from having to respond. "Alright guys, you ready to do this?" We both nodded. "I just want to go over the scene blocking with you and then we'll bring in the extras and start shooting."

After we'd figured out where our marks were, the extras came in and we were ready to roll tape. I tried swallowing my nerves and pushing them from the forefront of my mind, but it proved to be an impossible feat. I had so much riding on this movie and I knew Frankie did, too. Hell, everyone here did. I didn't want to be the reason—yet again—that someone walked away hurt and disappointed.

A heavy feeling pressed down on my chest making it difficult to breath. I'd been doing well handling the stress up to this point. I'd either surfed, gone to my AA or NA meetings, talked to my sponsor . . . whatever it took. But the urge to toss back a few shots was almost overwhelming in that moment. As we waited for the cameramen to set up, I reached into my pocket for my sobriety chip, trying to draw strength from the knowledge that only *I* could control my emotions and my stress responses.

"Quiet on set," Niles yelled. Everyone stopped murmuring and the second assistant cameraman walked into the scene with the clapperboard.

"Scene three, take one." *Whack.*

"Action," Niles said.

The extras started bopping around and dancing like they were partying hard to music, when in actuality it was completely quiet on the set. Frankie strutted across the room to a table set up with liquor bottles that likely contained nothing more than colored water. It was the first I'd noticed the booze. I stood unmoving, unable to look away.

"Cut," Niles yelled. "Someone grab Calder a cup. He's a college kid at a frat party. Where the hell's his drink?"

A production assistant rushed to pour a "drink" from one of the bottles on the table into a red Solo cup and handed it over to me.

I gulped. Sweat broke out on my brow and my heart started racing. I tried to draw in a deep breath without making it obvious.

"Quiet on the set."

"Scene three, take two." *Whack.*

Just like the last time, everyone started moving around and silently partying. Frankie once again strutted across the dance floor and I tried focusing on the sway of her ass and hips to help me get into character, but the red Solo cup felt as if it weighed a thousand pounds in my hand.

Frankie reached the table, mixed herself a drink, and turned to face me. She leaned against the table, stirring her drink with a straw and giving me a sultry look. It was almost enough to distract me, but the bottles behind her might as well have had glowing neon signs on them.

I pretended to sip my drink and walked over to her, the way that'd been discussed earlier. I managed to hit my mark—I didn't manage to remember my line.

"So, were you just going to stand across the room . . ." I trailed off and Frankie looked up at me expectantly. *Fuck.*

"Cut!" Niles moved from behind the camera. "Everything okay, Calder?"

I felt like such a fucking idiot. First scene and I was already causing issues. "Yeah, sorry. I'm fine. Just first-day jitters. I'm good now." I dug my hand in my pocket, turning my sobriety chip over and over and over, trying to calm myself.

"Okay. Good." He nodded and turned away from us to bark orders at the crew about getting the scene set up again.

I pursed my lips and made eye contact with Frankie. "Sorry," I said, chagrined.

She looked at me with concern in her bright eyes and then her gaze darted down to my hand in my pocket. Placing her fingers around my wrist, she squeezed, her big eyes full of sincerity. "You've got this, Calder. You do. I know it's probably hard pretending you're in a party environment, but you can do this."

Frankie had no idea how much her words of support meant to me. She removed her hand from my wrist and nodded, giving me a small smile.

"Thanks. I needed that," I said.

"Quiet on the set," Niles yelled. I walked back over to my mark for the beginning of the scene.

"Scene three, take three." *Whack.*

The scene began again like it should, only this time instead of absorbing everything else going on around me, I focused on Frankie. There was nothing else in front of me except this remarkable woman, who was giving me fuck-me eyes while wearing too little clothing.

This time when I approached her, I was completely in character. I gave her my practiced smile, the one I knew had gotten me inside many a woman before, and delivered all my lines to perfection.

I had the same reaction to Frankie's character flaunting her attraction to me as I'd had during the table read. By the time the final line was delivered, I was dealing with a semi in my pants.

"And . . . cut! That was great, you guys," Niles said. "Let's do it another time, but I want to get some close-ups this time around."

I exhaled in relief. With one good take under my belt, I finally began to settle into my character and just go with it, rather than analyzing and overthinking every single thing I was doing.

Frankie reached forward and gave my hand a squeeze. "See—I told you you could do it."

Yes, she had been the one to believe in me when I was close to not believing in myself. I smiled at her before returning to my mark, pretending that wasn't a complete and utter mindfuck for me.

chapter eleven

Frankie

"You have arrived at your destination."

I turned off the GPS feature on my phone and tossed it into my purse, which lay open on my passenger seat, the contents almost spilling out. I gripped the steering wheel like it was a dark and stormy night plucked right out of a horror movie—not like it was a sunny and warm California day on the Malibu coast.

It was our day off and Calder and I had decided to run lines together again. The remainder of our week filming together had gone better than I could have ever hoped. He'd been nervous at first and had flubbed his lines but soon found his rhythm, becoming the character and fully embodying all of the emotions each scene required. We were able to feed off one another's energy to deliver some really powerful moments.

So when Calder invited me over to his beach house to run lines with him, I should have said no. He really didn't need the practice. But something stopped me from saying it. Before I'd even given it much thought, 'yes' had come tumbling from my mouth.

"Are you going to sit out there all day?" Calder's amused voice reverberated through the speaker above the gates where I was idling.

Embarrassment warmed my face. He'd obviously been

watching me for a while. "Sorry," I said through my open window. "I was just double-checking my phone to make sure I had the right address," I lied.

He chuckled. *Buzz.* The gates in front of me began opening slowly. "You've got the right place. Come on in."

God, he made me nervous. Well, *he* didn't make me nervous. My reaction to him did.

I was in the perfect position to launch my career into the big time and aligning myself with someone like Calder wouldn't be smart. Sure, I now could see that there was much more to him than the "bad boy" the press portrayed him as, but perception was reality—at least in the entertainment business. Besides, Calder didn't strike me as a one-woman kind of guy, and I was most certainly a one-man kind of girl.

With clammy palms on the steering wheel, I drove through the gates and parked in front of a contemporary-style, white concrete home. I grabbed my bag off the seat and made my way up the stairs to the front door. Calder was already there waiting for me, dressed in a pair of shorts with a white graphic t-shirt stretched across his muscular chest. It was a definite effort to keep my eyes on his face and not let them dip down to sneak another peek.

He smiled at me, looking relaxed and in his element this close to the water—like at any minute he would pull his t-shirt over his head, grab a board, and head into the ocean. Or maybe the shirtless part was just wishful thinking.

"You find the place okay?" he asked, stepping back to let me through the door.

"Yup, Siri had no trouble."

He chuckled. "Thank God for technology, right?"

"I'd be lost without her . . . it?" I laughed. "I dunno . . . when I first moved to L.A., I used it any time I'd go anywhere on my own. Even if I'd already been there a bunch of times before."

"Can't say I blame you. L.A. can be a viper pit—wouldn't want to end up in the wrong area." His eyes clouded for a second, and though it was just for a second, I caught it nonetheless.

Eager to change the course of our conversation, I glanced around the beach house. It was as contemporary in design on the inside as it was on the outside with a wall of glass overlooking a large deck that sat high above the ocean. The sunlight gleamed off the relatively calm waters of the Pacific. It was open concept with the kitchen set farthest away from the glass walls but exposed to the entire main floor living/dining room area. I did okay money-wise, but I was nowhere close to being able to afford a place like this. Yet. "Nice place you have here."

"It's not mine. My dad rented it for me when I got out of rehab . . . thought it would be good if I wasn't close to my regular haunts."

Shit. I'd unknowingly stumbled into that one. "That was thoughtful of him, I guess." I didn't know what Calder's relationship with his father was like. He never talked about him on set unless someone else brought him up, and even then the conversation always revolved around the films his dad had worked on.

Calder rubbed the back of his neck with one hand and it bunched up the muscles in bicep. "I think he meant well, it's just . . ."

He trailed off and though I shouldn't have pushed him to finish, I couldn't seem to help myself. I wanted to know more about this man.

"It's just . . . ?"

"Aw hell, at least come have a seat before I bare my soul to you," he said half in jest as he walked over to the living area. The massive glass had been pushed to each side, allowing a warm ocean breeze and the sound of the waves to filter in.

I took a seat on the large beige couch and Calder sat down beside me. I was keenly aware of his proximity, his leg only inches from my own.

"My dad and I have an okay relationship. When my mom moved to Europe, I stayed here with him. I don't know . . . he tends to throw money at his problems. I guess that's what has always worked for him in the past." He shrugged like it wasn't a big deal, but the tightness around his eyes gave him away.

"What do you mean that's what worked for him in the past?"

"When he and my mom split, he paid her to go away. If he has any legal problems, he pays to make them disappear. Calder screws up and needs rehab? He pays. He needs to keep me out of the press? He pays to set me up here."

I put my hand on his knee and squeezed. "I'm sure your father really was concerned about you keeping your distance from temptation." I was going for reassurance, but the moment I made contact with him, the air around us became charged with tension. Of the sexual variety.

Calder stared down at where my hand was placed on his leg, though he didn't say anything. Self-conscious, I pulled my hand away and brought it to my lap.

I was quickly falling under Calder's spell and I knew—I *knew*—he wasn't aiming for it. On more than one occasion when we'd been locked in an intimate gaze, he'd pulled away, looking more than uncomfortable.

He bounded up off the couch and headed straight for the kitchen. And there it was again.

"Can I get you something to drink?" he asked, looking back at me with one hand on the stainless-steel fridge door.

"What do you have?"

"Well, let's see. There's a plethora of juices, water, soda . . . nothing stronger than that, I'm afraid." He chuckled lightly and pointed to himself. "Recovering addict and all." Calder tried to play it off, but it was apparent there was a level of shame he always carried with him.

"I'll take some juice—orange juice if you have it."

"One orange juice and one strawberry-kiwi juice coming right up."

He went about his business in the kitchen and I used the opportunity to study him. The muscles under the bronzed skin of his arms flexed as he pulled the glasses out of the cupboard and began to pour. I knew he was only pouring juice, but all of his movements were so fluid—graceful yet somehow still powerful.

I pretended to be looking at my phone when I saw him pick up both glasses to head back into the living area. "Here you are," he said, passing me the orange juice.

I took a sip and set it down on the table in front of me. Calder sat back down on the couch beside me, a little closer than was comfortable. I was acutely aware of the mere inches separating his thigh from my own.

Get a grip. It wasn't like I hadn't been this close to him on set when we were filming. There was something different though when you were doing your job with a bunch of witnesses watching your every move. I knew what to expect—knew what his character would say next, when he was supposed to touch me and how. This was unchartered territory and I didn't wing it well.

I cleared my throat and leaned over to grab my script out of the bag I'd brought with me. "Any scene in particular you'd like to start with?" I asked.

"I know we joked about it before, but I do think we should work on the scene where they first kiss."

I blinked rapidly but didn't say anything for a minute. "Oh . . . um, okay." I set my script on my lap and leaned forward to grab my glass, taking a sip of my juice.

"Haven't you ever kissed a co-star before?" I coughed, choking on my juice momentarily. "While filming, I mean."

"Uh, yeah." I set the glass back down on the table.

"Well, it'll be just like that. No difference."

My eyes widened. Sure, no difference. *Yeah, right.* "Okay then . . ."

Calder chuckled in a half amused, half cocky way that made me want to smack the self-assured smirk off his face. "I can tell you're nervous, Frankie. We don't have to actually kiss, but it's an important scene for your character. This is where she makes the decision to be with me and pretend that everything in her life is normal." I swallowed past the lump in my throat as it dawned on me how my own life was imitating art in that sense. "It's the catalyst for the entire story," he finished, squeezing my knee in the process. I was able to feel exactly where his fingertips had pressed into my skin, even after he removed his hand.

He had a point. Although my character had tried picking up Calder's character at a frat party, she was only ever looking for quick hook-ups, finding that was the key to keeping her mental health issues hidden. This scene where she gave herself wholeheartedly to a man was a leap of faith for her.

"You're right. Okay, let's start there." I thumbed through my script until I found the right spot.

"All set?" he asked with a dazzling smile.

"As ready as I'll ever be."

We'd been running the scene for a bit, trying some different things, improvising on some lines, changing our voices to see what we thought worked best. We hadn't even made it to the part where we were supposed to kiss yet.

"Let's run that last section right before the kiss again. I think we have everything up until that point down, and I liked what you did that last time," Calder said. I was surprised at how focused and serious he was. I'm not sure why, since I'd seen him on set. Maybe it was because, for the most part, he came off as being really easygoing, like not much fazed him.

"Alright. You start off." I nodded at him to let him know I was ready.

"I'm not interested in just a night or two with you. I already know that part will be insane. I want to explore what's in here." Calder placed his hand over my heart, just above my breast. "I want to see what this connection between us can be."

"I don't know what you're talking about," I snapped at him, pulling his hand from me and flinging it down in between us.

"You can keep trying to lie to yourself, but I know you feel it. And if the only way for me to get you to admit it is to not sleep with you, to not kiss you . . . as much as it's torture for me, too . . . that's what I'll do."

"You're imagining things." I crossed my arms over my chest.

"I'm not and you know it." He cocked an eyebrow at me.

I sighed and dropped my arms to my side. "How can you

be so sure?" I whispered, letting the vulnerable side of my character show.

"Before my mom passed away, she told me I'd know when I met 'the one.' She said it won't be like it is with anyone else. I won't be able to get that person out of my head, that no matter how much time I spend with her, it won't ever seem like enough. That there will be some invisible force drawing us together."

I watched as Calder leaned in, not all the way, but enough that I found myself leaning toward him, too. His eyes became hooded and I licked my lips as the distance between us closed even more. He bent his head and started to shut his eyes—

I popped up off the couch. "Why don't we take a break?"

Calder exhaled and ran a hand through his hair. "What did you have in mind?" He pushed himself off the couch to stand in front of me.

My body was still buzzing with his proximity to me. I spun around to gaze out the window. "I didn't really have anything in mind, but I could use a breather." I didn't add that it was because I'd been in danger of hopping onto his lap and throwing myself at him.

He came to stand beside me for a moment, hands on his hips, staring out at the ocean. "Let's go surfing."

"Surfing?"

"Yeah, surfing. I remember you said you wanted to learn. I can teach you."

Visions of Calder shirtless, inches away from my body in the water, had my heart thumping inside my ribcage. "You don't have to teach me."

"I want to. It'll be fun."

I shook my head. "I'm not sure you'll think it's so fun when we're an hour in and I can't even manage to stand up on my surfboard."

He shrugged. "No one is perfect their first go-round. Doesn't mean it can't be fun."

"I don't have anything to wear. I didn't bring a swimsuit."

He pursed his lips for a moment. "I have an idea. Follow

me."

I trailed behind him as he led me out onto the spacious deck. The sound of the waves meeting the shore was even louder here. It was relaxing and made me forget why it was a bad idea to go surfing with Calder.

At the corner of the deck was a small pool house. Calder opened the door and switched a light on inside. There were some pool equipment and chemicals on a couple of the shelves, what appeared to be some deflated beach toys, and hooks on one wall with several different wetsuits hanging from them.

Calder pulled one down at a time, holding them away from his body to examine them, then returned them to the hook if they weren't what he was looking for. It was a minute before he found one he liked and tossed it over his shoulder. "Looks like this one will fit you."

"What am I supposed to wear underneath?" I asked, skepticism ringing out in my tone.

"Wear your bra and underwear. They'll stay dry." He paused for a moment and a lopsided grin spread across his face while his eyes got a wicked gleam in them. "I'm assuming you're not going commando right now?" He arched a brow.

I matched his grin and leaned forward to pull the wetsuit from his broad shoulder. "Wouldn't you like to know."

I left Calder gaping behind me in the pool house while I went to change.

chapter twelve

Calder

We arrived at Zuma Beach and I still couldn't help but wonder whether Frankie had been joking about the commando thing or not. We'd chatted back and forth on the way down here, but it was never far from my mind.

Frankie stood behind the Jeep now and I passed her the surfboard she'd be using today. The wetsuit fit her like a damn glove, showcasing her petite curves and firm, slender body. I tried not to stare too hard at her. I was probably creeping her out.

Grabbing my surfboard, I turned to face her. "We'll start out on the sand and I'll show you how to get up on the board. Then we'll head out into the water." She pursed her lips and gave me a quick nod. "Don't be nervous." I reached out and squeezed her hand.

Her gaze shot up to meet my own and she held it for a beat then smiled and pulled her hand away.

Right. That probably wasn't the smartest thing to do when I was trying to keep my distance from her.

We walked across the cement parking lot until we reached the warm sand of the beach. I tossed my board down and motioned for Frankie to do the same.

She followed suit and put her hands on her hips, surveying

the board like it was an object from another world. "So . . . where do we start?" she asked.

"First thing I'm going to have you do is get down on your stomach on the board. See that line that runs down the middle?" She nodded. "I want you to center your body with that line. You've gotta be far enough down on the board so that your toes touch the back of it. That's your sweet spot."

"Alright, that I can do." She glanced over to my board lying a few feet away from her own. "Why is my board so much longer than yours?"

"I have a shortboard. You're learning on a long board—they're easier to paddle and since it's wider, it'll be easier for you to balance once you get up."

"Ha. *If* I get up. And that's a big *if*."

I shook my head with a grin on my face. "Oh no. We're not leaving here until you get up on that board. It doesn't have to be for long, but you will get up. I've never had a student fail on me and you won't be the first."

I saw her body stiffen at my remark. "Taught a lot of girls to surf, have you?" She'd tried to keep her voice casual, but there was an underlying tension to her words.

"You're the first, actually. It's only ever been buddies of mine in the past."

"Oh."

Before I was able to respond, the sound of a dog barking dragged my attention away from Frankie to the beach behind me.

A chocolate lab was bounding across the sand toward us. Hendrix was running behind it, trying to keep up. When the duo reached us, it made a dash right for Frankie, jumping up on its hind legs, leaning against her, tail wagging and tongue hanging out. Smart dog.

She used both hands to scratch behind the dog's ears. "Aren't you sweet," she said to the dog, a huge grin on her face.

"Who's this?" I asked.

"That's my partner in crime, Zeppelin. I use him to talk to chicks on the beach." He wagged his eyebrows in good-natured humor.

"Frankie, this is Hendrix. Hendrix, Frankie." I motioned between the two of them.

Frankie laughed. "You mean to tell me your name is Hendrix and you named your dog *Zeppelin?*" She laughed even harder now.

"A little cliché, isn't it?" I ribbed him, joining Frankie in her laughter.

"What can I say? My parents were seventies rock fans and it extended to me by way of osmosis." He shrugged but was smiling.

"What are you guys smoking up there in Canada?" I taunted him.

"Huh. Says *you.*" It struck me for a moment that he was right. "Shit. I'm sorry, man. I didn't even think—"

"Don't worry about it," I reassured him. "I walked right into that one."

Frankie looked between the two of us, biting her lip, seeming unsure as to how I would react to the dig.

"Still, I feel like an asshole."

Right at that moment, the dog let out the biggest fart and the tension that lay thick over us vanished.

"Ew, Zeppelin. What are you feeding this dog?" Frankie teased, stepping away from the dog and holding her nose.

We all laughed. "He sure knows how to charm them," I said.

Hendrix just shook his head in dismay. "I gotta jet. Have to meet my agent to discuss a sponsorship opportunity. It was good to meet you, Frankie."

"Likewise," she said, her forehead crinkled in confusion.

"Hendrix competes in motocross." I motioned to him with my head.

"Competes? Ha! I'm two-time reigning champion of the X Games," he said with a voice full of pride.

"Wow. That's impressive," she said. Hopefully she didn't think it was *too* impressive.

He turned his attention to me. "Hit me up next week.

Maybe we can get together and hang out."

I nodded. "Sure thing. I'm on set all week, but we can probably work something out." I paused for a second, wondering if I should extend the olive branch further. "You're welcome to come by and check it out if you want."

"Yeah, come on by," Frankie encouraged.

He shrugged. "Sounds good. I've never been on a real live movie set before. Might be cool to see what it's all about."

"Awesome. I'll touch base with you next week then," I said.

"Perfect. It was good to meet you, Frankie."

"Likewise," she said.

"Come on, Zeppelin." He waved the dog over and the serial licker complied, following Hendrix as he jogged away.

I looked at Frankie with a big smile on my face. She'd told me how much she'd always wanted to learn to surf and I was happy that I got to be the one to teach her. "Ready to do this?" I asked.

"I guess." She crouched down and lay on her stomach on the board.

Damn. She really did have a nice ass. I shouldn't be looking but it was staring up and taunting me, wrapped in the tight wetsuit material. "Okay, there's four steps. First, put your hands right next to your chest then push all the way up." I demonstrated with my hands and she did the same. "Now go back on your knees, bring your front foot forward, leave your back foot where it is and stand up on it."

I demonstrated the action on my own board and Frankie studied my movements with intensity. "You give it a shot now," I said, getting up off my board.

She did pretty well, though she'd need to be more comfortable with her movements and make them more fluid to stand a chance of getting up on the board. I glanced down to her feet then walked over so that I stood directly behind her. Without thinking, I wrapped an arm around her waist from behind and leaned into her so I was able to move the inside of her feet with one of mine.

"Spread your feet a little farther apart and make sure the

line on the board is in the middle of your feet. Now bend your knees."

She did so before I could remove my hand from her and back up, causing that fine ass I'd been admiring earlier to push into my pelvis. Frankie inhaled sharply when she made contact. We stood locked in that position for a minute, both of our chests rising and falling from our heavy breathing.

"Is that it?" she asked in a small voice.

I dropped my hand from her waist and stepped back, adjusting myself in the process. "Uh, yeah, just put your arms out for balance and that's it," I said to the back of her head.

"Got it. Arms beside my chest, push up, lean back, then stand up, arms out." She sounded like she was giving herself a pep talk. It was somewhat adorable.

"Let's try and do it all in one motion this time."

I made her practice over and over again, to the point that I think she was ready to tell me to piss off if we didn't step foot in the ocean soon. I relented finally and told her to grab her board and head in.

She smiled widely, which simultaneously made me want to smile and left a heavy feeling in my chest because I shouldn't— and couldn't—do anything about it.

chapter thirteen

Frankie

This was so friggin' frustrating. Clearly, I wasn't born to surf. I must've tried to get up on the damn board at least thirty times, and every time I ended up falling into the ocean, spewing water from my mouth when I finally made it back above the surface.

"Relax, Frankie. It's not an easy thing to do. Being tense and frustrated isn't going to help you," Calder said.

Deep down I knew he was right, but I was a perfectionist by nature and it irked me that I was unable to get the hang of it. I turned my head to face Calder. He hopped off his own board and swam over to stand behind me, holding my board so he could help me try to catch a wave. "I'm so close and I just can't get it. It's maddening."

"Here. Put your hands on top of the board. You need to relax." I did as he asked and before I knew what was happening, his hands were on my shoulders massaging me. "Your muscles are so tense. You'll catch your wave. You've got the movements down, just try not to overthink it."

It was hard *not* to be tense. His hands felt like a brand on me. I both reveled in the feeling and wanted to pull away, sure that this exquisite torture would end in pain somehow.

"Alright," he said, removing his hands after a minute. "You're good now. This time, try it without being inside your head so much. Feel the board underneath you. Feel—don't think."

I nodded and hopped on my board, lying on my stomach and exhaling a deep breath, releasing all of my pent-up frustration, both sexual and otherwise. I deployed the same technique I normally did when on set before a take. I emptied my mind and let instinct guide me.

A large swell was coming up behind me and Calder gave me a small push, letting go of the board at just the right moment. "Go, go!"

I pushed up on my arms and leaned back on my knees then wobbled a little but managed to catch my balance. I used my hands to push up from the board slowly, coming to a crouched position on my board . . . and I stayed there.

Exhilaration raced through my body as I traveled along the top of the wave. Wind and saltwater spray whipped across my face as I teetered using my outstretched arms for balance. I couldn't believe I'd finally managed to do it. I was so filled with joy it felt almost as if I would burst.

I turned my head to smile excitedly at Calder. He was swimming toward the shore, watching me with a huge child-like grin across his face. I threw my hands up over my head in a victory motion and promptly lost my balance and fell into the ocean.

That would teach me to think I'd conquered Mother Nature.

I could barely touch the bottom where I was, so when I emerged from the water I swam the short distance to my surfboard, crawled up on it, and straddled my legs around it.

Calder reached me moments later looking as happy as I'd ever seen him in the short time we'd gotten reacquainted with one another.

"That was killer," he said and hefted himself up onto the surfboard so he sat facing me, straddling it too. I used my hands to balance on the board as he climbed on so I didn't embarrass myself and fall off. Calder's surfboard was attached to the rope strapped to his ankle and bobbed in the water beside us. "You did awesome. If you hadn't turned to look at me, you would've ridden that one to the shore." He leaned forward to hug me, closing the gap between us. It was a friendly hug, and I returned it by wrapping my arms around his muscular back. He stiffened and it made the already hard back muscles under my hands even harder. The mood quickly transformed from jubilation to one fraught with sexual tension and need.

I pulled back but Calder's arms remained around me, and I found my face inches from his. I stared into those eyes that were bluer than the water we were floating on, my breath heavy in my chest, and he returned my gaze with half-lidded eyes. My heartbeat had picked up its pace and my breathing had become shallow.

I moved my hand up to his long, blond hair, which was matted to the side of his face, and played with it between my fingers. I'd never really been attracted to a guy with longer hair—until Calder.

His hand cupped my jaw. "Frankie . . ." he trailed off in a husky whisper then brought his mouth to mine in a gentle kiss. I was surprised that someone with his physical strength could manage something so tender.

My eyes darted up to his in surprise and his blue irises seemed to be questioning whether or not it was okay to do it again. I gave only the slightest of head nods and he leaned in again, pressing his lips to mine with the same soft touch but holding them there longer this time.

I pushed my fingers into the wet, sunkissed strands of his hair. He moaned, deep vibrations coming from his chest, and the tension between us snapped. Within seconds, his tongue pushed into my mouth and my other hand ran over his back, delighting in the feel of his hard muscles flexing underneath the wetsuit fabric as he ran his hands up and down my sides.

He tasted like saltwater and spearmint, and I vaguely remembered him chewing gum on the way over. My insides heated at the way he took ownership of the kiss, leading our tongues in a perfectly choreographed dance. The surfboard undulated below us as the ocean brought us closer to shore. As the wind picked up, a large wave jostled us, forcing our mouths apart.

We both sat there straddling the board, gazing upon each other with heated eyes. I swear the rims of his irises were darker than I'd seen them before.

A beat later, Calder broke the spell, squeezing my shoulder in a friendly gesture with a casual smile on his face. "Ready to do that again?"

"Yeah, sure," I said, a little disappointed that he was referring to the surfing and not the kiss. His quick transition from a heated, lust-filled moment to this 'best buddies' attitude had left me confused.

I was able to get up on my board a few more times before fatigue set in. I wasn't particularly out of shape, though I didn't have the fitness level Calder seemed to. He'd been in the water as long as I had and didn't have any less energy than when we'd first set foot on the ocean's sandy bottom.

I finally begged off, feeling bad that he'd spent so much time schooling me when I was sure he was eager to ride the waves himself.

I sat on the sand with my towel wrapped around me, enjoying the feeling of my sore muscles and the exhaustion that plagued them. And though my body may have been content being sedentary, my mind was far from it. I was happy Calder had shifted gears after our kiss and not made it into a big deal. It was a one-off. I needed to keep my head in the game and remember I had a job to do. I couldn't afford to get caught up in him. There wasn't room in my life for a wild card like Calder Fox.

Instead of dwelling on it, I leaned back on my hands and watched as his powerful body navigated the surfboard over the top of the waves. This man belonged on the water. Sure, he had the California surfer boy good looks, but it was obvious this was something special for him—that it both exhilarated him and brought him an inner peace that seemed difficult for him to find otherwise.

My thoughts were confirmed as he emerged from the water and jogged toward me across the sand. The lines of tension normally etched into his forehead and around the corners of his eyes were absent, his blue orbs sparkling with delight and pure contentment.

"That's it for today?" I asked. He really hadn't been out there that long.

I held out a towel for him. He took it and sat down beside me with his arms draped over his knees. "I feel bad leaving you out here to watch. Besides, I forgot to bring something to pull my hair back."

A warm sensation filled my chest at his thoughtfulness. The hair sounded like an excuse to me, so I was pretty sure he'd left the happy home of the ocean because of me. Although I relished the feeling, it was a little unnerving too.

"You didn't need to worry about me. I enjoyed watching you out there. It's clear you've been doing it for a long time."

"Yeah, but you must be getting hungry. We haven't eaten all day."

Now that he mentioned it, I *could* go for something to eat. Regardless, I didn't want to go out somewhere to eat with Calder. That would be asking for trouble. I'd been paying more attention to the tabloids since we'd started working together to make sure Calder was on the straight and narrow. I knew they still followed him around and I didn't need the attention that a picture of the two of us together would produce, knowing the media would spin it into a torrid affair. The paparazzi seemed to be just lying in wait, like wolves stalking their prey, for Calder to relapse.

"What did you have in mind?" I asked.

"There's a restaurant not too far from the beach house that has some awesome Mexican. We could get takeout."

Takeout. Perfect. "Sounds like a plan." I didn't think I'd make the drive all the way from Malibu back to L.A. without something in my stomach.

"Let's go rinse off in the beach shower, and then we can get going." Calder rose from the sand and stood over me, drying his hair with his towel in one hand. I had the fleeting thought that this must be what he looked like drying off after a shower—minus the wetsuit—and I felt my cheeks heat.

He reached out with his other hand to help me up and I took it, ignoring how much I liked the physical contact.

He gave me the once-over when I was standing. "I think you might've gotten a little too much sun. Your cheeks are red."

Unable to help myself, I giggled. "Could be," I said as we headed off to the car.

chapter fourteen

Calder

"Oh my God, I'm so stuffed." Frankie sank back into the kitchen chair and patted her stomach.

By the time we'd arrived back at my place and finished the Mexican food, I'd managed to get the memory of kissing Frankie to stop playing on a continuous loop in my head. Just barely, though. Riding the waves had done me good, no doubt. But as soon as I was jogging toward her on the beach afterward, the sensation of having Frankie's lips on my own was front and center in my mind again.

"The best, right?"

"For sure. I don't think I'll be able to move for another two hours," she said with a laugh.

I tried not to put too much hope in that statement. I'd enjoyed hanging with Frankie today—more than I'd enjoyed being with anyone in longer than I could remember. It was almost a foreign feeling to me, the contentment of being in someone's company who seemed to genuinely enjoy being in mine. Not because I was the son of a famous director and actress, but because I was me.

Frankie stretched her hands above her head, showcasing a strip of bare skin where her shirt had ridden up. She yawned, and then when she realized I was watching, her face flushed and she put her hand over her mouth.

I raised an eyebrow. "Must be the scintillating conversation?"

"I'm so sorry. No, I think it's just that my body has about had it after all the time we spent in the water today."

I'd like to have Frankie's body.

Jesus. Where did that come from? Get a grip, Fox. "Are you driving back to L.A. tonight?" I asked, attempting to keep my mind from wandering too far down that path.

She yawned again and her green eyes watered a bit. "Yeah, my place is there."

I nodded, two quick jerks as the tension in my jaw intensified. I pictured Frankie tired, driving in the dark down the Pacific Coast Highway and nodding off at the wheel. My stomach clenched as the image of a car wreck seized all rational thought. I knew I was projecting. I realized the likelihood of that happening wasn't that great, but it didn't abate the dread coursing through me.

"Maybe you should stay here for the night," I remarked as casually as I could muster, what with my balls all the way in my stomach.

Now she looked as panicked as I felt. "There's no reason to. I'm okay to drive."

"Look at you. You can't stop yawning. L.A. is over an hour away—and that's only if there's no traffic." As if by my command, she yawned again. "See?" I crossed my arms over my chest and it didn't escape my notice that she regarded them for a moment.

"I can't stay here. I don't have any of my overnight stuff with me." She crossed her arms over her own chest and quirked an eyebrow.

"You can borrow one of my t-shirts and a pair of shorts, if you like." I paused for a moment. "You don't strike me as a glam girl that needs all your lotions and potions to survive the night."

She dropped her arms to her sides and pushed her chair away from the table to stand. "Gee, thanks."

Fucking foot-in-mouth disease. I swear I'd been suffering from it since I'd gotten sober. Frankie was making her way over to the coffee table in the living room, probably to retrieve her purse, but I caught up with her before she got that far. I grabbed her arm above the elbow and she spun to face me.

"Please, Frankie. Don't drive home by yourself tonight. I just . . . if anything ever happened, I couldn't live with myself. I'm only trying to look out for you."

I practically sounded like I was begging, but I didn't give a shit. It was all true. I needed to know she was safe.

She swallowed hard, those green eyes wide with a touch of concern in them. "Okay," she nodded. "I'll stay. I can see that it's important to you."

I blew out a deep sigh of relief. "Thank you."

She nodded, still seeming a little unsure. "Since I'm staying, did you want to watch a movie or something before bed?"

Damn. Hearing Frankie say that word and the implication that we'd both be headed to sleep in the same bed at the same time had my dick twitching in my pants.

I cleared my throat. "Yeah, sounds good to me. Let me go pop some popcorn and then we can pick something. Unless you're full?" A smile lit up her face like I'd just told her she'd won an Oscar. "What?" I asked, perplexed.

"I'm never too full for popcorn," she said.

"Right? You can't watch a movie—"

"—and not eat popcorn," she finished for me.

I stood grinning at her like a fucking idiot for a bit before she broke the spell.

"I'll go see what our options are." She gave me a small sort-of smile and turned to make her way to the couch.

"Perfect," I said, not really sure if I was saying it *to* her or *about* her.

chapter fifteen

Frankie

"You ready to turn in?"

My eyes snapped open to see Calder standing over me as I lay on the couch. Jeez. This guy was forever finding me asleep on couches. I must have dozed off for a minute near the end of the movie.

"Clearly." I laughed a bit and pushed up off the couch. Calder stepped back to give me room to get up.

"Come on. I'll get you something to sleep in."

I followed him to the stairs and tried not to pay attention to the way his shorts gripped his muscular ass as he made his way up the steps. He turned his head to look at me about half-way up and almost caught me sneaking a peek. "There is one thing I forgot to mention . . ."

I may have been half asleep, but I could tell by his tone of voice that I wasn't going to like whatever he 'forgot to mention.'

"And that is . . ."

We reached the top of the stairs and he led me into what was obviously the master bedroom. A large California king bed was centered on one wall with dark mahogany night tables on either side. A sleek chaise lounge sat in one corner of the room, which was warm and inviting in a sleek, modern beach house way.

Calder turned toward me, hands on his hips, his face grim.

"There's only one bed."

It's possible my jaw actually did hit the floor. "How can that be?"

"It's only a two-bedroom house, and when I got here I turned the other bedroom into a gym." He shrugged. "Working out helps clear my mind . . . keeps me between the lines."

My ire deflated with that comment. "So what are we going to do?"

"I can sleep on the couch. No worries."

I felt a little like an idiot and a lot like a priss. The bed was huge—it wasn't like I'd be pressed up against his body all night.

Unfortunately.

No. Not unfortunately. Besides, we were both adults. This wasn't *that* big of a deal.

"You don't have to do that."

Calder raised his hands in a placating gesture. "I don't want you to be uncomfortable, Frankie."

"I'm fine. We're adults. No biggie." I shrugged, almost believing my nonchalance myself.

"You're sure?" He ducked his head down a bit and looked at me from under his brows.

I nodded. "I will need to borrow a t-shirt or something, though."

"That I can do." He walked over to a dresser, rummaged through it for a minute, and pulled out a shirt for me. "Here, wear this one. I can grab you some shorts, but I have a feeling they'll just end up on the floor anyway."

My eyes flared at his words and my skin heated.

"That came out *so* wrong." He laughed, his face taking on a slight pink tinge. "I meant that they'd slip right off. Not because of me. I wouldn't be taking them off or anything. It's just, your waist is so tiny and my shorts . . ."

I chuckled. "That's okay, Calder. Quit while you're ahead."

"Probably a good idea," he said.

He tossed the shirt to me and I walked to the door where I'd spied the ensuite bathroom. Once inside, I stripped my shirt and bra off and slipped Calder's t-shirt over my head. I pulled the cotton fabric up to my nose and inhaled.

Mmm. It smelled just like him—like ocean and outdoors. I took a moment to enjoy it without him knowing what I was doing.

Alright, this was getting creepy. I let the shirt fall. There was such a discrepancy in our sizes that his t-shirt ended up skirting my knees. I debated whether or not I should remove my shorts. Calder had said no funny business and the truth was, I believed him. Plus, the t-shirt went down past my shorts so Calder wouldn't be getting a view of anything anyway. I unbuttoned my shorts and shimmied them down my legs, then folded my clothes and left them in a neat pile on the marble counter.

I opened the door to find him beside the bed. He had one hand on the white comforter like he was about to crawl underneath. His head snapped up and he dropped the comforter when his eyes locked on me.

If I'd been holding anything, I would've dropped it too.

He stood there wearing only fitted grey boxer briefs with a prominent bulge and the expanse of his tanned, muscular chest on full display. Every female part of me was left wanting with desire, but I was finally able to rip my gaze away.

He stood stock-still, staring at me with heavy-lidded eyes, his hands squeezed into tight fists at his sides. "Wow, Frankie . . ."

I gulped. "Not really my best look, but . . ." I shrugged, trying to play off his comment, unsure how to take it.

"No, you look . . . I don't even know what word to use. Tempting would fit." I blushed and looked down at the ground for a moment. "Sorry, I'm making you uncomfortable."

"No, it's fine," I said, waving him off and making my way over to my side of the bed.

"I've never seen a woman in any of my clothes before. Who knew it would be so hot?" He laughed and it brought the intense atmosphere down a notch. That was until we both got into bed.

The same bed. Under the same covers.

We'd gotten in facing each other because we were talking—which was fine. But now that we were lying half-naked and I could have reached out and splayed my hands over his hard chest, you could've snapped the tension in two. Our heavy breathing was the only sound in the room.

I shifted in my spot. "Well, good night," I said in a small voice, then rolled over and turned off the bedside lamp.

Every bit of my skin felt charged like a live wire. I tried to ignore the sensation and closed my eyes for some much needed shuteye. Within a minute my eyes were open again, staring out at the reflection of the moon on the ocean.

Calder shifted on the bed behind me. I wasn't sure if he'd turned away from me or if he was still facing me, though I swear I felt his eyes boring into me from behind. I was unable to remain still. A blanket of sexual need cloaked the bedroom. How the hell was I going to get any sleep tonight? At least we were shooting a night scene tomorrow so I wasn't due on set until the afternoon. Maybe I'd have time for a nap if everything with my mom was okay.

I'd texted her earlier to let her know I wouldn't be home, offering no further explanation. I was old enough that I didn't have to check in with her anymore, but I didn't like worrying her if I could avoid it. She didn't handle stress well and worrying about me had been known to set her off. Fortunately, she'd been out having dinner with a couple of friends and hadn't bothered to give me the third degree.

I lay there, a strange mix of tired and wired all jumbled together. I needed to move. Maybe I had a case of restless leg syndrome or something. Though if that were the case, it hadn't developed until I was sharing a bed with one of Hollywood's hottest bachelors. More likely it was a case of restless vagina syndrome.

I turned over onto my other side so I faced the center of the bed, trying to do it without disturbing the mattress below me in case Calder had somehow managed to fall asleep.

When my head nestled once again in the pillow, what I saw almost stole my breath. Calder lay on his side facing me, the covers down by his waist, his muscled chest on full display. His hooded eyes were focused on me, and though the room was only illuminated by the silvery glow of the moon, the need and intensity pouring out of them was easy to see.

My nipples beaded underneath Calder's t-shirt, aching to be touched. My clit throbbed in anticipation as I pictured what that would feel like. Would he be gentle and lightly caress them, or would he manhandle them like a savage? Either sounded good to me.

We lay staring into each other's eyes until the weight of everything unsaid was almost unbearable. We hadn't discussed the kiss. In fact, it was as if it had never happened. As I lay there, my body inches from his, the need to talk about what had transpired became too overwhelming.

"Calder, about what happened—"

"Shhh, Frankie. Just go to sleep," he said in an even tone that belied the intensity of his stare. He didn't take his eyes off me for one second while he spoke. I wasn't even sure he blinked.

"Don't you think we should—?"

"You need to get some rest. There's plenty of time to discuss this later."

Disappointed, I pursed my lips and closed my eyes, choosing to focus on Calder's rhythmic breathing beside me. I didn't know how long it was before I eventually drifted off, but I did.

I should've known when Calder changed the subject that he wouldn't mention it again. Because when I awoke the next morning, we were back to pretending nothing had ever happened.

chapter sixteen

Frankie

The following week I sat in my trailer waiting to be called to set when there was a knock on the door.

"Come in," I said in a loud voice.

My manager, Brock, came up the steps. "Hey, Frankie."

"To what do I owe this surprise?" I asked. I didn't have a meeting scheduled with him so I was sure something was up.

He tossed a magazine down on the coffee table in front of me.

"What's this?" I leaned forward off the couch to take a look. I picked it up, unimpressed when I saw a grainy picture of Calder and me leaving the restaurant with our Mexican take-out. "You've got to be shitting me," I said with an exasperated sigh.

"I got a call from Calder's manager, Chelsea, when this hit the shelves."

I quickly scanned the article, which questioned whether or not our meeting over the weekend was a professional one or not. "Great, this is just what I need."

Brock raised a brow. "Is there any truth to this?"

"Pfft. You know me better than that. I'm not dating Calder Fox." I tossed the magazine back down on the table in front of me, dismissing his claim.

"Well, that's what I'm here to talk to you about."

I scrunched up my face. "What's there to discuss?"

Another knock sounded at the door. I figured it was someone calling me to set. "Come in."

My eyes widened when I saw Calder enter the trailer, followed by an attractive lady, probably a decade or so older. He gave me an apologetic grin and came to sit beside me on the couch. As always, my body felt like it'd been plugged into an electric socket when he was near.

"Hey," he said, nodding to the magazine sitting on the coffee table in front of us. "Can you believe those assholes?"

"I just found out," was my uber intelligent response.

"Frankie," Brock called my attention back to him. "Earlier when Chelsea called me to let me know about this, we got to talking about how we should handle it. We need to run it by each of your PR people first, but we had a thought." He glanced warily at Chelsea standing beside him.

I felt like we were two children being scolded as they both stood over us with Calder and me looking up at them.

"So . . ." I said, looking at Calder to see if he had any idea what the hell was going on. He shrugged.

"Brock and I both feel that there may be some benefit to the press thinking that you two are a couple, and that perhaps we might . . . go out of our way to keep them thinking that."

Wow. Just . . . wow. I was not expecting that. I'd assumed we were here to discuss how to spin it to the press so they would think we were *not* a couple.

There was stunned silence in the trailer for a moment before Calder spoke up. "Why in the fuck would we want to invite the press to start poking around?"

Chelsea sighed. "For a few reasons—not the least of which is that Frankie will help to clean up your image."

"Maybe so, but I'm not interested in ruining hers." Calder was glaring at Chelsea, but she didn't even flinch under the intensity of his gaze.

"That's actually part of it," Brock spoke up. "We've reached out to some of the fans and found that you're coming off a little too perfect, Frankie. Buttoned up and unrelatable even. A supposed fling with Calder might help soften your image." He rocked back on his heels, making it clear he was uncomfortable saying anything to me.

I didn't blame him. That kind of hurt.

"There's nothing unrelatable about Frankie," Calder insisted.

Brock turned his gaze to him. "I know that, and you know that, because you've worked with her. But the ticket-buying public doesn't. They've only ever seen the polished to perfection side of her in interviews and on red carpets."

I took a little solace in that.

"Landon's not going to like this," Calder said to Chelsea and then turned to me. "He's my PR guy."

I nodded.

"I think once I explain, he'll be on board," Chelsea responded. "This film has a lot of Oscar buzz already and you guys haven't even finished shooting. The more attention we can bring to it—and specifically, to you two—the better. The fact is, people *will* buy tickets just to see the two of you together on screen if they think you were a real couple while filming."

I blew out a breath. I knew everything they were saying was the truth. Well, except the part about me coming off like a stuck-up bitch. Jeez.

"I don't like it," Calder said in a firm voice.

Ouch, that stung. Was the idea of being tied to me in the press really that abhorrent to him? It wasn't that long ago that he'd had his tongue down my throat. Not that we'd discussed it, or even come anywhere close to that happening again.

I wasn't sure what to say so I just kept my mouth shut.

Chelsea sighed, giving me the impression she was used to dealing with the stubborn side of this usually laidback guy. "That may be the case, Calder—"

"The paps already follow me around like I'm carrying a winning lottery ticket they want to pickpocket me for. I'm not going to drag Frankie into that kind of mess."

A warm sensation spread through my chest at his admission. It had me feeling a little like it wasn't me he had a problem with but that he was trying to protect me. Not that I should care. I needed to keep reminding myself of that.

Brock spoke up. "There's a definite downside to this scenario and that would be it," he admitted.

"You've been quiet through all this. What are your thoughts?" Calder asked me.

"What did you have in mind?" I asked, moving my gaze between Brock and Chelsea.

A small smile formed on Chelsea's lips. "Spend some time together. Go out to dinner in public. Maybe go to some hot spots together. One of you get caught leaving the other's place in the morning," she said with a shrug.

"We're not asking you to make out in public or anything like that," Brock chimed in.

"You don't have to be physical in public . . . just make the press think you're being physical in private," Chelsea piped up.

I pressed my lips together, certain that my face must have been turning red.

"What's the studio going to think of this?" I asked. I didn't need to be pissing anyone off if I wanted to continue to build my career.

"As long as you guys do your jobs and produce an amazing piece of work, they aren't going to care whether or not you're dating—for real or pretend," Brock said.

We all sat there in silence while I contemplated what moving forward with this plan might mean. On the one hand, it would garner more press for the film—the old adage that 'there is no such thing as bad publicity' was unfortunately true in the movie business. Also, I enjoyed Calder's company, so spending time with him outside of work would be no hardship.

As far as I could tell, there were really only two drawbacks to this idea. The constant hounding from the press, and the fact that I didn't trust myself to remember it was all make-believe. This situation had the potential to get messy. What if I really did fall for him? As soon as this was all over, I'd end up with a broken heart and he'd move on with his life. I'd have been an unmentionable pit stop along the way, not the final destination.

I bounced my knee up and down as I sat there, needing to relieve some of the tension gripping my body.

There was one more thing I hadn't considered. Chelsea was right when she said this would help Calder's image and assist in getting his career back on track. Call me a sucker, but I found myself willing to risk my own peace of mind to help him live his dream. The Calder I'd come to know deserved the opportunity.

"I'll do it," I said.

chapter seventeen

Calder

If I was being honest, equal parts of me loved and hated the fact that Frankie had agreed to the whole ruse. This was going to be the ultimate acting challenge. How did I 'pretend' to like the girl I actually liked, all while trying to maintain my distance from her, yet continue to make it look like I wasn't? Hell, I *should* get an Oscar if I pulled this off.

We hadn't had any time in our filming schedules to hang outside of shooting, but I knew that was coming to an end. We were slated to do some outdoor shoots over the next few days, but with the weather not cooperating and the sets not ready for the studio shots because of some changes the director wanted made, we were going to find ourselves with a rare two days off in a row.

In an effort to distract myself, I had invited Hendrix to come watch today. In retrospect, it probably wasn't the smartest idea since we were filming a scene where Frankie and I were making out. I didn't need a bigger audience than I already had to witness me panting over my co-star.

"Earth to Calder."

"What's up?" I looked up from the surfing magazine I was absentmindedly thumbing through to find Hendrix leaning into the fridge, pulling out a drink.

"You want anything?" he asked.

"Nah, I'm good."

He nodded, grabbed a bottle of organic fruit juice, and sat in the armchair beside the couch. Long gone were the days when my fridge was full of any number of liquids that could get you royally fucked up.

"Everything okay with you? You seem a little distracted today."

"Yeah, I'm cool."

He pressed his lips together, looking like he didn't really believe me. "You struggling lately? How's sobriety?"

For fuck's sake. I'd quickly figured out that as a recovering addict, you were never allowed to have an off day. If you did, people assumed you were either using again or thinking about using again.

"No, it's not that. I mean, don't get me wrong . . . every day is a struggle, but I'm managing."

"What's up then? It's obvious something is going on."

I chewed on the inside of my cheek, not really wanting to talk to anyone about how I was attracted to my co-star.

When I didn't reply, Hendrix pressed on. "You can talk to me, you know. I realize we're not best buddies, but I'm not some douchebag who'd sell your story to the press."

I felt a little bad that he thought I saw him that way. I didn't. Not at all. I knew he was good people or Akoni wouldn't have given him the time of day. My heart clenched as his name passed through my mind, as it always did.

"I know you wouldn't. Believe me, if I thought you were, you wouldn't be here."

He laughed out loud and said, "I'll bet."

Knowing he had a competition coming up, I asked him how his training was going, successfully changing the subject.

An hour later, Hendrix and I were standing around on set waiting for the lighting guys to make a few changes when Niles sidled up with an attractive blond girl. Glancing down at Hendrix's visitor pass, he said, "Must be bring-a-visitor-to-work day." He laughed a bit at his own joke before continuing,

"Guys, this is Jess Chambers. She's a student at USC and won a contest for 'best film' in her class. As a prize, she gets to spend a week on set here with us to see how a big-budget production really works. Or doesn't." He motioned with his head to the guys who were still moving the lighting around the set.

I stuck my hand out. "Nice to meet you, Jess. I hope this week doesn't scare you right out of film school."

She laughed a little and shook my hand, then flicked her eyes over to Hendrix. That was new. Usually whenever I met someone for the first time, I had to deal with their disbelief at meeting 'the Calder Fox.' It was undeserving and unnecessary. I had to say—I kind of liked that she didn't.

"This here is Hendrix Monroe, a buddy of mine."

I'm pretty sure the rest of us in the room disappeared by the time those two shook each other's hands. Niles noticed too because he finally cleared his throat. "I need to speak with Calder in private for a moment. Jess, Hendrix . . . do you mind giving us a minute?"

They dropped hands, looking a little startled at having the real world intrude. "Sure thing," Jess said.

She walked off toward the area where craft services had set up with Hendrix following behind.

"Is everything okay?" I asked.

"That's actually what I wanted to ask you. How are you doing?" Niles rubbed his chin, looking at me like he was trying to figure me out.

"I'm doing alright. The better question is how do *you* think I've been doing?"

"I'm thrilled with what you've done so far. You and Frankie have good chemistry on film and have really brought it with some of the more emotional scenes we've done."

I wanted to puff my chest out with pride when I heard that. I'd put so much effort into this movie—more than I'd done for any job before. "I appreciate you saying that."

"I was just checking in to make sure the pressure wasn't getting to you. I know you've had your struggles over the past year—"

"You don't need to worry about that. I'm committed to my sobriety program. I'm not going to mess this opportunity up by using or drinking."

"Good to hear." He clamped me on the shoulder. "Frankie should be on set any minute. You ready to film this scene?"

Was I ready? Um . . . yeah. I finally had an excuse to kiss Frankie again, and even though it would be in front of a roomful of people this time, I'd been anticipating this since . . . well, since our last kiss. "I'm ready when she is."

"Atta boy." With another pat on the shoulder, he smiled and made his way over to one of the producers.

Frankie walked on set in a pair of boy shorts and a tight-fitting tank top. Damn. This was going to be a difficult scene to film, but not for any of the usual reasons. It wasn't a highly emotional point in the story. I didn't have to deliver some long, sweeping monologue. The scene wasn't a physically demanding action sequence. No, today's work involved Frankie and I filming our first kiss.

Well, it was our first kiss as far as anyone else was concerned. The two of us still hadn't discussed our 'real' first kiss. It was as if it had never happened. Just the way I liked it. I didn't need any drama and it was better than the alternative, which was to have Frankie pull the usual 'what does this mean' or 'where is this going' female routine.

"Hey, Calder. How's it going?"

I cleared my throat. Seeing Frankie in those painted-on scraps of fabric was going to make it difficult for me to not physically react to her. The last thing I wanted to do was pitch a tent on camera. "Not bad. How're you doing?"

She shrugged and pulled at the hemline of her shorts. "I'd be better if wardrobe added a few inches to these things. Jesus. You think they could've found something smaller?"

I glanced down at the expanse of her long, lean legs. Since she'd pretty much invited me to with her comment, I figured it was okay. "They don't leave much to the imagination, that's for sure." I chuckled.

She shifted her weight from foot to foot, obviously

uncomfortable in what she was wearing. "I saw Hendrix when I was coming in."

"Yeah, I hope that's okay. When I invited him to set, I didn't really think about what we were filming today."

She waved me off. "No biggie. It's not like it's the love scene or anything."

I laughed, though now I was feeling uncomfortable . . . down below. The last thing I needed her bringing to mind was *that*. I resisted the urge to adjust myself.

A moment later, Niles called everyone to attention and we headed to our marks. Sitting side by side on a dorm room bed, I couldn't help but think of the last time we'd been together on a mattress. She'd been so tempting lying next to me in nothing but my t-shirt, her bare legs peeking out of the bottom. It had been crazy hard not to touch her that night at my house. I deserved a fucking medal for the fact that I hadn't.

As Frankie shifted, the smell of her shampoo wafted into my nose and I inhaled deep. I loved her smell. Wait. What? What the hell was happening to me? Had I grown a fucking vagina when I'd gotten sober that I wasn't aware of? Christ.

Niles called 'action' and we were getting through our dialogue well. We'd only had to stop a few times to block the scene and change some of our positioning. I was trying to straddle the line of staying in the moment—in my character's headspace—while at the same time not be so into it that I embarrassed myself in front of everyone, including Hendrix. I'd never hear the end of it.

This was it. All I had to do was lean in and kiss her. I'd done it before. I could do this.

Only I couldn't.

When the time came, I froze, feeling the eyes of everyone on set boring into me. Talk about performance anxiety.

"Cut!" Niles yelled. He made his way over to us, looking grim.

"Is there a problem?" he asked.

I shook my head. "No, sorry. I spaced out there. Won't happen again."

"Okay, let's do this." He walked back to the monitor. "Places everyone."

I'd avoided Frankie's gaze until that point. She probably thought I was a total chump. When I mustered up the courage to look at her, she had a concerned expression on her face and leaned in so only I heard her. "Listen, I know it's weird because of what happened . . . on the surfboard . . ." Her voice wavered a little and then she said, "I know it's not like that for you and I get it. It's your character kissing me—nothing more."

She was so completely off base. It was totally like that.

I was afraid if I gave into the kiss, I wouldn't be able to control where my emotions might go. I knew what my physical response would be—I was already dealing with that on a daily basis. But kissing her again . . . how was I going to pretend that it didn't mean anything to me?

The situation was completely fucked. But so was my career if I didn't get my shit together.

Niles called 'action' and we went through the scene just as we had before. This time, however, I used every bit of the pent-up lust I'd been carrying around for her to make the scene sizzle. I cupped her face in my hand, leaning in, inch-by-inch, not too fast, not too slow. Her emerald eyes flared for a moment, her pupils dilated.

My lips touched hers softly at first—just a peck. I licked the seam of her mouth and she parted her lips slightly with a breathy exhale, bringing her hand into my hair and gripping it tightly. I didn't mind—truth be told, I liked it a hell of a lot. I parted my lips and pushed my tongue into her mouth, tasting her, exploring her. I think I broke the world record for semi to completely erect in point five seconds.

I shifted on top of her, one hand supporting her back, the other on the back of her neck until she was lying on the mattress. I pressed into her, knowing she'd be able to feel the obvious evidence of my arousal. We continued kissing, her hands exploring my back and my hair. I felt her weight shift beneath me and as her hips rose up to meet my own—

"Cut!"

My eyes whipped open. Damn it. I'd almost lost myself so completely in her I nearly forgot we were performing for the camera. Frankie looked as dazed as I felt, but instead of gripping me in a fit of passion, her hands were now on my chest, pushing me up and off of her. I slowly rose to a sitting position, bringing a leg up and dangling my arm off it in an effort to hide my noticeable hard-on.

"That was perfect, you guys," Niles said as he approached us. "We could really feel the chemistry. I think we got it, but how are you two feeling about it? Do you want to get another take?"

"No!" Frankie yelped, almost before he was done with his sentence.

I slid her a sideways glance. Would it really be that terrible? "I feel good about it, Niles. I think we nailed it."

"Alright then." He turned to face on the other side of the camera. "Let's get set up for the next shot."

Everyone else on set started bustling around, doing what they were paid to do. I caught a glimpse of Hendrix. He was still chatting up that Jess girl, but he must've been paying some attention because he gave me a knowing grin. Fucker.

Frankie moved to get up off the bed. I grabbed a hold of her wrist before she took off. "What are you doing later?"

She looked down to where I had my large hand wrapped around her tiny wrist, and I let it drop. "I don't know. It'll probably be late, so I'll just head home."

"Do you want to grab something to eat with me?"

"Um . . ."

"You need to eat, Frankie. And it's probably time that we allow ourselves to be seen in public together again."

She sighed. I tried not to take it personally, but her reaction still stung. "If you don't want to go through with this—"

"No, no, I do. It's fine. We'll go get something to eat. Sure."

Sure. I don't think I'd ever gotten that reaction before when I'd asked a girl out.

"Okay then, it's a date," I said without really thinking about it.

She leaned down so that her face was level with mine and looked me in the eyes. "It's *not* a date."

I pushed up off the bed, forcing her to back up, then moved into her personal space so that she had to crane her neck back to look at me. I leaned in, speaking right into her ear, "You keep telling yourself that, sweetheart." A shiver rippled through her body and I chuckled before pulling back and walking away.

I don't really know why I wanted to get under her skin, but in that moment I did. The way she was pretending there was no connection between us was starting to get under *my* skin. Even though I know it shouldn't.

Whatever. It probably had more to do with the male ego than her anyway—at least that's what I kept telling myself.

chapter eighteen

Frankie

Calder had insisted he drive for our "date" so I'd given him my address and now stood waiting on my driveway for him to show up. I didn't want him in my house. In fact, this was really the first time I'd allowed anyone outside of the few people who worked for me on my property. If I was getting together with someone, I'd always come up with some excuse why it was better if we met there, the same as my mom did with her friends. Over the past few years, we'd both gotten really good at making excuses.

But Calder had been insistent, and I figured there wasn't any harm in him pulling his car into my driveway for two minutes.

An engine purred not too far off in the distance. It was getting closer, then I heard it pause for a moment before pulling into my driveway. I'd given Calder a temporary code to get past the gate. A few seconds later, a low-to-the-ground white sports car wheeled around the sharp corner of the driveway and screeched to a halt a few feet from me.

Calder climbed out of the car with a smile and a mischievous twinkle in his eye. I swear, he really was an overgrown kid. With a six pack. And a significant bulge in his boxers. I suppressed a smile. I didn't want to find it endearing, but somehow I did anyway. I mean, what was there to like about a twenty-five-year-old guy acting like an adolescent?

He'd pulled his hair back and changed since I'd seen him on set and was now wearing a pair of worn jeans, ripped and frayed in places, and a casual buttoned-up black shirt. The dark shirt set off the blond in his hair. He looked good. He looked *too* good, and I knew I'd have to work at remembering that this evening was just a farce.

"Nice car," I said and placed a hand on my hip. "You drive a little like Lewis Hamilton in it though."

I had no idea why I said that—it wasn't like I followed racing. The only reason I knew the Formula One champ was because I'd had a non-speaking role in one of his endorsement commercials a while back. Great guy.

Calder chuckled and walked around the front of the car to the passenger side. "Thanks. It's a Porsche 911 GT3. One of the first ones released to the public."

He seemed pretty impressed with himself and I proved unsuccessful at fighting the urge to bring him down a notch. "Looks like one of those cars guys drive when they have short dick syndrome."

Calder grinned but didn't seem to take any offense. "I assure you, that's not a problem I have." With amusement in his eyes, he bent down and held the door open.

I strutted toward him, our back and forth making me feel brazen. "That's not how it felt earlier today when it was pressed against my hip." I snickered and walked around him to get into the car. Without warning, his arms wrapped around my stomach, pulling me so that my back was against his front, my ass against his groin. And if it hadn't been already, it was clear that no, he definitely didn't have that problem.

"You sure about that?" he said in my ear with a low, raspy voice that oozed sex.

I stood there for a moment, panting like I'd just run a marathon. Finally, my lust-addled brain cleared enough that I was able to respond. "Maybe I was mistaken. Doesn't seem like a problem for you," I said with a breathy whisper.

His hand spread across my stomach so that a few of his

fingers sat mere inches below my breasts. What I wouldn't give to feel his hands there. I closed my eyes as that image appeared unbidden in my mind, and I attempted to preserve it.

"I think of it as more of a solution than a problem." His voice was still husky and I found myself wishing he'd keep talking—I could listen to his deep timbre all night. Preferably with his naked body pressed against me.

Jeez, I needed to get a grip. "That thing is sure to cause problems . . . could complicate things."

He dropped his head so that his nose was nuzzled into the base of my neck and inhaled. My knees trembled. Actually friggin' trembled. He must have noticed because he gave a low chuckle that I felt reverberate throughout my entire body.

"Maybe I like complicated," he said, his thumb moving back and forth over my ribcage. I could have demanded that he take his hands off me. I knew I should have. But when he pressed his hardness further into me from behind, I found myself trying to stifle a moan rather than telling him to stop.

I pushed back—I couldn't help myself—and I heard his sharp intake of breath. His face was still nuzzled into my neck, and I continued to rub myself against him like a cat in heat. How attractive.

The sound of a car revving its engine out on the street brought me out of my haze, making me suddenly aware of what I was doing—and where—and with whom.

Not that we were in danger of anyone seeing us. My house was set well away from the road and surrounded by vegetation and a wall. That wasn't the point though. The point was that I was letting my co-star, with whom I was supposed to be having a "pretend" affair, touch me like we were lovers. Which we most definitely were not.

My body stiffened and Calder must have sensed the change because he stopped all movement. I was wrong to have responded to him—to let him think this was okay. Oh, I was sure he did this kind of thing all the time with women and that it was no big deal to him. But I didn't. For me, anything physical we might do meant something and I knew it wouldn't to him. He was just playing his role in this charade—whether it was behind the privacy of my front gates or not.

"We should get going. It's late," I said in an even voice, as if I hadn't just been grinding myself all over him like he held the patent for whore lure.

Calder didn't say anything, but he did remove his hands from me. I jumped into the car as fast as possible, unable to even look at him when he shut the door. I didn't want to give him the chance to question why I'd pulled away. Just as he hadn't wanted to discuss the kiss we'd shared, I couldn't have *that* conversation with him. I had some pride. Maybe not enough to prevent him from pawing me in my driveway, but enough that I would not be telling him that the reason I couldn't be physical with him was because that would lead to me having real feelings—feelings that I knew wouldn't be reciprocated.

He walked around to his side of the car and got in, then started the Porsche without a word. It wasn't until we pulled out onto the main road that he addressed me.

"You cool if we go to The Ivy?"

"Sure." It came out more like a squeak so I cleared my throat before saying, "That'll be fine."

I'd never actually been there, but if there was one place you wanted to be seen and photographed in Los Angeles, it was The Ivy. Which only validated what I already knew—this was all about furthering our careers. I wasn't mad at Calder for it. How could I be? I'd signed up for it, the same as he did. So why did it hurt so much when he proved me right and did exactly what we were supposed to do?

chapter nineteen

Calder

I spent the majority of dinner silently cursing God for even allowing the condition of blue balls to exist. Because as I was finding out regularly these days, it wasn't a bullshit excuse some frat guy made up to convince a girl to go down on him—it was a real-life situation. And it hurt. Like a motherfucker.

Dinner had been strained at first—the shadow of what had happened in her driveway hung over the table, blanketing everything in a shroud of uncomfortable darkness.

As per our usual M.O., we didn't discuss it. I wanted to. But I liked this girl and it was clear that she didn't want to talk about what was going on between us. I was putting it off as long as I could because I didn't want to scare her away, but I also knew we were avoiding the inevitable. I enjoyed my time with her too much and I didn't want it to end, so if it meant pretending I was oblivious to our growing attraction to one another, then that's what I'd do.

I had no choice but to suffer through the blue balls, but I needed to end the underlying tension at the table . . . stat. We were supposed to be on a date, and it was no secret that if you dined at The Ivy you were opening yourself up to reports from the patrons and staff, not to mention the regular paps that hung around outside.

To that end, I reached for Frankie's hand across the table and gripped it in my own the moment the waiter took our empty plates away. Her eyes widened and she took a quick inventory of the people at the tables around us.

"Tell me why you wanted to get into acting." I wanted to know more about her, and if I had to use the guise that we were on a real date to do it, then so be it.

She didn't remove her hand, which I took as a good sign. Though she didn't exactly look comfortable with it because I noticed her glance down at our joined hands several times before answering. "I was part of a school play when I was in sixth grade. Not through any choice of my own, mind you. The entire class had to participate. At first, I was terrified about being on stage in front of people. I thought it was going to be stupid, or cheesy or something." She shrugged and I sat and listened quietly because she was finally opening up to me and I didn't want to bring attention to that fact in case she closed herself off like she normally did. "Instead, when I got up to do my part, I enjoyed myself and the audience didn't make me nervous at all. In fact, their reactions to what was happening on stage were the fuel that drove me through the performance."

"Did you act in plays all through school?"

I nodded. "My parents started fighting when I was in eighth grade. It helped to disappear into the character . . . dealing with my character's problems on stage and in rehearsals allowed me to forget my own."

I figured I'd push my luck and see if I could get anything more out of her. "When you say your parents started fighting . . ."

"They're divorced now. Have been for a while."

I squeezed her hand and said, "I'm sorry." I knew what it was like to come from a divorced home.

"It is what it is." She shrugged. "My dad is happily remarried. I don't see him much. He lives in North Carolina now with his new wife."

"And your mom . . . is she remarried?"

I hadn't thought I was offside asking, but an unknown

emotion raced across her face. Terror was my first thought, but it was gone so fast—and covered up as only Frankie knew how to do—that I questioned whether I had manufactured her reaction in my head. "She took the divorce harder than my dad. She still hasn't really moved on."

"I can't relate. After my parents divorced, it was less than a year and my mom had already moved halfway across the world to marry her new man." I lifted my drink to my lips and took a sip.

"Ouch."

"Yeah. I mean, I don't fault her for it. She deserves to be happy, and she and her husband are definitely that. At least she didn't make me move to Europe with her." A vision of Akoni slashed through my mind. "Though sometimes I wonder if it would've been better for everyone if she had," I added before I could stop myself.

Now Frankie squeezed my hand. My gaze darted up to hers and I found only sympathy—no judgement, yet again. I held her gaze, which was no hardship . . . it was easy to get lost in her large, multihued eyes.

"Calder, I—"

The connection was broken when her cell phone started buzzing on the table beside her outstretched arm. She glanced down at the screen, and after seeing who it was she whisked her hand from mine and picked up the phone.

"Is everything okay?" she said in a low voice. I had to assume it was so the other patrons wouldn't overhear. She listened for a moment, twirling one of her stud earrings with her free hand. "Okay, calm down. Take a deep breath. Slowly. Hold it. Now exhale. Okay, now do it again." She waited a minute, presumably for the person on the other end of the line to do just that. "That's better. I'm leaving now. I'll be there soon. Just keep doing that until I get there."

She hung up and grabbed her purse that hung on the back of the chair, bringing it to her lap and shoving her phone inside. "I'm sorry, but I have to go." She pushed her chair back so she was standing. I did the same.

115

"Let me pay the bill and I'll drive you home."

"I have to go now. I'll catch a cab. I'm sorry to run out on you like this, but it can't be avoided." Without another word, she was hightailing it away from the table like it was doused in gasoline and someone had just struck a match.

I slunk back into my seat. Figures. Just when I was getting somewhere with her. It seemed Frankie was destined to remain a mystery—for now.

chapter twenty

Frankie

I sat in the make-up chair the next morning, praying they could do something with the bags under my eyes. My mom had been upset last night so I'd stayed up later than I would have liked given my early call time this morning. I was chit-chatting with my friend Jasmine as she applied what I was pretty sure was the tenth layer of cover-up under my eyes.

We'd met a few years ago on a set when she'd been assigned to me throughout production as my make-up artist. She was a sweet girl—not Hollywood at all—and so we'd hit it off right away. She was lamenting the fact that trying to date in Hollywood was the equivalent of hell on earth when I felt my phone vibrate on my lap.

I picked it up to see a text from Brock.

> *I'm stopping by the studio to see Amber later.*
> *She's recording a song for the Collateral Damage*
> *soundtrack. Any chance you want to swing by?*

"Oh my God," I said aloud.

"What is it?" Jasmine asked.

"My manager just invited me to sit in on a recording session with Amber freaking Marshall!"

Jasmine laughed. "Amber is a real doll. You'll like her." Of course Jasmine would know her. She'd probably done make-up for most of Hollywood's A-list.

I typed out my reply to Brock and hit send.

> *Um . . . do I want to go? Does a Beverly Hills plastic surgeon do boob jobs? Yes, I want to go! I'm a huge fan!! When & where?*

He gave me the details and as long as things went smoothly on set, I'd be able to make it. My phone buzzed again.

> *Invite Calder along.*

I had no idea if he'd want to, but I'd extend the invitation.

> *Sure thing.*

"Girl, you're gonna need to tell me why you have that smirk on your face."

I dropped my phone back into my lap and closed my eyes as Jasmine applied the base shadow to my eyelids.

"It's nothing." I was glad I didn't have to look at her—she'd know I was lying.

"Mmmhmm. Sure it is. It wouldn't have anything to do with a certain co-star of yours, would it?" I opened my eyes to find Jasmine with make-up brush in hand, hip cocked, hand at her waist.

"What?" I said with as innocent of an expression as I could muster. My eyes flicked to one of the producers who had just entered the room.

Jasmine shook her head and came at me with the brush again so I closed my eyes. "You and I are going out for drinks sometime soon, and you're filling me in. No arguments."

I laughed. "Alright. No arguments from me."

"Would you relax?" Calder glanced over in my direction and placed a hand on my knee that had begun anxiously bobbing up and down the closer we got to the studio. I'd dropped my car off and he had picked me up from my place, though now I wished I were driving to get my mind off where we were going.

"I can't. I'm nervous."

"Clearly," he laughed at my expense. "I don't get it. You're Francesca Leon. You've met all kinds of celebrities."

"Yeah, but this is Amber Marshall." I gave him a 'duh' look. When he gave me a 'so' look back, I said, "Amber Marshall, Calder."

He shook his head at me in exasperation. "Whatever you say, babe." We drove for another couple of minutes in silence while I thought of what I could possibly say to Amber when Calder cut into my musings. "Everything okay? You had to run out pretty fast after dinner last night."

"What . . . ? Oh, yeah. Everything's fine. Thanks." I smiled at him, and thank God for small favors because right at that moment we pulled into the parking lot of the studio. In the big scheme of things, it hadn't been a huge deal. My mom had been on the verge of one of her episodes and had needed me home. Nothing I wasn't used to.

I texted Brock to let him know we'd arrived then exited the car. Calder came around to my side and took my hand in his, winding his fingers through mine. "You're cute when you're nervous."

"This isn't funny," I said.

He tugged my hand. "Relax. She's just a regular person, same as we are."

I laughed. I *was* being ridiculous. I'd been around plenty of stars before. I took a deep breath and said, "Alright, let's do this."

Brock met us in the lobby and took us back to the studio Amber was recording in. When we entered, she was in the booth belting out a melody in a haunting tone. She sang of love put to the test and the fight to keep it. I was grinning so wide my cheeks hurt. Amber had such an amazing voice and it sounded as good in person as it did on the radio.

There was a man sitting at the control board with his back facing us. When she sang the last note of the song, he pressed a button and said, "That was great, Shortie. Why don't we take a break for a few minutes and listen to some playback?"

She smiled at him through the glass and nodded. Maybe I was imagining it, but the way she was looking at him . . . I don't know. It seemed like there was something there. The thought quickly left my head as Amber entered the room through the door to the right of the control board.

The first thing that struck me about her was how different she looked than when I'd seen her on TV. Her image in the media screamed sex and seduction with big hair and heavy make-up. But today her red hair was pulled back into a simple pony-tail, she wore very little make-up and was dressed in a slim-fit t-shirt and yoga pants.

"Hi guys. I'm Amber." She gave a small wave as she checked out the two of us.

"Amber, this is one of my other clients, Francesca Leon, and this is her co-star in the movie, Calder Fox."

Amber put a hand on her hip and directed her attention to Brock. "Really, Brock? It's not like I'd need you to introduce either of these two." She looked over to me. "I'm a big fan of your work."

Holy-lee-cow! Amber freaking Marshall just said she's a fan of mine. This was unreal. I closed my dropped jaw and recovered quickly. "I'm a huge fan of yours. I have all your music."

"Aw, you're so sweet. Guys, this is Deshawn. He's producing the track for the movie."

Deshawn rose from his seat and walked over to our group. His dark skin seemed to set off the sparkle in his equally dark eyes. He wore a baseball cap, baggie jeans and a t-shirt, and when he smiled it was clear why Amber might have been looking at him the way I thought she was.

Calder stuck out his hand and shook his in that way that cool guys do. "Hey, man," he said.

"Good to meet you both," Deshawn replied. "Did you want to hear the whole song?"

"That would be amazing," I said.

"I think this song is going to be big," Brock interjected.

"You have to say that," Amber said. "You're my manager.

Am I right, Francesca?"

I chuckled. "I've never heard him tell me I was going to star in a flop."

"Alright, you two. I didn't get you together so you could gang up on me. Let's hear the song."

Deshawn turned around and pressed a few buttons, and music immediately began piping out from hidden speakers within the room. The song started off softly and continued building and building until Amber was belting out the lyrics near the end. It really was an amazing song.

The music ended and Amber turned to face us all, biting her bottom lip and looking a little nervous—as if she actually cared what we thought. "So, what did you think?"

"I thought it was great," Calder said.

"Me, too. The chorus is really catchy. People will be driving themselves crazy singing it in their heads all day," I added.

"Oh, yay! I'm so glad you liked it." Amber clapped her hands in front of her.

She was so cute—nothing at all like I'd expected her to be. We ended up sticking around for another hour while she and Deshawn re-recorded a couple of parts that he wasn't happy with. I wasn't sure what was wrong with them because they sounded fine to me, but what did I know?

I was still giddy by the time Calder pulled into my driveway. It was late and the sun had long since gone down.

"Oh my God, that was so cool!" I turned to face him. "Thanks so much for bringing me home."

"Of course. I wasn't about to leave you at the studio fangirling over Amber." He laughed.

"I was not fangirling! Wait, was I fangirling?" I asked, suddenly concerned that I'd made myself look like an idiot.

Calder put a hand on my shoulder and squeezed it. "Maybe a little, but it was charming."

"Oh, okay." Calder removed his hand and I instantly wished that he hadn't.

"Come on, I'm walking you to the door."

I scrunched up my forehead. "You don't have to do that."

"I want to. I'm not going anywhere until I know you're safe inside your house."

Butterflies took up residence in my stomach at his thoughtfulness. Suddenly, this friendly outing felt more like a date with the awkward end-of-the-night goodbye scene soon to come.

I opened the car door and headed straight for my front door, Calder right behind me. I felt his stare like a brand on the back of my head. Pulling my keys from my purse, I inserted the key to unlock the door, but didn't open it yet. I wasn't sure I could trust myself not to invite him in if I did. When I turned to face him, without hesitation, Calder pressed into me, placing his hands above my head, effectively caging me in.

The scent of him—saltwater and outdoor—washed over me, and I met his gaze.

"I had fun with you, Frankie. I enjoyed seeing yet another side to you." He leaned in so our mouths were a hair width apart.

"I had fun, too," I said, way too breathy for my liking.

"There seems to be no end to the amount of fun we have together, and we haven't even gotten to the good stuff yet." I gulped. I didn't know what to say to that.

Calder didn't wait for a reply. He brought his mouth to mine and took my bottom lip between his teeth, pulling it, then bringing his lips back to mine. After licking the seam of my lips, his tongue entered my mouth, causing fire to dance in my veins and igniting every part of me. He pressed his hard body to mine, pinning me between the door and himself. The idea of being trapped had never been more appealing.

He sucked and teased and drove me to the brink of asking him to stay the night. Before I could form the words, he pulled away from me and started walking backward to his car, a small smirk playing on his face.

"Sleep well, Frankie," he said, and without another word, he got into his car.

He left me this worked up and he thought I was going to sleep well? Gah!

I turned the key in the lock and entered my home. Once

the door closed behind me, I heard his engine rev as he headed back down my driveway. I leaned against the door and stood there for longer than I wanted to admit. I tried slowing my racing heart and preventing all the thoughts in my head from focusing on the one place they seemed determined to go: Calder.

chapter twenty-one

Calder

I'd mustered every last ounce of willpower I had last night when I'd left Frankie standing outside her house. What I really wanted to do was kick in the damn door, carry her up to her bedroom, and bury myself balls deep inside her. Even now, the memory alone of how worked up she'd been from our kiss had me adjusting myself as I made my way over to her trailer.

I jogged up the steps and knocked on the door. When I heard Frankie call out, I entered to find her sitting at the kitchen table, looking down at her phone.

"Hey, you," I said. She glanced up at me and a smile lit up her face, making her jade eyes sparkle.

"Hey, yourself." She put her phone down on the table. "What are you up to?"

I walked over and sat across the table from her. "I figured we have some time to kill until they're ready for us so we could hang together."

"I'd like that."

"How are you? Recovered from meeting Amber last night?" I laughed at her surprised expression.

"As if. I was not that bad." She crossed her arms over her chest.

"I'm only kidding. So, what did you think of Amber?"

She looked up for a minute, seeming to think about it before she answered. "She was different than I expected. I mean, I should know better than to judge people by what you see in the media. She was just so *normal*. I don't know . . ."

"What?" I reached across the table and took her hand. There was something more she wanted to say, I could tell.

She shrugged and looked down at the table. "It's just that I've had a few reminders lately that you shouldn't judge people before you really know them." Her green eyes flicked up to mine. "I went into this job totally expecting you to be one way, but you've been nothing like that."

I squeezed her hand. "That's a good thing, I hope?" I held my breath as I waited for her to answer.

"That's a great thing, Calder."

I wanted to reach over the table and drag her onto my lap. I didn't though. Instead, I smiled, hoping that she was able to read how much what she'd said meant to me.

She broke away from my gaze and hopped up from her seat. "Hey, I found a set of cards in here. You want to play something?"

"Sure thing, if you think you stand a chance of beating me."

Frankie rolled her eyes. "As cocky as ever. Maybe I spoke too soon." She opened one of the kitchen drawers and rifled through the contents.

"Alright, we can discuss my cock if you want. Though I have to say, I'm surprised. I didn't take you for that kind of girl."

She whipped around to face me and her cheeks were bright red. "I did *not* say anything about your . . . you know." She motioned toward my lap with the deck of cards that were now in her hand.

I laughed, holding my stomach because it hurt so much. It was the cutest damn thing to see her so flustered.

"Just say it, Frankie. You know you want to discuss my cock."

She tossed the cards down on the table, took her seat across from me and pinned me with an incredulous gaze. "I do not."

"You can't stop thinking about my cock. Admit it." I pressed my lips together to try and supress my laughter.

"Would you stop saying it!" she said with a raised voice.

I picked up the cards and started shuffling them. "I'll tell you what. Let's play a game. I win and you have to admit you were thinking about my cock. And you have to say the word. If you win . . ."

"You never say the word around me again."

I chuckled. "Deal. Name your game."

Her eyes narrowed and she thought about it for a second. "Crazy eight countdown."

"Really? I was expecting some form of poker."

"I used to play it with my dad all the time when I was little. You know it?"

I nodded. "I do," I said, setting the shuffled deck in front of her. "I'll even let you have the first deal."

"Don't look so smug," she said, dealing the cards. "You haven't won yet."

Half an hour later, Frankie looked at me like a petulant child with her arms crossed over her chest. "You don't have to look so smug."

I grinned. "Don't be such a spoilsport. Now, I believe you have something to tell me."

She sighed, but didn't say anything.

"Come on, baby. A deal's a deal."

She uncrossed her arms and put them in front of her on the table. "Fine. I was thinking about your cock. Your long, hard, manly cock. I want to talk about your cock. All I want to do all day is discuss your cock. How it looks, what it feels like, how big it is. Cock, cock, cock. Satisfied?"

I groaned and shifted in my seat, trying to ease some of the pressure of said cock as it pressed against the zipper of my pants. "That was so fucking hot. I'm anything but satisfied right now. Try sexually frustrated."

Frankie laughed at my expense as someone from outside the trailer knocked on the door, announcing that it was time to return to set.

She got up off her seat and leaned down so we were face-to-face, and I couldn't stop myself from inhaling her lavender scent. Which did not help the situation below my waist. Not at all. "After last night, you only have yourself to blame." She kissed my cheek. "Coming!" she yelled and dashed out of the confined space, her laughter trailing behind her the entire way.

Neither of us was doing any coming at the moment, but I'd be sure to rectify that as soon as possible. That girl was going to be the death of me.

chapter twenty-two

Frankie

On the first of two days off, Calder drove us along the Pacific Coast Highway in his Jeep, surfboards sticking out the back, the top off the vehicle, the California sunshine soaking into our skin. He was taking me to a different beach this time and I was going to attempt to improve on my lacking, but somewhat improved, surf skills. Though he was always complimentary and encouraging, I knew I still had a long way to go before I'd feel confident on a surfboard.

Calder leaned forward and turned down the music. "You nervous?" he asked with a grin that told me he'd be happy if I admitted I was.

"A little."

"You'll be fine. The beach we're going to normally doesn't get too big of waves so it won't be anything you can't handle." His hand landed just above my knee and he gave it a squeeze. I felt that squeeze throughout my entire body.

I looked over to him and he smiled, making his blue eyes crinkle in the corners. He leaned forward and turned the music back up, Led Zeppelin's "Going To California" blasting through the speakers.

We rolled along, my hair whipping around my face like I was in a windstorm, both of us content to listen to the music. I'd kicked my flip-flops off and had my feet resting on the dash.

I was inspecting my dire need for a reapplication of nail polish when "Bridge Burning" by Foo Fighters came on the radio. I was keeping time to the music, tapping my feet, when I became aware that something was very, very wrong with Calder.

The Jeep swerved into the lane beside us briefly and we were lucky no one was there, though the guy behind us blared his horn to let us know he wasn't pleased. I sat up straight in my seat and spun to look at Calder.

He was breathing heavy with one hand white-knuckling the steering wheel, the other pressed to his chest. He was still looking forward, but it was obvious that he wasn't really seeing the road.

I reached for the radio to turn it down. Trying not to sound panicked, I asked, "What's wrong? Are you okay?"

He didn't answer me. Instead, he gripped his chest harder and began trembling, sweat breaking out on his face.

"Calder!" I yelled, desperate to get his attention. He looked over at me quickly and I'd never seen fear in someone's eyes like I did right then.

That's not true. I had seen it before . . . with my mom.

"Calder we need to pull off the highway." I was trying my best to stay calm. I glanced around and noted that there still wasn't anyone beside us. "I'm going to help you. Stay with me for a minute." I couldn't reach the turn signal, but I placed a hand on the steering wheel and helped him ease the car into the right-hand lane. By some small miracle, there was an exit coming up. "We need to get off at that exit. Do you think you can slow the car down and get us off the highway?"

He jerked his head in a nod. Sweat now dripped down his face and he was breathing so hard and so fast I worried he was going to hyperventilate.

"Alright, here's the exit. Let's ease the car off the road." I kept my hand on the steering wheel, just in case, and we took the lane off the highway. "Now, can you pull over and park for me, Calder?" I asked in a gentle voice.

He did as I instructed and as soon as the Jeep was stopped on the shoulder of the road, he undid his seat belt and jumped out of the car. We were on the side of a two-lane road surrounded by nothing but nature. Calder started walking along the side of the road and I followed behind, running to catch up to him.

"Calder, wait!" I yelled. When I reached him, I ran in front of him and stopped so he'd be forced to look up at me. He did and my heart lurched when I saw the fear still present there. I placed my hands on his shoulders. "You need to slow your breathing before you hyperventilate. Take a deep breath in, nice and slow, and then let it out just as slow." He nodded and tried doing what I asked. "That's it, keep doing that." I squeezed his shoulders.

After a minute or so, his breathing began to even out and he removed his hand from his chest.

"I feel like I'm going to throw up," he managed to say, his voice gravelly.

I nodded. "I know. It's all the adrenaline in your system. Just keep focusing on your breathing and it should pass in a few minutes."

I stood there with him until he was breathing normally and the golden color had returned to his skin. "Are you okay?" I asked in a soft voice.

"I don't know what the hell that was." He ran a hand through his hair, now damp with sweat at the roots.

"I think you were having a panic attack."

His facial expression contorted and he looked like I'd slapped him. "A panic attack?" He shook his head. "I've never had one of those before."

"I've seen my share . . . my mother gets them," I admitted.

"I don't understand."

"What were you thinking about before it happened? Usually something triggers them."

He looked to the ground for a moment, then his body stiffened and the color drained from his face again.

"Calder . . . what is it?"

He looked back up at me with pain in his eyes. "I was thinking about other places I wanted to take you surfing, and then that song came on . . ."

"Bridge Burning?"

"Yeah. That's the . . . that's the song that was on when my car hit the tree . . . when Akoni was killed. I didn't even remember that until right then. Why do I even remember that?" He looked up to me again with unshed tears in his eyes.

Oh, God. I sucked in a breath. Before I could stop myself, my hands flew out and I wrapped my arms around him, wanting nothing more than to ease his pain yet knowing I couldn't. He reciprocated, enfolding me in his arms and tucking his head into my neck.

"Who knows why we remember that stuff? We just do." I knew from experience that sometimes we remembered the oddest things about pivotal moments in our lives. To this day, I knew exactly what socks I was wearing when my parents sat me down to tell me they were getting a divorce.

He gripped me tighter, to the point that it was hard to breathe, but I didn't utter a word. It was clear I was his lifeline in that moment, and I wouldn't do anything to jeopardize it.

Eventually he pulled away, looking more like himself but still unsettled. His eyes had taken on a dull hue I'd never seen in them before.

"Would you mind if we skipped the surfing lesson for today?"

I shook my head. "Of course not."

Without making it obvious to him, I wanted to stay with him tonight. He was a recovering addict and something like this, well . . . I imagined it was going to bring up a bunch of stuff for him and I didn't want him seeking comfort in the bottom of a bottle. I wanted to be his comfort.

We hadn't talked much about it, but I got the feeling that he didn't have many people he could trust. He was one of the most visible people in the world yet still one of the most isolated.

With that realization, my heart wept for him and I felt like my chest was caving in on itself. It was a moment before I realized that we weren't all that different. I'd never given it much thought because I'd been working non-stop, trying to further my career. But I hadn't made time to befriend any of my co-stars in any of the projects I'd worked on, nor had I reached out to my old friends from back home. It wasn't that I didn't want to. Between looking out for my mom and my busy work schedule, those opportunities seemed to have passed me by.

"I'll make it up to you," Calder said, bringing me out of my thoughts. It took me a second to realize he was referring to canceling our surfing lesson.

"It's no big deal. How about we go back to your place in Malibu? We aren't that far from it, and if we stop at the grocery store, I can make you some dinner. We can just chill this evening." I was praying I'd sold him on my idea. I didn't want to come off as being needy, but I would if I had to. I was *not* going to let him be alone tonight.

"Yeah . . . yeah, that sounds good," he said. He gripped the back of his neck with interlaced fingers, looking down at the ground once again. "Think you could drive? I'm still a little shaken up."

"Of course." I glanced back at the Jeep, which I now realized was probably still running. "Come on," I said, reaching for his hand. He accepted it, gripping my hand tightly, and we walked hand-in-hand back to his vehicle. He seemed more settled now. Still, I couldn't help but worry that my company tonight wouldn't be enough to keep him from falling back into bad habits.

As I drove us down the highway, Calder searched his smart phone for something. He appeared slightly frantic, tapping his foot triple-time. He hadn't said anything since we'd gotten in the car so I had no idea what he was looking at, but based on the expression on his face, he seemed desperate to find it.

"Good," he said, more to himself than me, and leaned back into the seat, his posture a little more relaxed.

I used the opportunity to see if I could figure out what was going on. "What's good?"

My attention was focused on the road ahead, but I heard him take in a deep breath. I'd opted not to turn the music on this time. "There's a meeting not far from my house in a half hour. Would you mind if we made a pit stop there before heading to my place?"

"A meeting?"

Calder cleared his throat. "It's an AA meeting."

Duh. How stupid could I be? "Absolutely. Whatever you need." I glanced over at him. He appeared uncomfortable, fidgeting in his seat.

"Sorry. Not trying to be high maintenance or anything. If you'd rather go back—"

I reached for his hand that was resting on his thigh and clasped it in mine. "Calder—there's no shame in getting the help you need. None at all."

He was silent for a beat, then squeezed my hand in return. I glanced over at him again and he was staring at me like he was trying to figure something out, though I wasn't sure what. Me, maybe.

"I'll drop you off and go find a grocery store to get everything I need for dinner and then come back and pick you up. Does that work?"

I wasn't exactly sure how meetings worked, but I assumed they were confidential and an outside audience wouldn't be welcome.

He squeezed my hand and brought it to his mouth, running his lips across my knuckles. "That'd be perfect."

chapter twenty-three

Calder

I waited outside the non-descript building for Frankie to pick me up. I didn't want to be too optimistic, but it seemed I'd gotten over the worst of whatever that was earlier. It still shook me that I'd pushed the memory of that song being on when we crashed out of mind until today. Regardless, the meeting had helped center me. One big reminder I always walked away with from those things was that I'd gotten off lucky—there were people who'd suffered more than I had at the hands of their addictions.

I was about to text Frankie to see where she was when she pulled into the parking lot and brought the Jeep to a stop in front of me. She exited the driver's side and walked around the bumper to the passenger side.

"Sorry, I'm late. I took a wrong turn and had to backtrack."

"No biggie. You able to get everything you need for dinner?" I asked, taking the keys from her outstretched hand.

"I was. But don't expect anything too exciting. You eat fish, I hope?"

"Definitely."

"Okay, good. I didn't realize until I got to the store that I hadn't asked you, so I took a chance."

"Frankie takes a chance. I'll have to mark this day down on

135

my calendar as one to remember." Her hands flew to her hips in mock indignation. I grinned at her, then made my way to the other side of the Jeep.

When we were both situated in the car with our seat belts on, she responded, "Are you implying that I don't take any chances?"

I turned the key in the ignition and pulled away from the building. "Your words, not mine." Glancing over, I couldn't help but laugh at the affronted look on her face. I leaned over a bit to give her thigh a gentle squeeze so she'd know I was joking.

"I'll have you know that I do take chances. Just because I like to have a plan for things doesn't mean I don't."

I laughed wholeheartedly this time. "If you say so."

She smacked me across the upper arm. "I do."

"Alright, I want to know about the last big chance you took," I responded with a smug tone to my voice. When she was silent for a minute, I continued to taunt her, "Well, let's hear it. I want to know all about the wild and crazy things you've done."

"Give me a second . . . I'll think of one." She chewed on her bottom lip for a minute then exhaled a frustrated sigh. "I can't think of anything right now, but there are some. Trust me."

Truth be told, a part of me liked the fact that Frankie wasn't a risk-taker. She was stable and made decisions based on facts, not emotions—as far as I could tell, at least.

"Well, take it from someone who's taken too many chances in his life . . . they're overrated. Eventually, they catch up with you." Why the hell had I said that? We were having a nice conversation until I had to go and ruin it.

I glanced to my side. She seemed to think about my comment for a minute. "I think the key is to take the right chances. The ones your gut tells you are worth it."

"I'd never thought of it that way." I didn't tell her, but I had an inkling that she was right.

"You seem in a better head space now. How was the meeting?" she asked cautiously.

"It helped. Thanks for not making it an issue that I wanted to go."

She touched her hand to my shoulder and I afforded myself a quick glimpse in her direction. "Whatever you need, Calder. I'm here."

Funny thing was, I believed her.

"Well, what did you think?" Frankie asked.

I thought the meal she'd made was excellent. She was a damn good cook, but I couldn't resist the opportunity to tease her a bit. "The salmon was okay. I thought the asparagus was a little overdone."

She pushed me to the side with both hands and laughed. "Whatever."

We sat beside each other on a doublewide lounger situated on the large deck off the master bedroom that overlooked the ocean. The sun was beginning to set, casting a golden hue over everything. Frankie's porcelain skin looked like it was on fire from within.

When we'd gotten back to my beach house, she'd wasted no time before firing up the grill. She'd bought and used a cedar plank from the grocery store, which I'd never actually tried before, but the outcome was fantastic.

"That was some of the best salmon I've had," I said, truthfully this time.

"Thanks." She tilted her head and rested it on my shoulder, leaning against me.

I reached for her hand, intertwined her fingers with mine, and turned my head into her hair, inhaling so I could catch the gentle scent of her shampoo. I kissed the top of her head and then relaxed into her, happy to sit in silence and enjoy nature's show in front of us.

We were quiet and content—at least I was—for long moments until the sun had almost dipped below the surface of the ocean's horizon. It was then that Frankie spoke softly.

"Have you been close to using at all since you came out of rehab?"

My hand involuntarily twitched in hers and she squeezed

it in response. "Never closer than I was today after that episode."

I felt her nod against my shoulder. I was glad I didn't have to look at her when we were having this conversation. I knew it was coming. It was inevitable that if you were dating—or pretending to date, or whatever the hell this was—that the topic would need to be addressed.

"Maybe you should talk to someone about what happened today." Her voice sounded wary, like she wasn't sure how I'd react to her suggestion.

"What, like a shrink?"

She shrugged. "Maybe. I don't know. Someone who can help you sort out your feelings."

I didn't want to go see some fucking shrink. Some overpriced PhD sitting in a chair taking notes wasn't going to help me let go of the guilt I carried for causing my friend's death. Nothing could ever do that. I'd had my share of doctors in rehab and thankfully my celebrity status had gotten me out of having to see one every week after I was released. I could handle this. "I have my sponsor. I go to meetings. I was just unprepared when that song came on the radio. It won't happen again," I assured her.

She didn't say anything, so after a minute I looked over at her. She pulled her hand from mine and leaned a shoulder on the back of the lounger so she was facing me. "Do you want to talk . . . to me about it?"

Her eyes were earnest, and more than anything I wanted to confess everything to her. This thing between us was evolving, actually becoming something. I didn't know what, but before it became whatever it was going to be, Frankie deserved to know about my past. Even the parts I didn't want her to.

She brought a hand to my face, running her thumb along my cheek. "You don't have to . . . but you can talk to me, you know. If you think it would help."

I reached up and placed my hand over the top of hers, bringing it to my mouth and kissing her knuckles. Then I took a deep breath, and for the first time in a long time I decided to act like the adult I was supposed to be and face this head-on.

"The night that Akoni was killed we were out partying together. I'd dragged him to a club in Hollywood, which wasn't really his scene, but because we were best buddies he agreed to come along. Looking back, I think he was trying his best to be a friend to me."

Her face scrunched up for a second, but the compassion in her eyes remained. "What do you mean?"

"When we were together, we were still as close as ever. But as I started partying more—drinking heavily and getting into drugs, which were never his thing—we started seeing less and less of each other. Before, I'd go to his house every Sunday if I was in town. His mom would make us a ton of food and we'd hang out or go surfing after. I started missing out though because I was sleeping off a hangover or still passed out at some random person's house. I think the only reason he came that night was because he was trying to maintain our friendship."

"That just shows how close you were."

God, Frankie. She really wanted to believe the best about everyone. I wanted to believe it too. I knew the truth though. At the time, I'd been a self-absorbed asshole who thought no one and nothing could touch him. I was trying to make something better of myself now, but back then I'd only been thinking of me—if I was thinking at all.

I shook my head. "No, even when we were at the bar, I was pushing him to drink more than he normally would, busting his balls for being dead weight. The only reason I'd wanted to go there that night was because I was looking to score and I knew the guy with the best coke in Hollywood would be there dealing."

Frankie shifted in her seat but didn't take her eyes off me. "Were you using a lot back then?"

"Yeah, I was drinking and using every night, pretty much. Back then it was just about having a good time. Being young and having the world at your feet and all that bullshit." She sucked her bottom lip into her mouth and it was clear she was hesitant to say something. "What is it?" I asked.

"I was just thinking about how differently we grew up. My parents are divorced now, but for the most part I spent my adolescence in a regular, middle-class home." She paused for a moment, taking in my reaction before continuing. "You had access to things I would've only been able to dream about. You had money, a family that meant everyone knew who you were, a face that any girl would fall for. That's a lot for a kid to handle. I would have despised it if it had been me."

Frankie was the first person to ever say anything other than how lucky I should feel for being born into the family that I was. Her assessment was one hundred percent right. Growing up the way I did, though it looked like all anyone could ever want from the outside, was an illusion.

"I'm not trying to sound like a pompous jerk . . . but yeah, I had my struggles with it. There were a lot of friends I found out were only hanging around because of who my dad was, hoping to have an 'in' with him so they could star in one of his movies, or asking me to pass along a screenplay they wrote. There were girls who dated me for money or status . . . friends that hung around because I'd foot the bill a lot of the time. I'm sure you're familiar with the feeling now, but it's hard to know who to trust when everyone around you is just trying to get their own little piece of you." I ran my free hand through my hair. "I had to deal with that my entire life."

"Living under a microscope, never knowing anything different . . . I wouldn't wish it on anyone," Frankie said softly.

"It was more than that. People who didn't even know me treated me like I was something special . . . like I was better than them and deserved their adoration or something. It's unsettling to meet people for the first time and have them think they know everything about you when you haven't even learned their name yet. Do you know how many people throughout my life have told me what they thought I wanted to hear?"

"The price of fame," she said in an even voice.

"I suppose."

"So what happened that night?"

Pain lanced through my chest as memories flooded my

mind again and I pulled my hand from hers. Hurt flashed through her eyes for a moment, but I pretended not to see it. I was a good pretender when I wanted to be. Removing my gaze from hers, I looked back out to the ocean, which was an inky, dark blue now that the stars were gaining purchase in the sky.

"That night after I'd pushed some drinks on Akoni that he didn't want, snorted some rails, and downed way too many drinks myself, I wanted to head to a house party I'd heard about in the hills. There were always more drugs to go around those places and more willing women." My gaze darted over to Frankie. "Sorry."

"It's fine. Go on." She said it was fine, but her mouth was pressed into a thin line, making me think it wasn't, in fact, fine. Then again, I was too far in to turn back now.

I inhaled deeply before continuing. "He didn't want to go. Said it was going to be a bad scene and we were better to stay where we were. I was an asshole." Frankie placed her hand on my thigh. "I said I was going anyway. And I would have. But Akoni being Akoni insisted he'd come along. I was determined to drive and because I wouldn't let it rest, he said he would since I was in no condition to drive anywhere."

Frankie sucked in a breath. I couldn't bear to look at her anymore, so I turned to look out to the ocean's depths.

"Obviously, that didn't turn out well. Blood toxicology said that he was just over the legal limit when my car slammed into the tree."

Silence.

I wanted to bust out of my skin wondering what her reaction was. I was a chicken shit though, too afraid to turn in her direction.

I closed my eyes tight, the image of the car halfway wrapped around the tree forever imprinted on the back of my eyelids. That picture, taken by an onlooker, had circulated the media for weeks. I hadn't wanted to see it again, but I deserved to be tortured by what had happened and so I'd looked at it . . . a lot.

When I couldn't take the silence anymore, I turned in her direction. My stomach catapulted up into my chest when I saw the single tear that ran the length of her cheek.

"I can't imagine how much pain you were in after the accident." She sniffed and wiped the tear away. "What a burden carrying all that guilt around must be," she whispered.

"I deserve the weight of that guilt," I replied, my voice flat.

Frankie frantically shook her head. "Calder, your friend was a grown man who made his own decisions. Maybe everything you said leading up to that night is true, but it doesn't change the fact that *he* decided to drive that car."

Now I was the one shaking my head. "No. I put him in an impossible position. He was trying to protect me—from myself." I turned back toward the Pacific.

"Calder, look at me." She sighed. "Look at me," she said more firmly.

But I couldn't. I'd already caused so much pain, and for whatever reason, this conversation was hurting Frankie. I could barely stomach it.

Without warning, she cut off my view of the ocean by crawling on my lap and straddling me. She took my face in her small hands and forced me to look at her. All traces of her earlier sadness had disappeared and in its place was only determination.

"You listen to me. Everyone makes their own decisions in life. Your friend could've left you to drive on your own, or called a cab or a car service, or taken your keys and not given them back to you no matter how pissed you would've been. *He* made the decision to drive the car after he'd been drinking—not you. You can't blame yourself for someone else's choices—it doesn't matter what the end result was." Fire burned behind her eyes. I'd never seen her so intense. It was as if she was willing me to believe it.

"If it wasn't for me . . ."

"Calder," she whispered. "You have to forgive yourself."

Unshed tears burned behind my eyes and I inhaled a lungful of air to try and prevent them from spilling over. "I don't know how." My voice broke on the last word.

"Oh, Calder." Frankie leaned in and gave me a whisper of

a kiss on my forehead. There was so much compassion in her eyes it rocked me to my core.

"Your friend wouldn't have wanted this for you. Look what happened because you blamed yourself. You ended up in rehab. He wouldn't have wanted that." Another tear rolled down the porcelain skin of her cheek.

The self-loathing inside me was like a vice gripping my chest and squeezing tighter and tighter. I wanted something to keep the pain at bay, to numb myself so that I didn't have to feel—at all. Unbidden, I remembered the rush I'd get when the cocaine first hit my bloodstream, and it had my mouth watering in anticipation. I chewed the inside of my cheek, my eyes darting back and forth over everything surrounding us. My heart picked up speed, pounding out a staccato pattern inside my chest.

"No, no, no. Stay with me, Calder," Frankie said, gripping my face tighter. She leaned in and kissed my forehead again, then kissed one eyelid, followed by the other. "Stay with me," she whispered.

She continued peppering kisses across my face. Her tender touch and concern was soothing. Soon the pain inside began to ease, bit by bit. My heart rate slowed and I accepted the kindness and compassion she was showing me. Each touch of her lips gave me a tiny piece of myself back. Each caress deposited a tiny sliver of hope that one day I would find a way to forgive myself.

I cupped her face in my hands, and she responded by slipping her arms around my neck. Frankie brought her forehead down to rest on mine and I breathed her in as she exhaled, absorbing her goodness while stroking her cheek with my thumb.

I brought my lips to hers for a tender kiss. She returned it and pushed her tongue into my mouth and we kissed lazily. Her hands pushed into my hair, playing with the long strands, as I ran my hands up and down the sides of her lean torso.

She pulled away to pin me with an intense stare. "I'm here for you."

"I know," I whispered.

143

Our gazes were heated and I became abundantly aware that she was straddling me, only a few pieces of flimsy fabric separating me from her wet heat.

I pushed my hands into her hair and she moved those couple of inches forward until our lips met again. There was no hesitation—she parted her lips and my tongue plunged inside. The kiss was a slow boil, a simmer that got hotter and hotter.

I dragged my tongue up her neck to her earlobe, nipping at it and then sucking it into my mouth to soothe it. On a breathy exhale, she pressed down onto my arousal, grinding back and forth, driving me to the edge of need.

I removed my hands from her hair and reached for the hem of her shirt before whisking it up and over her head. Then I leaned back in the seat to take her in.

"What are you doing?" she whispered.

"Enjoying the view for a moment." I heard her rough exhale and I leaned forward to undo the back clasp of her cream-colored lace bra, then eased back again in the lounger.

"Take off your bra for me, Frankie. Slowly."

She appeared a little unsure but pulled one strap off her shoulder, slowly and purposefully like I'd asked. Then she repeated the same with the other side. She held the cups of the bra to her breasts, the rise and fall of her chest letting me know that she wasn't unaffected by what was happening. She lowered her arms and let the bra slide down until she sat on top of me, fully exposed. Her tits weren't large, but they were perfect. Small and firm and erect. A warm breeze rose up off the ocean and her nipples puckered even further.

"You are so beautiful, Frankie." Her eyes closed briefly at my endearment.

I leaned forward and without touching her anywhere else, placed my mouth over one of her nipples and sucked it in, swirling my tongue around the hard bud and flicking it back and forth. She moaned, pressing her weight into my lap. I dragged my tongue along her heated flesh and sucked her other nipple into my mouth harder than the last one, then let it go with a loud pop.

When I pulled away, Frankie crashed into my lips in a frantic kiss.

Pressed against the inside of my shorts, my dick was so hard it was painful. The friction she'd created with her grinding had me groaning into her mouth. With each push into my lap, my world was dwindling down to one single-minded focus—to get inside her.

Frankie pushed her hands into my hair, gripping it at the roots. My control slipped with every press of her core against my straining cock. The need to be surrounded by her heat annihilated any remaining pretense that I was a gentleman.

I pushed my hand between us, felt under her skirt for her underwear, and tugged so hard I ripped the crotch right out of them. She inhaled a quick breath then pushed down into my hand. Fuck me. She was so wet, my fingers were instantly coated. I pushed one finger into her tight passage and thought I might blow my load right there.

"Oh baby, I need in there now. Pull me out."

She didn't argue and began fumbling with the zipper and button on my shorts. When she had them undone, she spread the material open and gasped. "You're commando."

"Always," I said, stroking my erection, hoping to ease some of the discomfort of being harder than a fucking rock.

"But I saw you wear boxers to bed."

I chuckled low in my throat. "That's only because you were there."

"I usually sleep nude, too," she said in a husky voice.

"Fuck. Come here." I reached behind her neck and pulled her forward until our lips met in a savage kiss.

She pushed up on my lap until I was able to feel her arousal wet the tip of me. I reached between us again and held my erection straight up. She moved up on her knees a bit, arranging herself so that she was right over me, and pushed herself down on my cock, inch by agonizing inch until I was fully seated inside her.

The feel of her slick heat running down my cock was more pleasurable than any high I'd ever experienced when I'd been using. If I could bottle it up and sell it on a street corner, I'd be the richest fucker around and we'd all be addicts.

She sat unmoving as she adjusted to having me inside her, our panting and the ocean waves the only sounds surrounding us. I pulled away from her mouth and moved my hands to her waist, pressing my fingers into her smooth skin. She looked down at me, her dark hair framing her face, her green eyes hooded.

Frankie began moving, sliding herself up and down my length. I helped to set the pace with my grip on her waist, but she quickly took over, taking what she wanted. Her breathing was heavy as she slammed down on top of me, again and again. I moved my hands to cup her face as she grew even wetter around me. Leaning her forehead against my own, the intimacy and connection intesified until it was almost overwhelming. I'd never experienced anything like it.

She continued to rock back and forth on me, her skin becoming damp with perspiration. When her breathing became choppy, I knew she had to be close. I pushed one hand into her hair and moved the other in between us, circling her clit with my thumb.

Frankie arched her back and bore down on my lap—hard—grinding into me frantically until I felt her come apart around my cock. She was so stunning when she came. I returned my hands to her waist and held her just above me, pounding into her from below until, with a final jerk inside of her, I came apart as well.

I wrapped my arms around her back and pulled her into me. She slumped forward and rested her weight against my chest. With my arms circled around her tiny body, I enjoyed the feeling of still being inside her while the ocean breeze cooled my heated flesh.

I felt more relaxed and at peace than I could remember since . . . well, since forever.

"I'm on the pill," she panted, still trying to catch her breath.

"Huh?" I said, trying to regulate my own heartbeat.

"We didn't use a condom. I'm on the pill and I'm clean. Are

you . . . ?"

Fucking hell. I'd never had unprotected sex before—even when I'd been completely fucked up, I'd always worn a condom. The fact that protection didn't even cross my mind when Frankie and I took this step was concerning. My world seemed to dissolve into her alone whenever I got around her.

"I'm clean," I assured her. "I had to have an extensive medical before I was able to be insured for the film. I know I'm good."

I felt her release a relieved breath against my chest. "Good. I don't know what came over me. That was so irresponsible." She shook her head into my chest.

"Yeah, that's really a conversation we ought to have had before we . . . you know."

She leaned back until she sat up straight. "I'm going to go clean up." Pink highlighted her cheeks, and it was the cutest damn thing.

"Yeah, okay. I'll be inside in a minute."

"Okay." She pushed up off my lap and I slid out of her, immediately missing her slick, wet heat.

Frankie picked up her shirt and bra and while she made her way into the house, I zipped up my shorts. I couldn't help but wonder what this meant for us. Were we a real couple now . . . was this a one-time thing . . . what the hell did I even want?

I sat pondering for a few minutes and finally decided to forget about it for now. They were always trying to get us to live in the moment in rehab, so that's what I'd do. Take it as it comes—pun fully intended.

chapter twenty-four

Frankie

I looked at myself in the powder room mirror. How in the hell had that happened? One minute I'd been comforting him, and the next I was riding him. Talk about flipping the script.

I took a deep breath in and finger brushed my hair, then rubbed the make-up smudged under my eyes so I didn't look quite so freshly fucked.

This was okay. It was. I liked him. A lot. I'm pretty sure he liked me. This was the natural progression of things. I'd just take my cues from Calder as far as what he thought this was between us and things would be fine. After all, there was no reason we couldn't have fun together.

A knock sounded on the door. "Everything okay in there?" Calder asked from the other side.

I whipped open the door and was met with his startled gaze. "Fine. Everything is great."

He stepped forward and wrapped his arms around me, bending his head to place a chaste kiss on my lips. "Good. I thought maybe you were freaking out in there about what happened."

I brought my arms up around his neck. "Not at all." He placed a kiss on my cheek and pulled away.

"What do you feel like doing? We could download a movie . . . or we could just head to bed."

149

I wrinkled my forehead. "Isn't it a little early for bed?" I asked. Calder tilted his head down and looked at me from under his brows. "Oh, I see." I tried hard to keep the blush from creeping into my cheeks but I wasn't successful.

"Bed then?" He arched a brow and pulled me into him.

"Did I really have a choice?" I laughed.

He shrugged. "Not really, but I thought it'd be nice to pretend like you did." He kissed me quickly and darted for the stairs with me following close behind.

I had a feeling I'd follow this man almost anywhere.

The next morning after breakfast we were heading back upstairs to shower when I spotted a stack of boxes piled against one of the walls near the foyer. "What's all that stuff over there?" I nodded to the area in question.

"A bunch of crap different companies have sent me. I guess now that I'm off Hollywood's shit list, they're all back to wanting me to try their products."

I nodded my head in understanding. "It still boggles my mind that these companies send their stuff to the very people that can afford to buy them."

"The power of the marketing machine," he replied with a cynical edge to his tone.

One of the boxes caught my eye, so I went over to it and hunched down to get a better look. "This looks fun," I said. It was a karaoke set, complete with speakers, a mic, and laser lights that shone out of the top of it.

I felt Calder's presence behind me. "Karaoke?" It was clear from his tone that he was skeptical.

I laughed. "Yes, karaoke. It's fun. Have you ever done it before?" I turned my head to look up at him. He was gazing down at me, one hand rubbing the back of his neck. The expression on his face looked tortured.

It was then that I became aware that my eyes were level with the bulge in his pants. Embarrassment warmed my face and I sprung up to stand in front of him.

"Uh . . . no. Never tried karaoke."

"I used to go all the time before people started to recognize me when I was out. I miss it."

Calder walked around me and removed the boxes sitting on top of the large karaoke box, then bent to lift it like it weighed nothing. The way the physical exertion made the muscles in his arms flex sent a wave of heat straight to the center of my thighs.

"Let's get this bad boy going then. I want to see what you got." His gaze ran the length of me and I shivered under his intimate perusal.

"Are you sure?" I felt a little silly now as I pictured Calder and me singing karaoke alone in his Malibu beach house.

He shrugged. "I'll try anything once." He winked at me and turned around, heading into the living area.

This would be interesting. I wasn't sure Calder knew what he was in for.

I quickly learned a few things about Calder—he didn't like to read directions, and he wasn't one of those guys that could look at something and instinctively know how it works.

"Alright, I think I've got it now." He was trying to pair my iPhone with the karaoke player and wasn't having any luck.

I suppressed a snicker that I didn't think he'd find amusing.

He pressed something on my phone and, miracle of all miracles, music started blasting through the speakers. He brought one of the microphones up to his mouth. "Testing . . . one, two, three." His voice came through clear as a summer day.

He turned to face me. "Ready to do this?"

"Bring it."

"Who's up first?" he asked with a grin.

"Why don't you go first? You seem confident." He probably thought I was afraid to perform in front of him. I wasn't. I had a decent enough voice and I'd sung in front of people on many occasions. The only thing that made me slightly nervous was that it was *only* him who'd be watching me.

Whatever. I was a professional performer . . . acting and singing were just different mediums.

"Alright. I'll even let you pick the song," he said, bringing my iPhone over to me on the couch.

Even though there were two modes on the machine, it had been enough work for Calder to figure out this much. So we were only going to use my phone for the music—no lyrics.

"Do your worst," he said as I scrolled through my playlists.

"A-ha. Here it is." I sunk back into the cushions, ready to enjoy the show.

"I'm not singing some lame pop princess song. Please don't torture me with that shit."

I chuckled. "No worries. I had something a little more aggressive in mind anyway." I hit play on one of my favorite songs. It was one that Mason Nash, one of the hottest guys in hip-hop, had collaborated with Amber Marshall on last year.

Calder groaned. "Oh, man." He put up a bit of a fuss, but in the end he was a good sport. When he was done butchering the song, he set the microphone down on the table and, looking only a little sheepish, came to sit beside me.

"That was uh . . ."

"Terrible, I know." He laughed and took the phone from my hands. "Your turn now."

I picked the mic back up off the table and stood with it dangling from one hand, my other on my cocked hip as I waited while Calder scrolled through my musical selection.

He started laughing. "Perfect."

I rolled my eyes. God, what had he picked?

He pressed the button and I wanted to laugh when I heard the intro to one of Trace's songs sound out throughout the spacious room. There was no way that he'd know this, but Calder had unknowingly picked something right in my wheelhouse. I loved rap—like *loved* it—and I knew almost every word to every rap song on my phone. This was one of my favorites.

Instead of grinning at him like I wanted to, I bit my lip, looking worried. A smug smile grew on his face and I chewed on the end of one of my fingers while I waited for the intro to finish.

A second before the lyrics cut in, I raised the mic to my mouth and changed my body language from one of concern to aggression and then launched into the rap.

Come on and hear my revelation
Don't wanna miss this declaration
Cause this ain't no collaboration
You gone and lost my cooperation
Throwin' at me every allegation
I guess I'm guilty by association
I can see the correlation
Must not've had much of a foundation
Your response was my confirmation
So consider this our termination
You're just scared, shorty, why can't you admit
That you don't think I'm worth puttin' up with this shit.
So just keep on hidin' behind all those lies
Instead of lookin' at what's on the inside
I thought we were soulmates, that's what you had said
But the goin' got tough and you got goin' instead
You messin' with my mind
Make me want to scream and shout
Took their word over mine
The fuck's that all about?
You say we're too different
Girl, you know that ain't true
But when it all goes to hell
That's the story you wanna turn to
Did you forget what we did, what we said
That was more than a fuck that happened in your bed
Do you think, do you care,
Do you sit alone and stare
At the wall, at the mall, or do you think of me at all,
doll?
Fuck the chills and the thrills, fuck the butterflies that
I get
Every time you're near, I fear, so I just say 'fuck it!'
Cause it's obvious to them and to us that I must not be
enough
Or you wouldn't run to the one, yeah that one, you're
probably fuckin'
So darlin' can you hear, loud and clear that I've had

*my fill
Of this mother-fuckin' fun? Girl, we're through, we're
done.*

The music ended and the silence that enveloped the room
was almost overwhelming. Calder sat on the couch staring
straight ahead at me, his mouth hanging open, eyes wide.

I thought I'd killed it, having not missed a word and using
my hands and body movements the same way I saw them do in
the video. But as I continued to stand with him not speaking,
doubt crept in.

"Are you going to say anything?" I asked softly.

"You were so . . . so . . . gangster." There was awe in his
voice and he pushed up off the couch and came over to me,
placing his hands on my hips. "That was so badass and hot it's
not even funny."

I blushed, feeling heat sink into my cheeks. "Thanks," I
said and dropped my gaze to the floor.

"I'm serious. Where did you learn to do that?"

I shrugged and looked back up at him. "I told you. I used
to do karaoke a lot. Sometimes I'd do a rap song."

We held each other's gazes for a moment then he pushed
a hand into my hair. He guided me back until my knees hit the
couch and I was forced to sit down. Within seconds, he had me
flat on my back, pinned down underneath him.

"Now it's time that I make you pay for that little stunt,"
he said, grinding his hips into me and burying his face into my
neck.

"Who, me?" I said in a sugary sweet voice.

"You're not as innocent as you look," he said, trailing his
tongue from the base of my neck up to my ear.

A full-body shiver hit me and Calder chuckled. He removed
my clothing, piece by piece, and then proved to the both of us
that I was most definitely not as innocent as I first appeared.

chapter twenty-five

Calder

I walked into the dive of a diner Alisha and I usually met at. It wasn't one of the usual celebrity hangouts so I didn't have to worry about the paps stalking the place. As long as I wasn't followed here I was good, and so far I'd been lucky that I never had been.

Sitting in the corner booth, Alisha noticed me making my way over and smiled, giving me a small wave. She was an attractive lady in her early thirties with long black hair and green eyes. She'd grown up in Beverly Hills, the daughter of one of L.A.'s biggest screenwriters, which was probably why she'd been assigned as my sponsor.

As I took a seat in the worn leather booth across from her, she patted the top of my hands that lay in front of me on the table. "You're looking good, Calder. This job you're on must agree with you."

"It feels fantastic to be working again—and to be taking it seriously. How have you been?"

"Good. Jim and the kids are away visiting his parents up in San Fran. I couldn't get the time off work so I had to stay behind." She pushed her bottom lip out in a fake pout.

"How are you handling being alone?" I asked, immediately concerned that her family being away might leave her feeling on edge. Alisha had been sober for eight years, but I imagined that the temptation never really went away.

She waved me off. "I'm fine. Believe me, you'll see for yourself one day when you have a family that sometimes alone time can be a good thing." She laughed, then added, "Even if you are in recovery."

"Yeah, well . . . I'll take your word for it." I couldn't picture myself as a family man. Not any time in the next decade or two anyway.

She chuckled as the waitress came up to our table. "What can I get you two?"

I nodded to Alisha to place her order first. "I'll just have a coffee please."

The waitress turned her attention to my side of the table. "Same for me."

She nodded and walked back behind the counter, grabbed the coffee pot, and returned to our table, filling both our mugs before pulling some creamers from her apron and tossing them down onto the table. "Let me know if you need anything else."

"Will do." I smiled and began the process of doctoring up my coffee. When we were both satisfied with our creations, I took a sip and relaxed back into the seat.

Alisha looked at me with a serious expression on her face and it was clear we'd moved past the chit-chat portion of our meeting. "So . . . how are you doing with your recovery?"

I pressed my lips together and nodded. "One day at a time. Some are easier than others, but no slips."

"Glad to hear it," she said, squeezing my hand again.

"Being on set most of the time helps to keep me occupied. When I'm not there, I've been either working out or surfing."

"Good. It's important for you to find ways to redirect your urge to use when it comes. Sometimes it's a matter of taking one minute at a time, not one day at a time. I'm glad you've found a healthy way to deal." She lifted her coffee to her lips and took a large sip.

"I can't go back to being that person after what happened to Akoni." Tears pricked the back of my eyes as emotion welled inside me. I wondered if there'd ever be a time that I wouldn't come close to losing it at the mention of his name. Probably not—which was how it should be. I didn't deserve the solace.

I knew what question was coming next before she even asked it. It was always the same. "Have you reached out to Akoni's mom yet?"

Shame and sorrow flooded every cell in my body. I was *such* a chicken shit. When he was alive, I'd stop by her place a couple times a month for her homemade Loco Moco. And not only had I not attended the funeral because I'd been in the hospital recovering from the accident, but I hadn't been able to bring myself to visit her after he died. I couldn't bear witness to her repulsion when she set eyes on the man that had caused her son's death.

"No, I haven't." My voice broke on the last word.

I knew Akoni had helped his mother out with money. He had a bunch of younger brothers and sisters, and since his dad died a decade earlier, his mother had struggled to get by. I'd sent a couple of checks to her in an effort to help out, or to try and assuage the guilt . . . I'm not sure which. But when they'd both been returned, I took the hint and didn't bother her again.

Alisha narrowed her eyes. "Calder, you know that a part of the recovery process is facing the ones we've hurt and making peace with the past."

"I know that," I snapped, squeezing the coffee cup in my hand so hard I thought it might shatter under the pressure.

"You need to face that demon before you try to drown it at the bottom of a bottle." She looked at me in earnest and there was genuine concern there. I knew she only wanted what was best for me.

I exhaled loudly. "I know you're right. I know it. I just . . . I'm not ready yet. Someday, but not yet."

She pressed her lips together and nodded. "Okay then. Are you ready for a relationship?" she asked, arching a plucked brow.

"Come again?" I lifted my cup to my mouth and took a sip of the steaming liquid.

"I saw you in the press this week with your co-star."

"Oh, that. That's nothing—just for show." That was a lie, but it was how it had started between us so I went with it. I didn't want to listen to another lecture.

She didn't look like she believed me. "Really? It looked like more than show to me."

"That's kinda the point." I didn't want to discuss Frankie with her. I already knew what her opinion would be—that it was too soon for me to be in a relationship with someone. That I needed to concentrate on myself right now and I didn't need the drama and emotional mess of a relationship. Good for me that Frankie and I hadn't discussed having one then.

Unfortunately, she just crossed her hands in front of her and leaned back into the seat with narrowed eyes, waiting for more of an explanation.

I dug a hand into my hair, gripping the roots. "Frankie and I aren't a couple. We're pretending to be to get some extra press surrounding the movie."

It sounded so underhanded when put that way. I could tell myself any number of things to make me feel like what we were doing wasn't really that bad. Celebrities pulled shit like this all the time . . . a well-placed call to the media about where they'd be dining that evening, an "accidental" release of a sex tape, wardrobe malfunctions, you name it. We were only playing the same game as everyone else, with the same set of rules that had been in existence in Hollywood for decades.

"We didn't plan it, but the press got a picture of us and started inferring things so we figured we'd go with it and use it to our advantage. In the end, they'd just go and make up their own story anyway. It's better if we're the ones spinning the story, not them."

Alisha brought her mug to her mouth and took a slow sip, still studying me. "I understand the what and the why, Calder. I grew up in the business, too." She paused for a moment like she was considering whether she really wanted to say what was on her mind. "Are your feelings for Frankie pretend?"

Damn it. Of course she'd ask that question. As much as I

wanted to, I couldn't lie to her. She didn't need the details, but I knew that in order for her to support me as my sponsor, I needed to be truthful with her about what was really going on. "My feelings for Frankie are . . . complicated."

"Which means?"

I heaved out another sigh. "Which means that I'm not really sure how I feel about her." That wasn't totally true—my dick sure as hell sprung to attention when she was around. "I like her. A lot. She likes me. I think. We haven't really discussed it," I admitted.

"Sounds like this situation has the potential to become problematic. People could get hurt."

"I'm not going to hurt her," I vowed. And I meant it. I'd already done enough of that to the people closest to me in my twenty-five years—I couldn't stomach any more.

Alisha sighed. "I know you believe that. And maybe you won't." She leaned forward and looked me straight in the eye. "What about *you* getting hurt? How are you going to cope? Have you thought about that? You already admitted you have feelings for this girl. If they continue to grow and she doesn't reciprocate, then what?"

I sat biting the inside of my cheek, gathering my thoughts. She wasn't saying anything I hadn't thought of myself. Like the true addict I was though, I couldn't seem to help myself.

"I feel good around her. She sees me for me, and not as 'Calder Fox.'" I made air quotations when I said my name. "I know it's a risk, but I've gone into this with my eyes wide open."

"I hope you're right, Calder. But if this does go south, don't forget you can call me for support—twenty-four-seven."

"I know, and thank you for that."

We finished our coffee and chatted about more mundane topics, but Alisha's warning continued to plague me. I hoped it remained just that—a warning and not a prophecy.

chapter twenty-six

ᴄFrankie

"Why don't we head over to your place after this to hang out?"

All my muscles tensed and I sucked in slow, deep breaths. I knew the subject of going to my house was bound to come up at some point. I just hadn't figured out exactly what to say when it did.

"I haven't seen your place here in Los Angeles yet. Why don't we head there?" I hoped he'd take me up on my suggestion.

We had the day off and Calder and I were out in L.A., eating at a restaurant. This would be our public appearance for the day. While we hadn't discussed it outright, it seemed that the more our relationship—or whatever this was—developed, the less we wanted the press involved.

Having finished what was on his plate, Calder pulled the napkin off his lap and tossed it to the side of his cutlery. "We're usually at my place in Malibu. You must want to spend some time in your own space. Besides, I'm sure you miss your mom. You're always checking in with her on the phone when we're together."

So he'd noticed. My heart raced as I tried to think of something—anything—I could use as an excuse to keep us far from my place. It wasn't like he'd have any idea something was up just by spending time in my section of the house, but I'd never had anyone there to hang out. Besides the cleaning lady, my assistant, Angela, was the only one who'd ever been there.

Calder gave me a quizzical look and leaned across the table, taking my hand in his. "Is everything okay?" he asked.

I nodded. Having come up empty, there wasn't much I could say without making it obvious I didn't want him over. "Everything is great. Sure, let's go over to my place." I smiled at him, but the gesture felt forced and I was sure he could probably tell.

"Cool. Let me settle the bill and we'll head out."

He motioned to our server and after he'd paid the check, we left the restaurant, hand in hand. Within seconds the paparazzi were swarming us, shouting our names and inane questions like, "Do you love her?" and "Has she met your father yet?" We kept our heads down, refusing to comment or even acknowledge their presence like we always did.

When we finally reached the car, Calder helped me into my side and hurried around into the driver's seat. The photographers surrounded the car on all sides, leaning over the hood to take pictures of the two us sitting there. I mean, really? How interesting was that?

"All set?" Calder asked after he'd situated himself and started the car.

I nodded my affirmation. Calder leaned over and placed a hand around the back of my neck, bringing me forward. He kissed me, just a chaste kiss that lingered a little longer than normal, and pulled away. The photographers outside went crazy, snapping off pictures and jockeying for better positions. That picture would be splashed all over the tabloids and the internet by day's end.

He started to pull the car out of the parking spot. "Let's see if I can get out of here without hitting one of these assholes."

We'd been hanging out at my place for a couple of hours without incident and I was beginning to relax, although I couldn't shake the nagging feeling that I was lying to Calder by not telling him about my mom. He was the first person I'd ever felt that way with. He'd been so open and honest with me about his own struggles—it seemed deceptive not to share my own with him.

I volleyed back and forth about whether I should tell him. I felt like I could trust him, but what if I was wrong? It would be my mother who would suffer the consequences of my decision to confide in him, not me. What if he started using or drinking again and for some reason blurted it out? Addicts were unpredictable at best.

"So when do I get to officially meet your mom?"

Calder's question pulled me from my thoughts. An eerie feeling descended on me, as if he could read my mind.

"You want to meet my mom?" I asked, genuinely surprised by this.

He shrugged like it should have been obvious he'd want to meet the mother of the girl he was dating. Banging? Having a pretend yet somewhat real relationship with? Whatever. He had acted as if it were no big deal. Which for me, it most certainly was.

"Sure. She's a big part of your life and you two are obviously close. I don't want her thinking you're dating the douchebag the press has made me out to be in the past." He paused for a moment, reflecting. "Though I was a douchebag back then."

I reached across the patio table where we'd been relaxing outside and squeezed his hand, giving him a sympathetic smile. "Don't do that to yourself. Stop bringing up the past and just leave it where it belongs."

He pressed his lips together. "Why are you trying to avoid me meeting your mom?"

They say the best offense is a good defense so that's the strategy I decided to employ. I crossed my arms over my chest and leaned back in my chair. "I haven't met either of your parents yet. In fact, besides Hendrix, I haven't met anyone in your life."

"First off, my mom lives in Europe—which you know—and my dad is on the other side of the world directing a film." He tipped his head down and looked at me. "Second, besides Hendrix, there really isn't anyone else in my life. Except for you.

When I got sober, I realized that everyone else was only hanging around for the party or to get something from me. I lost the dead weight after rehab."

A deep aching sadness slammed into me like a tidal wave hitting a breaker wall. The man sitting across from me who had one of the most recognizable faces in the world, who had everyone clamoring for his attention, was by all accounts, alone. And he knew it.

Tears welled up in my eyes. Not tears of pity, but of sympathy. I knew in that moment that I had to be honest with him about my mom.

Calder's forehead wrinkled. "Hey, what's wrong?" He rose from his chair and came around to my side of the table, squatting down on his haunches beside me. "Frankie, talk to me. What's going on?"

"I want you to meet my mom, but there's something you need to know."

"Okay . . ." He nodded his head slowly.

"If I confide in you, I need to trust that you won't tell anyone."

"Of course. If you tell me to keep my mouth shut, I will." He reached out to take my hand in his.

"The easiest way to tell you is probably to show you." He scrunched his face up, not understanding what I meant. "Come with me."

Calder followed me out of the house and down the path toward the entrance to my mom's. My heart beat so fast I felt lightheaded and was concerned I wouldn't even make it there.

I'd never told anyone about my mom. Anyone. The amount of trust I was placing in Calder was immense. I was confident he wouldn't tell anyone else . . . but what if he judged me? Or my mom?

We arrived on my mom's doorstep and I knew the door would be open even though she wasn't home. She'd mentioned earlier that she had plans with a couple of her friends and she never locked it unless I was going to be away from the house, too.

I gripped the handle so hard my knuckles were white. "This is my mom's place," I said, turning to face him.

"Right . . ."

Drawing a lungful of air, I turned the handle, pushed the door open and motioned for Calder to go in ahead of me. He eyed me as he walked past, then turned his attention to the inside of the house.

He gasped. "My God." He shuffled in sideways—he had no choice with his broad shoulders in order to get past some of the neck-high piles. His eyes were wide by the time he reached the living area, darting from one pile of junk to the next before he finally said something. "Your mom's a hoarder." His voice contained some measure of disbelief, and call me crazy, but I didn't hear any judgement or censure in it.

"Among other things. Now you know my big bad secret," I said, trying to make light of it, but feeling like I was full of lead on the inside.

Calder turned to look at me. "How long has this been an issue for your mom?" he asked.

"It started when my parents divorced and after both my grandparents died, one after the other. A couple years later is when it really ramped up. She has other issues, too . . . anxiety, some slight OCD tendencies . . ."

Calder covered the five or so feet between us in two giant strides and wrapped his solid arms around me, embracing me in tight hug. "Have you been dealing with this on your own? What does your dad say?"

I squeezed him back, happy to be able to talk to someone about it for once. I didn't want his pity, but just having someone else in my life know made it feel less like a burden—made me feel less alone.

"My dad doesn't know. My mom made me swear not to tell him. You're the only one who does. I'm trusting you with this."

He pulled away from our embrace and placed both hands on my shoulders, dipping down so he was eye level with me. "I would never tell anyone. Thank you for putting your trust in me."

I pressed my lips together and nodded.

Understanding washed over his face and he straightened up to his full height. "This is the reason you've gotten phone calls and run off on a few occasions."

Though he wasn't asking a question, I answered anyway. "Yes."

"You can't do this all on your own, Frankie. You need some help here."

I glanced around the room. "She has a therapist she sees and she's done really well under his care. When she takes her medication, it helps a lot."

He turned to survey what little you could see of the room. "Even so, you shouldn't have to deal with this on your own."

"I have no choice, Calder. I can't risk letting anyone else know. If they sold the story to the press . . . she'd be so mortified and ashamed . . . I don't know what that would do to her."

He put his hands on his hips and turned to face me again. "I understand. I just hate to think that you're all alone in this." He sighed, then wrapped his arms around me and kissed the top of my head. "I guess the good news is that you've got me now. If there's ever anything I can do to help you with this, you have to promise me you'll let me know."

I put my hands to his muscular chest and tried to push away, but he only held me tighter. "Calder, you have enough stuff to deal with on your own. You don't need to make this your problem." I felt all the muscles in his body stiffen.

"I'm not letting you go until you promise me, Frankie. Me worrying about you isn't good for my mental state either. Say it. Say you promise." His tone left no room for argument.

"I promise," I whispered, overwhelmed by him wanting to help me.

"Good. Now that that's settled, what do you say we go for a dip? I'm hot and there's this really sexy girl I've been hoping to see in a bikini." He pulled away from the embrace and I laughed.

"Did you bring your swimsuit?" I asked.

He shrugged with a wicked gleam in his eyes. "No, but just

because I want to see you in a swimsuit doesn't mean I need to be in one."

"I'm fairly certain I don't want the first time my mom meets you to be while you're skinny-dipping in my pool."

He laughed. "I can picture it now."

"Well, keep picturing it because that's all it'll ever be." With a chuckle, I spun on my heel and sashayed my way out of my mom's house with Calder close behind, knowing he meant what he'd said.

He had my back.

Calder and I were nestled on the couch together, in the middle of a *Sons Of Anarchy* binge, when I heard my mom come through the front door. I hadn't mentioned anything about Calder to my mom. I knew she had to have seen the press coverage, but she hadn't asked, so I hadn't offered.

"You home, kiddo?" she called out as she made her way to the back of the house. "I wanted to show you what I—Oh, I'm sorry. I didn't know you had company." My mom stood in the entrance to the living room with some shopping bags in tow, her gaze darting between Calder and me.

I suppressed an eye roll, knowing full well she would have seen Calder's car out front and known someone was here. Extracting myself from his hold on me, I got up off the couch. Calder followed suit. "Mom, this is Calder." I motioned behind me with my hand. "Calder, this is my mom, Gianna."

My mom pressed her lips together, a small grin playing on her face. "It's nice to meet you, Calder. I saw you at the premiere party for Frankie's last film, but we didn't have an opportunity to meet."

Calder walked around me with a big smile on his face. His arm was outstretched and my mom took it willingly. "Pleasure to meet you, Gianna," he said as they shook hands.

"What are you two up to?" she asked. It was obvious that she was more than a little curious.

"We're in the middle of a Jax marathon," I said.

"Pfft. Speak for yourself. I'm watching for the Harleys and the violence," Calder said, and my mom and I both laughed.

"What did you want to show me?" I asked her.

"I picked up a couple of dresses that were on sale. I was going to show you. Nothing that can't wait."

"I was just thinking of asking Frankie if she was getting hungry. I could run out and grab something if you want to join us, Gianna?"

My mom looked stunned for a moment. "Um . . ." She glanced over to me. I think she was trying to gauge what I thought of Calder's offer. I nodded at her. "Sure, if you two really don't mind."

"It's fine, Mom." I smiled at her. She seemed relaxed and at ease. I treasured these moments with her.

"What do you ladies feel like?" Calder asked.

"I'm open to anything," I replied. I ignored the way Calder's eyes heated when he looked over at me.

"How about some good 'ol American burger and fries?" my mom said.

"A woman after my own heart," Calder said. He draped an arm around my mom's shoulder and placed his hand over his heart, fluttering his eyelashes in mock rapture.

Again, he had both my mom and me in stitches.

"Alright," he said when we'd both calmed down. "Let me grab my phone off the coffee table. I'll take your orders and leave you girls to the fashion show."

"Thanks for not judging her."

We'd all inhaled our food and my mom had returned to her place. The conversation over dinner had been full of laughs and flowed without effort. I'd been worried about how Calder would act around my mom, knowing what he did about her, but it seemed my concern had been unfounded.

He arched a brow. "You think me—of all people—would judge her?"

"I wasn't sure how you would react."

He closed the distance between us and clamped each of his hands on my upper arms. "I know better than anyone how not being able to deal with your emotions can affect you, and I understand that if she had a choice and could, she'd be healthy."

He shook his head. "There's no judgement here."

I exhaled in relief. He'd handled himself well when I'd shown him my mom's place, but I couldn't be sure how he was going to feel now that he'd had some time to think about it. I was afraid I'd see a glimpse of superiority from him or condemnation in his interactions with my mom. But there was none of that. There was only the real Calder—the one the press and the fans never got a chance to see—the one who gave everyone a chance and didn't think he was better than anyone else. The one who loved life and wanted to live it to its fullest. The one who, deep down, I think, just wanted someone to love him . . . for him.

"I knew there was a reason I liked you so much." Placing my hands on the couch in front of me, I leaned forward to where he sat and brought my lips to Calder's. With no warning, he pushed me back down onto the couch and hovered over me, pinning me with not only his body but his heavy-lidded gaze.

"I want to hear more about these reasons you like me," he said as he dropped his face into my neck, sucking and licking his way up to the shell of my ear.

"I'm not sure your ego needs the boost," I said in a voice way too breathy to be convincing.

He nipped on the spot where my neck met my shoulder and I yelped. "Padding a man's ego is always a good thing, baby. Now tell me another reason you like me so much."

I shook my head. "Nope, not going to do it." Calder scooted down the couch farther until his head was even with the juncture of my thighs. I saw the rise and fall of my chest from my heavy breaths as I watched him inhale deeply and then bite me on the outside of my shorts. "Calder!"

He looked up at me with lust in his eyes. "You smell fucking divine, baby." In seconds, he'd unbuttoned my shorts and pulled them down and off my legs. I watched silently, afraid that if I said anything he'd stop. He leaned in and placed his warm tongue on the outside of my lace undies. He sucked and nuzzled me until the lace was soaked and my hands were in his hair, gripping tightly. Then he pulled away.

"Now, you were saying . . ." He cocked an eyebrow.

No. No. No. I wouldn't give him the satisfaction of breaking me. I would not! I couldn't manage any words, so I shook my head back and forth, biting my lip.

Calder chuckled and leaned in again, gently running his tongue along the lace. I gripped the fabric of the couch in my hands and squirmed to try and get him to put more pressure on my clit.

He backed away and leaned over me, supporting himself with his hands on either side of my waist. "Sure you don't feel like sharing? Tell me one thing and I'll take these off." He pushed a finger under the waistband of my underwear and then pulled back and released, snapping it against my skin.

The momentary sting heightened my arousal and my core pulsed in anticipation of having his face between my legs again. "Fine. You're fun, okay? Satisfied? Now take them off."

He gave me a lopsided grin and slowly—too slowly—pulled the lace down my legs, tossing them behind him without a second glance. He wrapped both of his large hands around my ankles, taking one leg and placing it on top of the couch and moving my other foot to rest on the floor below so I was completely exposed to him.

He gazed down at my pussy adoringly. "So beautiful," he said, his voice full of awe. His gaze flicked up to mine. "You move your feet from where I put them, you try to close your legs at all and I stop. Got it?"

Sucking my bottom lip into my mouth and inhaling a big breath in anticipation, I nodded slowly, never taking my eyes from his.

He leaned in and swiped his tongue over my swollen bud. Fire shot from all my nerve endings, spreading throughout my lower belly. I moaned, and though the urge to move my legs was immense, I resisted, knowing I'd feel like I was going mad if he stopped. He continued to drive me to the brink, lapping at my clit and inserting his tongue into me. I watched with fascination as he did it over and over again until I felt like I was going to explode.

And then he stopped.

"Calder!" I yelled as he brought his head up to rest on my belly.

"Now. What else is it you like about me?"

Was he serious? I gave him a what-the-fuck staredown and he just chuckled at me. Asshole.

"Come on, baby. Tell me one more thing and I'll let you finish. I promise, you won't inflate my ego too much."

I leaned my head back against the couch, staring up at the ceiling, and pressed my palms to my head. "You're hot, Calder. I never get tired of looking at you, you look good in anything you wear, your body belongs on a male model calendar, and I'm turned on pretty much every minute that we're together. There. Now make me come."

I glanced over and his grin was so wide I thought it might split his face in two. "Gladly." He winked and lowered his head, then did exactly what he said he would do. Whether or not I'd inflated his ego was hard to tell, but as I'd find out shortly after my orgasm, I'd been highly successful at inflating something else.

chapter twenty-seven

Frankie

I hadn't seen my mom much lately between spending all my time on set or with Calder when we weren't working. Today we didn't have to report in until late because we were filming a night scene. Calder had opted to go to an AA meeting so I thought I'd pop over to my mom's for an overdue visit.

We'd only spoken briefly about Calder since the night she'd met him. I had the feeling she didn't want to pry, and I was happy not to have to deal with questions I didn't have the answers to.

I stood outside waiting for my mom to answer her door while the California sunshine beat down on my back. A minute later, she cracked it open an inch. When she saw it was me, she opened the door fully. No matter how many times I told her that she didn't have to worry about it being anyone else, she still answered the door the same way. I suppose it was habit by now, but no one was getting past the gates at the front—she had nothing to worry about.

"Well, this is a surprise. Come on in, sweetie." She turned and shimmied her way through the narrow passage between the piles until she reached the living room, me following behind. "You aren't filming today?"

"I have to leave in a little while. Thought I'd stop by for a visit before I left." In truth, I much preferred when she ventured over to my place to hang out. I didn't want to make her feel bad or guilty though, and I would if I always demanded we spend time at my place in order to avoid hers.

"How's filming going. How's Calder?"

I wasn't able to supress the smile that stretched across my face at the mention of his name. "Calder is great and filming is going well. I have a tough scene coming up tonight though. It's an emotional point in the story and I don't want to screw it up."

"You'll nail it, sweetie. You always do." She smiled widely at me and sat on the small space available on the end of her couch. I settled on the edge of the coffee table in front of her.

"Thanks, Mom. What have you been up to the past couple of days?"

"I had an appointment with Dr. Barker. I spent yesterday volunteering down at the homeless shelter. The day before last, I met a couple of friends for lunch." She shrugged. "I just got in from picking up my weekly haul of magazines." She motioned with her hand to the stack beside her.

My mom had her own issues, God knows she did, but she still found it in her to help others. I'd never given it much thought, but I knew her example was one of the reasons I never judged her or others for their struggles. I tried to deliver the same amount of support and compassion to others that I'd seen her give over the years.

"And you've been feeling okay?"

She nodded. "I haven't had any more episodes. Seeing Dr. Barker has been really good for me."

I leaned forward and reached for her hand. "You make sure you let me know if that changes, okay? I worry about you."

She patted my hand that was still gripping hers. "I know you do. You worry enough for the both of us." She gave me a small smile, and there was a tinge of sadness and guilt in her eyes. "Now, I want to know everything else that's going on with you. You've been spending so much time with a your co-star that I've barely seen you." She grinned at me playfully and I knew there was no animosity there.

I hadn't filled my mom in about the situation with Calder.

She didn't know we'd started out faking it for the cameras and that now it was . . . well, it was whatever it was. We hadn't broached that subject yet and now that the time to do so was here, I realized I was worried about what my mom might think of our plan to try and play the press to our advantage.

Swallowing my anxiety, I took a deep breath and told her everything. All of it. Well, except the sex part. I sat anxiously after I finished, bopping my knee up and down, waiting for her censure.

"Are you happy?" was all she asked.

"At the moment . . . yes."

"What does that mean?"

"I don't know what's going to happen with us—we haven't discussed it. But I love spending time with him, and I believe he's a good person and has the ability to change. I think he already has changed in a lot of ways."

She pressed her lips together for a moment before responding. "If you're happy, I'm happy, sweetie. In the end, that's all a mother wants for her child."

For the first time since I could remember, I felt carefree. There was no other way to describe it. I was content. I wasn't trying to look ten steps ahead. I didn't find myself manufacturing every scenario of what could go wrong in my head and thinking of ways to mitigate the risk. Who knew what might happen in the future, but right now I was happy and I was going to enjoy it while I felt this way. I'd stopped taking anything and everything so seriously. I welcomed the change that I hadn't even known I'd needed and I told my mom so.

"Wonderful," my mom said, leaning forward and squeezing my knees.

"So what magazines did you pick up?" I said, eager to change the subject. I grabbed the latest copy of *People* off the top of the pile beside her.

"The usual. My daughter wasn't sharing with me about what was happening in her personal life, so I figured the press might help fill in the blanks."

I rolled my eyes and laughed. "You know you can't believe

half of what you read in these things." I started thumbing through the pages of the magazine.

"I had nothing else to go on. What's a mom to do?" she said playfully. She picked up another gossip rag and started glancing through the pages. After a few minutes, I heard her gasp and then snap the magazine closed, pressing it into her lap.

A feeling of uncertainty crept over me and left me feeling on edge. "What is it?" I asked her.

She shook her head. "It's nothing."

"It's not nothing, Mom." I reached to snatch the magazine from her lap, but she held on tight. "Let me see the magazine."

"There's nothing to see, sweetie."

I clenched my teeth. "You're lying. Let me see it." I tugged on the magazine, now with both hands. If the damn thing ripped, I'd just piece it back together. I pulled hard enough that I finally pried it out of her lap.

"Frankie, give it back to me—"

"Mom, whatever is in here I'm going to hear about eventually when either Brock or my PR firm calls me." I flipped through the pages as fast as I could, searching for anything that would explain my mom's reaction.

Seven pages in, I found what I was looking for. My stomach dropped like a lead weight as I stared at a picture of Calder and an attractive lady sitting across a table from each other—a booth, actually—her hand encompassed in his. The headline read, "Did the Fox snare another one?"

The magazine fell from my fingers and dropped to the floor.

"Sweetie, I'm sure it's not what it looks like."

Thoughts of Calder's scandalous past and the various stories I'd seen about his womanizing ways—ways he'd fully admitted to—came to mind. "It's not out of the question," I said and looked up to my mom.

She reached forward and placed her hand on my knee. "You just said so yourself that you can't believe any of what you read in those things."

I knew she was right. But the seed of doubt had already been planted, and now my overactive imagination and Calder's past were working in tandem to ensure that small seed was being fed exactly what it needed to flourish.

I pushed up from the coffee table. "I need to get ready to go to set."

"Before you assume the worst, talk to Calder. I'm sure there's an explanation."

I nodded, unable to say anything past the lump forming in my throat. My mom gave me a sympathetic smile and I turned to leave.

The entire time I was getting ready, I tried my damnedest not to think about the article. I told myself that the press didn't know what they were talking about, so there wasn't any reason to give it any headspace. That didn't explain who the girl was though. The press could make up a story, but they hadn't made up the fact that the two of them had been together and looked pretty cozy while doing it. A picture might be worth a thousand words, but this particular one yielded a thousand questions.

When I got in my car, I noticed I'd missed a call from Calder. I twisted my lips as I debated returning the call. This was really a conversation that needed to happen in person. I glanced at the time on my cell. We wouldn't be talking before filming, that was for sure. I was running dangerously close to being late as it was. I tossed my cell in my purse, deciding I'd deal with Calder after we were finished with our scenes for the night.

I stewed as I drove to the set, trying my best not to think about it, but something was nagging at the back of my mind. It wasn't until I'd arrived that I fully realized what it was.

I was mad at Calder, yes, but more than anything I was pissed that I had no right to be pissed. Sure, we'd slept together—more than once—spent a bunch of time together, and shared things with one another that weren't widely known . . . or in my case, weren't known to *anyone* else. But we'd never actually discussed what that meant to the other, or even talked about being exclusive. If Calder really was seeing someone else, it definitely signaled to me that he wasn't someone I wanted to be linked to romantically. But did I have the right to be mad about it? I wasn't sure I did.

I followed the crew's directional signs to the makeshift parking lot and pulled in beside Calder's Porsche. Taking a deep breath, I tried to harness all of the emotional angst I was feeling in hopes that it would provide some good fuel when I was filming this difficult scene tonight.

I knew that after we finished tonight the time had come . . . Calder and I finally needed to face head-on what was going on between us.

If there even was an *us*.

chapter twenty-eight

Calder

I glanced at my watch moments after Niles yelled it was a wrap. Shit. Five A.M. No wonder I felt like crawling into a hole and hibernating for the foreseeable future.

"That was a long night, but you really nailed that scene," I said to Frankie as we walked side-by-side on our way to the parking lot.

"Yeah, thanks. You, too," she said in a voice devoid of any emotion.

My guy radar was pinging every which way. Something was up with her tonight. While she'd been nothing short of flawless in the performance she'd given earlier, something was off. She hadn't engaged in conversation unless I spoke with her first, and when she did respond to me, her answers were clipped.

Once we were out of earshot, I wrapped a hand around her upper arm and brought her to a stop. "What's going on with you?"

"Nothing I can talk about here." At least she hadn't pretended that nothing was wrong, which was what most women seemed to do. Then they'd get pissed when you weren't able to figure out what the problem was on your own.

"Where can we talk then?"

She pulled her arm away. "It's been a long night. Let's just go to bed and we can deal with this after we've both slept for at least eight hours straight."

"I'm all for being in a bed with you, babe, but I'm not sure how much sleeping we'll get done." Nothing. No reaction. Not even a small lift of the corner of her lips. "Something's up with you and I want to know what it is." I crossed my arms over my chest, ready for a fight.

"I'm not doing this here." She walked away from me and anger rose in my chest.

As tempted as I was to say 'fuck it,' race off in my Porsche, and avoid whatever was about to go down between us, I forced myself instead to follow after her. Me being alone with my agitated feelings later on wasn't a good idea. I had no desire to fall into bad habits that might make me want to use again—more than I already did every second of every day.

No. The new Calder was trying his best to be upfront about his feelings and face everything head-on. To deal. Even when everything in me was screaming to walk away and do whatever it took to strip it from my mind.

It was with that in mind that I followed Frankie to her car, and when she got into the driver's seat of her Mercedes, I swung open the passenger-side door and sat down on the cool leather.

"What are you doing?" she asked with a scowl on her face. "I'm tired. I want to go home."

"We can either do this here, or you can start the engine and I'll be joining you at your house. The choice is yours."

She used the heel of her hands to massage her forehead. I knew she was losing patience with me, but I didn't give a damn. I wanted to know what was going on with her.

"Well, what's it going to be?" I asked when she still hadn't answered me a full minute later.

She blew out a frustrated breath. "Fine. An article hit the newsstands today with a picture of you and a brunette looking all cozy at some restaurant. The headline implies that you've gone back to your old ways and are pulling one over on me."

What the fuck? "What magazine?" I asked, irritation clear

in my tone.

"Does it matter?"

"And you believe this?" I asked incredulously.

"You're holding hands," was her response. "I'm not sure what to think."

"This is bullshit. I want to see what the hell this is all about." I reached into my back pocket and fished my phone out. When my browser window came up, I typed in the web address to one of the tabloids. It barely took a minute to find what Frankie was talking about. I clicked on the picture to enlarge it on my screen.

I heaved a sigh of relief—I had nothing to worry about. Not that I had been fucking around on Frankie, but I was happy to see that what they'd posted had an easy explanation.

"That's my sponsor, Alisha."

Frankie had been sitting with her arms crossed staring blankly out the front windshield, but her gaze snapped over to me almost before the words had left my mouth.

"Your sponsor?"

"Yeah. My sponsor. Who also happens to be happily married with kids, I might add." Now that was out of the way, I felt the anger inside me building over the fact that she would so easily believe a story fabricated by someone trying to sell some fucking magazines. "You really thought I would do that?" I asked, my tone lethal.

Frankie uncrossed her arms and gripped the steering wheel tightly. "I didn't at first. I don't know. I had planned to talk to you, to get the story from you before I jumped to conclusions, but I was so tired by the time we'd finished our scenes that I didn't want to discuss it. I thought it'd be better to wait until we'd both had some rest."

That explanation gave me a small sense of relief, but not much. Did this woman not realize that I was completely batshit crazy over her? Had I not made it obvious?

"I know you're tired, but let me ask you something. What is this to you?" I motioned between the two of us with my hand.

Frankie's eyes flared for a second and she seemed to be

caught off-guard by my question. "This? As in us?"

"Yeah. Us." I liked hearing her refer to the two of us that way.

She shrugged. "I don't know. What is it to you?"

"Oh, no you don't. You're the one who doubted my integrity . . . you get to go first."

She pressed her lips together for a moment but didn't argue. "I have no idea." Her hands went flying up in exasperation.

"We've been avoiding this conversation for too long. I know it's late . . . or early. Whatever. I'm not getting out of this car until we figure this out and come to a mutual understanding."

"I don't know what you want me to say, Calder." Irritation crept back into her tone.

"When you first saw the article, how did you feel?"

Her knuckles turned white as she gripped the steering wheel even tighter. Eventually, she let go altogether and shifted her body to face mine. "Hurt. Angry. Jealous. Betrayed." She stopped for a moment, biting on the inside of her cheek. "Then I questioned whether I even had any right to feel those things. So then I was pissed at myself."

Now we were getting somewhere. "Why did you feel that way?" I pinned her with my gaze. She just stared back at me, saying nothing. "Why, Frankie?"

"Because I care about you. Because I don't want to see you with anyone else. Satisfied?"

A warm feeling invaded my chest. "Very."

"Good. Happy to pad your ego. Now, get out of my car so I can go home and get some sleep." She wouldn't meet my gaze and turned back around to face the steering wheel with her arms crossed over her chest.

"Look at me, Frankie," I said in a low voice that brooked no argument.

She gave me a sideways glance but didn't turn her head. I reached forward and turned her chin so she was looking at me.

"I'm glad you feel that way."

"You are?" she whispered.

I nodded slowly, maintaining eye contact with her. "If I thought for one second that you were seeing someone else, I'd lose my shit." I leaned over the console and slammed my mouth onto hers, taking what I hoped I'd made clear was mine.

She pushed her hands into my hair and moaned when our tongues met. I nipped at her lower lip, then sucked it into my mouth. She tugged on my hair until the point of pain. I pulled away quickly. Confusion was etched on her face.

"Drive," I just about growled.

"What?" She was panting, her chest rising and falling with the action.

"Drive. Now."

She didn't question me again, starting the car and reversing out of the spot.

"Go right." She pulled out of the makeshift parking lot where we'd been shooting and followed my directions. It was still dark out, the sun had yet to make an appearance to start the day, but it wouldn't be long.

I had no idea where we were going, and I really didn't fucking care. Privacy. That was my only goal as I adjusted the rock solid erection straining against the confines of my jeans. Frankie was silent as she maneuvered the winding roads of the hills surrounding the city.

"Take that road," I said, pointing to a narrow street that veered off to the right. When we'd driven another minute and come across nothing, I told her to pull over. She did as I asked and put the car in park, then cut the engine.

There were no streetlights to illuminate the inside of the car and the only sound was our labored breaths, heavy with anticipation.

"Come here," I ordered. Her head snapped in my direction and I was able to make out the whites of her eyes. As was typical of her, Frankie started to say something but I cut her off. "Now."

I adjusted the seat until it was pushed back as far from the dash as possible. She climbed up off her seat and made her way over the console until she was straddling me. She wore a casual cotton skirt and I tried not to focus on the fact that there wasn't much separating the two of us. That was hard given that all the blood was currently rushing down below my waist.

Dawn had just started to break seconds before and every-thing was washed in a dark blue light. I cupped her face in my hands because I wanted her undivided attention when I said this. I needed her to believe me.

"It's time we talk about exactly what is going on between us. I know this started out as a ploy to play the press, and on some level I guess we're still doing that. Somewhere along the way it turned into more for me. My favorite time of the day is the time that I'm spending with you. When something funny happens, the first thought in my head is that I want to call or text you to tell you about it. When I'm inside you—God, Frank-ie you have no idea. I swear to you that must be what heaven feels like."

She sucked in a breath and her eyes widened for a fraction of a second. I caressed her cheek with one of my thumbs and she brought her hands up to grip my wrists while I still held her head in place.

"What I'm trying to say is that I want this to be real. It al-ready is for me, but I need to know if you want the same thing, baby."

She took a moment before answering, searching my face for something—sincerity maybe. "I want it. I want this to be real."

The moment the words left her lips, I took her mouth un-der my possession. She moaned and pressed down into my lap, causing me to buck up off the seat, wanting—no, *needing*—the friction against my cock.

I palmed her tits over the top of her shirt and she gasped and threw her head back. I ran my tongue along her neck and went straight for her earlobe, knowing that was a sure-fire way to drive her crazy.

She sighed and I trailed my nose back down her neck, in-haling her scent as I went, then brought her nipple into my mouth. I pressed down with my teeth, nibbling against the layers of cotton. She writhed against me, crying out in a sound that was clearly part pain, part pleasure.

"I need to be inside of you," I mumbled against the swell of her chest.

"Yes," she panted. She brought her head back down and looked at me with half-lidded eyes. Moving back a bit on my lap, she reached for my shorts and undid the button with almost frantic jerks before pulling the zipper down. She spread the opening of my shorts wide and my erection sprang free— at last. My preference for commando had come in handy once again.

Frankie gripped the base firmly with her hand. "You're so hard," she said with reverence and ran her hand up my shaft, swirling the liquid on my tip with her thumb.

I reached below us and hit the button to lower the back of the seat so that it was almost horizontal. "Get on your stomach underneath me."

Without coaxing, she did what I asked and we awkwardly maneuvered ourselves so that we'd switched positions. Frankie lay on the leather seat, ass up, with her hands gripping the top of the headrest.

I didn't say a word as I pushed her skirt up to her waist, spread her legs with my knee as far as they would go—which wasn't far since we were in her car—and wrenched her underwear to the side. She gasped, then tilted her ass up in invitation. With my other hand, I guided my cock into her slick passage until I was fully pressed into her.

"Ah, God," she cried, then shimmied herself side-to-side, willing me to move.

If I wasn't careful, I was going to blow my load right away. I sucked in a lungful of air and tried to maintain control over my body.

It was difficult when the next thing out of her mouth was, "Give it to me, Calder. Give it to me hard."

Screw making this last. With comments like that coming from her sweet little mouth, I couldn't be held responsible if I was a two-pump chump.

I shifted so I was fully on top of her, my chest pressed to her back. I placed one hand above her shoulder and the other beside her waist then pulled the length of my cock out and slammed into her. She let out a cry of pleasure and it stoked the raging inferno inside of me. She felt as magnificent as always—hot, wet, and ready. I adjusted my angle as I drove into her, hitting her G-spot, and her cries became more frantic.

"Calder! Oh my . . . oh, God."

So. Fucking. Wet. "That's right, baby. I want to hear you screaming my name in three—" Slam. "Two—" Slam. "One."

Frankie cried out my name and her core pulsed against my cock as she came.

The tingling started at the base of my spine and I continued to pummel into her at a punishing pace while she rode out her orgasm. Frankie moaned her satisfaction and pressed her forehead into the seat as I slammed into her over and over again. I couldn't hold back any longer and pushed into her one final time, jerking my hips in an uneven pattern until there was nothing left.

I slumped forward onto her and nuzzled into her neck. Shifting my weight on one forearm, I played with the ends of her hair. I pushed her dark locks to one side and planted a kiss on the back of her neck, resting my lips there for a moment and breathing her in.

The windows were covered in condensation. Dawn's light was visible, however, and I took it as a good sign that the beginning of a new day was heralding my new beginning with Frankie.

chapter twenty-nine

Frankie

I lay with my head on Calder's lap, enjoying the feel of him absentmindedly playing with my hair while he watched the sports report on the TV in his trailer. Closing my eyes, a small smile playing on my lips as I reveled in the feeling of contentment that washed over me.

Since our talk, my time with Calder had been like a dream. I'd never seen him smile so much or appear so content. In general, he was a laid-back, easygoing guy, but before we'd had our talk, there'd been times where the cloud of the past hung low overhead, casting shadows over everything.

Lately, that hadn't been a problem. I knew I was getting to see the best parts of him, the Calder he could be when he wasn't letting the oppressive weight of the guilt he carried weigh him down like an anchor dragging the bottom of the ocean. He was beginning to forgive himself, and that brought me more bliss than anything else could have.

Calder was doing great. My mom was managing her issues as well as I'd ever seen her. Filming of the movie was going better than I could have hoped. Things were looking up for everyone.

Bang. Bang. Bang. Someone rapped on the trailer door. "You guys are needed on set," said a faceless voice from outside.

"Duty calls, babe," Calder said, leaning down to plant a kiss on the tip of my nose.

I pushed up off the sofa and ran a hand through my locks. Hair and make-up would touch me up before filming the scene, but I hated to mess up all their hard work.

I raised my hands above my head, stretching out my limbs. The blouse I wore rode up and Calder ran his fingertips across the strip of skin. I giggled. "We don't have time for that right now, and I don't think sexual frustration is going to help your performance today," I teased.

"Quickies are underrated, you know." He leaned forward and placed a chaste kiss on my lips.

"You'll have to prove it some other time." I returned his kiss with one of my own and purposely brushed my breasts against his chest as I turned to make my way out of the trailer. My boobs may be small, but they were mighty.

Calder growled. "Now you're in for it." He chased me out of the trailer. I ran down the steps as fast as I could, laughing, and then booked it in the direction of the set.

He caught up with me in seconds, heaving me up over his shoulder.

"Calder! Put me down! You're going to ruin my hair and wrinkle my outfit."

He laughed and smacked my ass with his hand. "This will teach you to tease me."

I squirmed on his shoulder, but he had an iron grip. Eventually I succumbed, content to lie limp until we reached our destination. I didn't *really* mind. Any time Calder had his hands on me it was welcome.

But the poor hair and make-up people were going to wonder what the hell I'd gotten up to between takes.

We were filming a dinner scene. It was the first dinner that our characters were hosting as a married couple for some friends of theirs, and it would provide the first glimpse to the audience that all was not as it seemed on the surface with my character.

Though dinner scenes may have looked easy and even fun

to film, I'd always found them to be challenging. You had to eat and drink for hours on end, and when you weren't eating, you had to pretend that you were without clinking your dishes or silverware around. The food on the plate and the amount of liquid in the glass had to be the same for each shot, and you had to pass the food around and act "natural" while remembering your lines. All in all, not some of my favorite scenes to shoot.

I sat at the opposite end of the table as Calder, waiting while the props master finished what he needed to do with the table. Finally, Niles directed everyone to get in their places and yelled 'action.'

"So, Morgan, what do you and Kyle have planned for the holidays?" I asked, then brought my fork to my mouth and took a small bite of the roast beef on my plate.

"We're off to his mother's place with the kids this year. I'll have to pack my patience if I'm going to put up with all her backhanded compliments."

I laughed and the guy playing Morgan's husband delivered his line. "Come on now, Mo. She's not that bad. You married her only son, that's all. Nobody will ever be good enough for me in her eyes."

She dropped her cutlery onto the table and turned in his direction. "Kyle, she still treats you like a child. She washes your underwear when we go to visit, for God's sake."

Kyle shrugged and took a slug from his drink and Morgan turned back around to me. "Speaking of children . . . when are you two going to start a family of your own?"

I smiled coyly, like it called for in the script, and looked over at Calder.

"Let's not rush these things," he responded. "I'd like to enjoy my wife first before we add a bunch of kids into the mix. Besides, I'm having fun with all the practice we're getting."

The table erupted in laughter and Calder picked up his drink to take a sip. Seconds after the liquid had entered his mouth, he spit it out everywhere, pushed his chair from the table, and shot up out of his seat. The look on his face—a mix of anger and fear—had the tiny hairs on my arms standing on end.

He turned toward everyone standing behind the cameras. "Who the hell put real alcohol in my drink?" he shouted.

Oh shit. My stomach sank and bile rose into the back of my throat.

No one said a word. The silence seemed to roar in my ears louder than Calder's yelling just had.

He reared his hand back and slammed the glass down on the floor, the sound of the shattering glass echoing throughout the room. He pushed both of his hands in his hair and his face crumpled in anguish before he spun on his heel and took off.

It was a moment before anyone moved. Presumably, they were all in shock like I was. It had all happened so quickly, it took my head a moment to wrap my brain around it.

I pushed out of my chair and ran to catch up with Calder. He was long gone, but I ran to his trailer hoping to find him. I had to make sure he was okay. I needed to know how he was handling it.

I pounded on his trailer door but there was no answer. Without waiting any longer, I yanked open the door, afraid of what I would find.

I found nothing. He wasn't there.

I racked my brain, wondering where he could have gone. The only other place I could think of was my trailer. I raced down the steps of his and across the lot to my own, taking the stairs two at a time. Again nothing.

I wrapped my arms around my waist, gripping my stomach and willing myself not to throw up. Adrenaline coursed through my system in a mix of fear and uncertainty.

Where could he have gone?

I yanked my phone off the kitchen table and dialed his number.

Voicemail. "Calder, it's me. I'm worried. Please call."

I sank down onto the couch clutching the phone to my chest, tears burning in my eyes. Where in the hell was he and what was he doing?

The possibilities were too scary for me to consider.

chapter thirty

Calder

As I sat on my kitchen floor cradling a bottle of vodka between my legs, I rocked back and forth, desperate to push the obsessive thoughts of drinking from my mind.

"Fuck. Fuck. Fuck!" I screamed to a house full of silence. With my elbows on my knees, I gripped my hands in my hair until it hurt, looking for any distraction from the temptation gripped between my limbs.

Why had I stopped at that liquor store? What if the press had been following me? I hadn't paid any attention to my surroundings. No, I'd been hell-bent on one thing—getting my hands on a bottle.

A distraction. That's what I needed. Anything to take away this feeling, this craving, this absolute *need* for a drink.

I heard the front door open and close. Shit. I'd forgotten to lock it when I came in. I knew who it was before she showed her face. Though a small part of me was happy she cared enough to track me down, I cared enough about her that I didn't want her seeing me like this. She'd gotten to know the new Calder—there was no telling if she'd still like me after she became reacquainted with the old Calder.

"There you are," she whispered as she came around the side of the large center island and saw me on the floor. Her gaze darted to the bottle between my legs and she sat on her knees in front of me, reaching for the poison. "Oh, thank God it's not open." She pulled it away and stood to place it on the counter behind her. I fought the overwhelming urge to grab her wrist and stop her. She sat on her knees in front of me again, gripping my face between her hands. "You haven't . . ."

I shook my head. "No," was all I could manage with a raspy voice.

"I'm so sorry. I don't know what to say. What can I do?" she asked, holding me.

I wrapped my arms around her in return, squeezing her hard, and inhaling her familiar scent. It brought me some measure of comfort, but it only dulled the constant itch under my skin to the point where it was almost bearable.

"Where's your sobriety chip?" she mumbled against my neck.

It was in my car. Truth was, I'd stopped carrying it around after I'd started spending time with Frankie. I hadn't needed to rely on it anymore—I had her. It didn't matter anyway because fingering a fucking sobriety chip wasn't going to cut it right now. Not after I'd gotten a taste of what I was missing. It was a Pavlovian response—the memories instantly slamming into the forefront of my mind. The way I felt so happy and free when I was drunk or high, the fun I used to have, the fact that I didn't have to feel anything undesirable when I was under the influence . . . at least not anything I didn't want to.

"Calder?"

I heaved a heavy sigh out. "It's in my car. But it's not going to help now."

"Tell me what I can do." Frankie was a fixer. She wanted to fix this—to fix me—but what she failed to realize was that she couldn't. My fate was in my own hands. My own incapable hands.

"Nothing," I croaked out in a broken voice.

I felt her shake her head against my body. "I don't believe that. There has to be something. Please tell me."

I didn't respond, just gripped her tighter, and a minute

later I felt her hot tears wetting my shirt. I grabbed her shoulders and pushed her away from me. Tears streamed down her face and she looked afraid. So afraid.

"Why are you crying?" I searched her face for answers.

She fisted my shirt in her hands. "I can't stand seeing you in this much pain. Tell me what I can do. We can talk, or we can do something to distract you until you're in a better place. Just tell me. Anything. I want to help." She released a sob and snuggled back into my chest. I wrapped her in my arms, wishing I could protect her from the pain I was causing.

I had a family that loved me, but they had lives of their own. I'd never had anyone fight for me the way Frankie was trying to now. I'd never felt deserving of someone's fight—until her. If someone like Frankie thought I was worth saving . . . maybe I really was.

"There's nothing you can do. I'm not sure there's anything *anyone* can do."

"What have you done in the past when you wanted to drink?" she mumbled against my chest.

I bent my head down and gripped my hair in my hands. "Surf. Go to a meeting. Try to keep myself busy. Watch the minutes tick by on the clock and thank God when another one passed and I hadn't given in to temptation."

She pulled back from me with hope in her eyes. "Let's do one of those—any of those!" Her voice was almost frantic now.

"It's not going to make any difference. I'm destined to repeat all the same mistakes. You should just go." I tried to put some finality in my tone, but my voice only came out strained. She shook her head from side to side. "I'm not going anywhere."

"I don't want you to be another victim!" I yelled.

She looked up at me, her eyes swimming with confusion. "Of what?"

"Of me." I choked back a sob and pressed the heels of my hands into my eyes.

"Oh, Calder. No." She gently stroked my cheek with her hand.

I pulled my hands away from my eyes and squeezed them

shut. "I've left so much damage in my wake." My voice broke at the end.

"Baby, you have to forgive yourself. You can't keep doing this . . . continuing to punish yourself for something you had no control over."

"You don't understand—"

"I understand perfectly." She gripped my face in her hands, meeting my eyes head-on. "You know better now. So do better. That's all you can do. That's all any of us can do," she insisted.

I felt the weight of her words, the truth of them starting to sink in, and it provided a small amount of solace. But instinct had me trying to push back the relief. No matter what she said, there was no denying that I was deserving of all the self-loathing.

Frankie tried to soothe me, peppering soft kisses all over my face. First, my forehead, then down to my nose, and back up to each of my eyes. She followed along my cheekbones, eventually reaching my chin, and finally bringing her soft lips to my mouth. I pulled my head away. The pain that flashed across her face lanced into my chest, spilling out my insides.

"Frankie . . ." I said in a pained whisper. Old habits were rearing their ugly head, making me want to take what she was offering—to use her to push away everything I was feeling.

"Let me help you." She ran a hand up my thigh until she cupped my growing erection over the top of my shorts, squeezing.

I brought a hand to her wrist. "No."

"Please. Let me distract you. Let me help take the pain away." I shook my head and diverted my gaze, not wanting to see the earnest and somehow still seductive expression on her face. "It's okay," she said, rubbing my hard length. "Use me for this. I'm offering."

I released her wrist and shoved my hands into my hair. The urge to bury myself in her and forget what I was feeling was so powerful. While I sat internally debating what to do, Frankie had undone my jeans. My hips jerked up as her hand made contact with my cock and pulled it out. If my dick had a vote, it was obvious what it would have been, given that it was standing ramrod straight.

I half-heartedly pushed Frankie back by the shoulders, which she resisted. "Frankie, no . . ."

She shrugged out of my hold and bent her head to my waist. "Let me do this for you." Without further comment, her warm mouth enveloped the head of my cock, her tongue circling the tip. I groaned and leaned my head back against the cupboard behind me.

Her hand fisted the base and ran up and down my length while her mouth continued its assault. It felt so fucking good. A better man would've pushed her away. I wasn't that man. Not in that moment. And so I let her continue, even pushing my hands into her hair to guide her efforts up and down my shaft until I was close to coming.

"I need inside you," I ground out, my voice low.

She rose up out of my lap, wiping her mouth with the backside of her hand as she did. Fuck, that was hot.

"Stand up," I commanded. Her eyes widened for a moment before she did as I instructed. "Take it all off." Without a word, she pushed her shorts and underwear down off her hips until they pooled at her feet on the tile floor below. Next, she lifted her shirt over her head and unclasped her bra behind her back, letting the straps fall down her arms until the lacy number joined the pile of clothing. She shoved them all to the side with her foot.

I sat perusing her perfect body from below . . . her thin waist and perfect tits—all natural. Finding a girl who hadn't had her tits done in Hollywood was a lot like searching for the Holy Grail. Good fucking luck.

"Touch yourself." Frankie's face blanched momentarily, but she recovered her game face quickly. It was obvious she hadn't known what she was offering when she'd said she wanted to help me push the savage need I was feeling to the background.

I wrapped my fist around the base of my cock and started stroking with a light touch. She moved her hand to the center of her thighs and rubbed in small circles. Her nipples contracted into hard points and a soft sigh left her lips.

"Does that feel good?" She nodded, her eyelids growing heavy. "Keep going." My voice was rough and raw.

Minutes later, I wasn't thinking about how good the alcohol had felt when it first hit my tongue, or how I longed for the feeling of euphoria that snorting a rail would give me. I was concentrating only on Frankie and the smell of her arousal, the slickness that coated her fingers.

I stood from the floor and removed my shirt first, letting my shorts fall to the floor and pushing them off to the side with my foot. I stroked myself for another minute and when I was unable to keep my hands off her any longer, I leaned in and brought one of her tits to my mouth. I sucked it in hard, biting down on her nipple as I released it from my mouth. Frankie yelped and I ran my tongue over the taut peak to soothe the pain. Her hands dove into my hair, holding me to her chest. I moved to her other breast and repeated the gesture. She groaned.

I placed my hands on either side of her small waist and turned her so she was facing away from me. "This is gonna be rough," was all I said before I lifted her up onto the marble counter of the island. Her feet were left dangling, but because I was so much taller than her, it was ideal for me—her open core was perfectly lined up at my waist.

I stepped closer and ran the head of my cock up and down her slick heat, coating the tip with her arousal. She wiggled a bit but she couldn't get a foothold to gain any leverage. I smacked her ass and she stilled. She was glistening, and as much as I wanted to pound into her, I needed to taste her first.

I spread her legs further apart and held them open with both hands, then ran my tongue from her clit all the way to her slit, pushing my tongue inside. She tasted like heaven—sweet and musky at the same time. I repeated this several times and she moaned again and again. When I sucked her clit into my mouth hard, she screamed, trying her best to buck up off the counter. I pushed the weight of my forearm down on her back, holding her there, and continued to suck until she was on the precipice of coming.

Then I pulled away from her, stood up, and slammed into her in one fluid motion. She came instantly, crying out, her pussy clenching my cock as I stood there basking in the euphoric feeling. When she'd come down from her orgasm, I pulled out and slammed back in. Then I did it again . . . over and over. I was relentless, giving her no time to recover.

This was the Calder I remembered. The selfish one. The one who took what he wanted with no regard for anyone else's needs or feelings. Some perverse part of me enjoyed the resurgence of my former self.

I reached forward and grabbed Frankie's hair, forcing her to arch her neck and her back. She cried out in pain momentarily, but she didn't object and she didn't ask me to stop. I gripped her silken strands as I continued my assault on her, jackhammering in and out. My other hand palmed her ass roughly, striking it every so often, leaving an angry red handprint each time I did.

The base of my spine tingled and I knew I was close. When the orgasm overtook me, I jerked her toward me—hard—pushing my cock in as far as it would go, holding it there until I was drained completely.

I leaned over her, panting for a minute, before the scene in front of me became clear. The red marks on Frankie's ass, her neck craned back, her hair wrapped around my fist. I immediately let her hair go and pulled out of her, backing up until I hit the counter behind me.

"I'm so sorry," I whispered.

I was beyond disgusted with myself. I'd just used Frankie like I'd used so many women in the past. Like she meant nothing . . . was nothing. As if I had zero respect for her, when the truth couldn't be farther from that.

I watched as she pushed up off the counter and slid down until her feet met the cool ceramic beneath. When she turned to face me, I could see that her eyes had been watering before she quickly wiped underneath them.

197

"Did I hurt you?" I asked so quietly that I wasn't sure she would hear me.

"No, no, no." She shook her head and took a step toward me, which had me retreating and moving down the counter to get away from her outstretched hands.

"You didn't hurt me. It was rough, yes. I wouldn't want it like that every time we're together, but if that's what you needed, I don't mind."

She doesn't mind. *Jesus.* Why was she sacrificing herself for me? I massaged my temples. I was the lowest of the low, taking advantage of someone as sweet as Frankie and sullying her like that.

Her hands wrapped around my wrists and pulled my hands down from my face. "Calder, listen to me." I looked into her eyes, afraid of what I might see. There was only determination—none of the condemnation or anger that I deserved. "You didn't hurt me. If I didn't like what we were doing, I would have told you to stop. I want to be here for you. I want to be what you need. I care about you and you need to let me do that."

No—fuck no. I wouldn't let myself corrupt her. There was no way someone like Frankie could have possibly enjoyed what I just did to her. She had to be lying.

"I can't do this to you," I whispered, pushing her away from me. I walked over to her discarded clothes and tossed them at her, then picked up my shorts and pulled them on. "You're too good for me. You need to go."

When she said nothing, I glanced over. She stood stock-still with a stunned expression on her face, peering down at the clothes lying around her feet. "Why are you doing this?" she asked. When I saw the tears in her eyes as she directed her gaze at me, my knees almost gave out. I wanted to crumple into myself, but I'd have to wait until she was gone.

"I told you earlier. I'm not letting you become the collateral damage of my bad decisions. It's destined to happen. It's better that you get out now, before you really get hurt."

"You're just pushing me away because you're scared, Calder. Don't do this."

"Get dressed!" I said too loudly.

She reluctantly began putting her clothes on. Her bottom lip was trembling and it took everything in me to stop myself from soothing her by running my thumb along it.

"Do you know what kind of man you're dating, Frankie? I mean, do you really? I'm an ex-junkie and a drunk. I don't take much seriously. I'm selfish and self-absorbed and take what I want, as evidenced by what happened here—"

"But you've changed, Calder. You—"

"I used to bang almost anything with a pussy. It didn't matter who it was or how many at one time." The color drained from her face. "That's right. Porn stars, fans, other junkies. I'd be so high it's a wonder I always remembered to use a condom. Sometimes there were two or three of them at once. I hurt everyone I was close to—if I didn't kill them." My voice was raw. Speaking the truth about myself was no easy task, but she needed to know. She *had* to know.

"I've never even had the balls to visit Akoni's mother since he died. I'm responsible for her son's death and I'm too afraid to face her."

"You have to deal with this stuff, Calder, or it's going to keep eating you up inside. You'll never be able to move on."

"I don't deserve to move on!" I screamed. "That's the point!"

"You deserve happiness, just like anyone else!"

"I don't need you to make me your little charity project, for fuck's sake."

Before Frankie could respond, the shrill ring of her cell phone sounded from her purse. Her eyes closed briefly before she said, "That's my mom's ring. I have to get it."

She hunched down and rifled through her purse until she found her phone. "Hello?"

I couldn't hear what her mom was saying but judging by how the remaining color in her face vanished, it wasn't anything good. She listened for a minute, her forehead wrinkling. "I'll be home soon. Stay there."

It wasn't how I envisioned getting her out of my house, but

it would work.

She straightened and placed the strap of her purse on her shoulder. "I have to go."

"It's for the best anyway. I need to call my sponsor, Alisha. She's the only one I can talk to that will really understand what I'm going through."

Frankie's head snapped back like I'd struck her. She pressed her lips together for a minute, appearing to gather her composure. "This conversation isn't over."

"It is. So are we," I said in a voice empty of all emotion.

One single tear fell from her eye, and in that moment I hated myself as much as I had right after the accident. I would only ever cause pain in the lives of those who cared about me. My only consolation was that I was saving her from even worse heartache down the road.

Frankie reached for the bottle of vodka on the counter and tucked it under her arm. Without another word, she spun on her heel then walked out of the kitchen and out of my life. She was still the majority shareholder of my heart though.

chapter thirty-one

Frankie

I slammed the paper down on the table. "Fucking press."

"I'm not sure I've heard you say the 'F' word outside of a script before," Brock said, concern in his voice.

I glanced back down to the piece of "journalism" sitting on the trailer's coffee table and had to work hard to regulate my heartbeat. They'd reported on Calder running off set, with the angle that he was once again becoming unreliable and had probably started using again.

"If I was Calder, I'd bring a defamation suit against those assholes." I crossed my arms over my chest, my hands in tight fists.

Brock came and sat beside me. "How do you know they're not reporting the truth?"

I swung my head in his direction and pinned him with a lethal glare. "He is *not* using again." I sounded confident. I wanted it to be true, but really, how would I know? It had only been a day, but Calder continued to freeze me out. He refused to answer any of my texts or calls. My frustration level was at the boiling point and I was about to erupt like Mount St. Helens.

"Either way, it doesn't sound like it's your problem anymore," Brock said and patted my knee.

"Thanks for the reminder." I had filled Brock in on everything that had gone down—minus our time between the sheets, though I was pretty sure Brock was assuming that was the case anyway.

I knew what Calder was doing, and there was only a small part of me angry with him for it. The bulk of my heart was breaking for him. He was so scared. The incident on set had shifted something in his thinking, and the terror he felt had been written all over his face when he'd tried to scare me off and push me away. What he didn't know was that I didn't plan on going anywhere.

Niles had figured out what had happened. Apparently, one of the set guys had mistakenly given Calder the wrong cup. Said guy was no longer employed by the studio obviously, but the damage had already been done.

Brock glanced at his watch. "You're due on set any minute. Come on. I'll walk with you. I've got some time until my next meeting."

Today was the first time in . . . I'm not sure there had been another time . . . but today was the first time I didn't feel like being on set and sinking my psyche into a character that didn't really exist. I knew I needed to keep my eye on the long game that was my career and not be so short sighted as to let some guy I'd been seeing for a small amount of time waste the opportunity this movie had given me. I knew that. But somehow my heart didn't seem to care. What I'd had with Calder hadn't been big on longevity, but it'd been huge on meaning.

I got up off the couch and made my way out of the trailer, following behind Brock until we walked side-by-side to the golf cart that would taxi us over to the set we were filming at that day.

Brock put his arm around my shoulder and squeezed me into his side. "It'll all work out, you know. It always does."

I nodded, unable to say anything when I wasn't so sure. At least one of us seemed confident.

We turned the corner around one of the large sound stages and the golf cart came into view. It was just about to pull away when the driver noticed us approaching and stopped to wait.

Calder sat in the front beside him. All the air left my lungs when I saw the stony expression on his face. Without acknowledging me, he turned back around and faced forward.

"Figured I'd wait for you," the driver said with a smile as Brock and I climbed onto the back seat of the cart.

"I appreciate that. Thank you," was all I could manage. I sat there gripping the metal rail of the cart the entire ride. Calder sat behind me, mere inches separating us, and yet I'd never felt so far away from him.

The cart came to a stop in the middle of the small-town USA set. Brock patted my free hand before I hopped off. The knuckles in my hand holding onto the rail ached as I loosened my grip.

Smoothing out my shirt and pants, I avoided eye contact with Calder as I waited for Brock to exit. Calder set off in the direction of everybody else, and Brock and I followed behind at a slower pace to widen the distance between us.

"What scene are you guys filming today?" It was obvious my manager was trying to take my mind off the past few awkward minutes. That would be near impossible to accomplish, but I appreciated the effort.

"The one where we get in a fight and I take off in the car like the mentally unstable character that I'm playing."

Brock let out a small chuckle. "Well, that should be good for you. Releasing some aggression toward your co-worker," he said in a low voice so Calder wouldn't overhear us.

"You said it, not me." Despite how I was feeling, I couldn't help but give him a small smirk.

A second later, we'd reached the crowd where everyone was throwing around orders about what and who needed to be where.

Brock patted me on the shoulder. "I'll leave you to it. Break a leg, as they say."

"Or someone else's," I quipped before winking at him and making my way over to Niles to see what his thoughts were for the scene. Calder was already there speaking with him.

"Frankie, how are you feeling about today's scene?" Niles asked.

"I think a scene like this is just what I need." I smiled widely at him and glanced quickly over to Calder, who had kept his eyes on Niles, even though I was the one speaking.

"Glad to hear it." He nodded. "I was just filling Calder in on how we'd like things to go down here today. You two will go through the script on the sidewalk. Frankie, after you say, 'You're going to regret this,' you run to the car and pull out into traffic." He pointed to a nearby sedan parked at the side of the road. "Any other questions, you two?"

"None from me," I said. It was easy enough, even in my agitated state. Say lines, get in car, drive away. Do it all while being angry. No problem.

Calder didn't speak, choosing to nod his head instead.

"Good. Head on over there and one of the producers will show you your marks."

I gladly walked over to where Niles had indicated. I couldn't stand seeing Calder's complete apathy toward me. Maybe it was childish, but I'd rather ignore him than give him further opportunity to pretend I didn't exist.

A couple of hours later, we'd run through the take well over ten times. A few times because Niles wanted to try some different camera angles, once because one of the extras driving a car accidentally honked his horn, and another because Niles didn't feel that Calder and I were giving it all we had.

I knew I'd been holding back, afraid that if I really let go, my actual feelings where Calder was concerned would come bubbling to the surface and infiltrate my performance of the character. This take I'd decided not to worry about all that. I was going to let the full breadth of the emotions I'd been holding inside find their way to the surface and use them to fuel my performance. And it made all the difference.

I was nailing this take. I felt it in the energy of the people surrounding me, and I was able to read it on Calder's face and in his reaction to me as we went through our lines.

"You're going to regret this!" I screamed, pushing him for good measure. I raced to the car like I'd done a bunch of times before, turned the key in the ignition and careened into traffic with my foot pressing down on the gas pedal.

I saw something flash in the corner of my vision, but before I could process what it meant, there was a loud noise. And then, only darkness.

chapter thirty-two

Calder

I saw the car crush the driver's side of Frankie's car, heard the familiar crunch of metal, and felt absolute, abject horror like I'd never known before. Not even when flames consumed the flesh of my best friend and I was forced to watch before passing out.

My lungs squeezed every drop of available oxygen out of them and I fell to my knees. Bodies were running to the street, though they were all a blur to me. I wasn't able to make one person out from another. They were all nameless, faceless entities. I opened my mouth in a desperate attempt to suck some air into my lungs, but to no avail. My lungs burned and black spots crept into the edge of my vision, my head swimming in dizziness. I pitched forward, just barely getting my hands out in front of me before falling completely over.

The last thing I remember was the sounds of sirens, cutting through the shouts of everyone around me.

"Mr. Fox, can you hear me? Mr. Fox, if you can hear me, please open your eyes."

I didn't recognize the voice, but I tried to do as he'd asked. I barely had one eyelid open when I remembered the way Frankie's body had jerked around inside the car when it was hit. My eyes sprung open and I pushed up off whatever I was lying on with only one thing on my mind. I had to get to her.

"Frankie!"

A pair of strong hands met my chest and pressed me back down. "Hold on. Are you okay?" I looked up to see that the voice belonged to one of the production assistants.

I shoved him off of me and sat up. "I'm fine, damn it!"

It took a moment to get my bearings. I glanced around at the chaos surrounding me to see that a pair of ambulances had arrived on set. I stood up on still shaky legs.

"I think maybe you should sit down. We need to have you looked at."

I ignored him and raced over to the ambulance closest to me. The back doors were open but no one was inside, so I went around to the side of the vehicle to find the paramedics attending to an older gentleman on a stretcher who was clutching his chest.

Whirling around, I ran over to the other ambulance just as the doors were shut from the inside. I banged on them, but no one answered. Jumping up, I was able to glance through the window and see Frankie lying motionless, blood trickling down her face.

My stomach revolted at the image, causing bile to rise up to the back of my throat. The ambulance slowly started to make its way through the crowd of people on the street.

"Fuck." I needed to get to her. It was complete pandemonium. People were barking orders to one another, and some of the women were openly crying. I raced back to where the golf cart had dropped us off, finding a few of them still parked in the same area. I jumped on the first one I came to and pressed the gas pedal to the floor. I had to get back to my car. I needed to know she'd be okay.

Slowest. Mission. Ever.

When I finally made it to the hospital, which felt like five long fucking hours later, I ran into the emergency room waiting area, scanning the room for anyone that looked familiar. "Frankie, Frankie!"

A nurse popped out from behind the large reception desk,

giving me a stern look. "You can't be running around yelling in here, sir. Keep it down or I'll have to call security."

I gripped both her shoulders and brought my eyes level to hers. "Can you tell me where Francesca Leon is?"

She pushed away from me with thinned lips. "I can't divulge private information, sir. Why don't you go outside and set up camp with the rest of the press. I'm calling security." She turned to leave.

"No, wait! Please. Look at me. You must recognize me. Please. I have to see her."

She spun around and gave me the once-over through narrowed eyes. She took an extra second examining my hair and then realization dawned over her features.

"You . . . you're Calder Fox. Oh my!" She pressed her hand to her chest.

"Exactly. Now please. Can you tell me where she is?"

She nodded, her eyes wide. "Last I heard, she was down the hall." She pointed to the double doors with a large sign that screamed 'Authorized Personnel Only.' "Take your first right, second door on your left. I'll buzz you in."

I was already moving before she'd finished the sentence. "Thank you," I yelled behind me. I stood in front of the doors, shifting my weight from foot to foot. The buzzer finally sounded and I pushed through the doors, hurrying down the hall, dodging stretchers and hospital workers until I reached the door she'd directed me to.

I stood gripping the handle, my heart hammering against the inside of my rib cage. It wasn't until that moment that I considered the fact that I had no idea what awaited me on the other side of that door—no knowledge of what condition Frankie was in.

Unbidden, the image of snorting cocaine popped into my head, making my tongue salivate and my forehead sweat.

Fuck. I felt like my body and subconscious were working together to push me off my path to recovery. As the idea grew in my mind, I tried desperately to push it away by thinking only of Frankie. Picturing her beautiful face, her wonderful spirit, and remembering that she needed me right now. Being fucked up beyond oblivion would not help her.

I turned the handle and entered the room. The first thing I noticed was the doctor and nurse who stood in the corner, looking over some paperwork. They glanced over to the door when I entered.

"You can't be in here," the doctor said and began making his way over.

"It's okay. He can stay." I recognized that voice. I turned to see Niles standing in the other corner, his hands pressed into his pockets. How in the fuck had he beaten me here?

My gaze darted over to the hospital bed. Empty.

"Where . . ." I swallowed past the painful lump in my throat. "Where is she?" I pushed a hand through my hair.

"She's off getting some tests done," Niles responded.

"She sustained a rather serious contusion to her head," the middle-aged doctor said. "Right now she's unconscious."

My gaze flicked over to the doctor. "Why is she unconscious?"

He pressed his lips together before answering. "Sometimes when the body has sustained a shock or trauma, the mind will shut down until enough healing has occurred, at which point the patient will regain consciousness. We're hoping that's what's going on here."

I took a step closer to the doctor. "And if it's not?" I held my breath as I waited for his answer.

"There isn't any reason to jump to conclusions at this point. We're running more tests, but we expect her to make a full recovery. We'd like her to regain consciousness sooner rather than later, however it's not too much of a concern that she hasn't. We'll continue to monitor the situation and deal with things as we need to."

It wasn't exactly good news, but it wasn't the worst news either. I turned my attention to Niles. "Where is her mom?"

He looked as if he'd aged a decade in the past couple of hours—the stress of all that was going on evident in his features. I hadn't thought until now what this would mean for the movie. Not that I gave a shit about any of that. "I called the number we have on file and there was no answer. Frankie's manager tried reaching her too, but wasn't able to get a hold of her."

Hmm. That seemed odd. I knew from spending so much time with Frankie that she and her mom kept in close contact. I pushed the thought aside as I grabbed a chair that sat against the wall and dragged it next to Frankie's hospital bed. I wanted to be right here waiting when she woke.

A while later, an orderly came in to remove the empty bed.

"What are you doing, man?" I asked with panic in my voice. Niles came to stand behind me and placed a hand on my shoulder.

"The patient will be back in a minute. We're just going to roll her bed in rather than transferring her."

I nodded at him. "Oh, okay."

A few minutes passed and the door opened. Some nurses pushed the bed into the room, but I couldn't see her because it was being pushed in backwards. They maneuvered it into its spot, rejigged some of the monitors, and with a pensive smile at me, left the room.

Drawing in a large breath, I focused my attention on the person in the hospital bed. Oh God.

Tears pricked the back of my eyes. Frankie lay there looking pale and weak. Her eyes were closed and her face was banged up—angry red and brown welts were already starting to form on her forehead and one cheek. Her hands lay on her lap, and I surveyed the length of her body. Nothing else seemed to be amiss, at least from the outside.

I gripped her hand in mine, dragging my thumb over her wrist in what I hoped was a comforting motion. Whether it was for her or me, I wasn't sure. I felt her pulse thumping underneath and let out a sigh of relief.

"How the hell did this happen, Niles?" I wasn't able to disguise the anger in my voice.

"I'm not sure. From the reports I've gotten so far, the extra driving the car was going faster than he should have and it looks like he may have suffered a heart attack at the wheel."

"He's lucky she's not injured worse." Rational thought had no place in my brain at that moment. I didn't care that if that was the case, then technically it wasn't his fault.

"We're all lucky, Calder."

Hours later, I hadn't left Frankie's bedside. I was alone in the room now, and I sat up straight in an attempt to stretch out my back muscles. I massaged my neck as images of my car accident and Frankie's near-miss bombarded my mind. I squeezed my eyes shut. Old instincts of wanting to bury the pain and numb myself rose to the surface. I wanted to do some-thing—anything—to make them go away.

I bolted up from the chair and started pacing around the room, clenching and unclenching my fists. Shouldn't she be awake by now? Where the hell was her mom?

I couldn't stay pent up in this hospital room anymore, staring at Frankie looking so frail and weak, knowing there was nothing I could do.

I needed to go to a meeting. Or go surfing. Anything to get my mind off the self-destructive track it was currently barrel-ling down.

I gave Frankie one last look, feeling another stab of pain in my chest at my inability to do anything for her, and bolted from the room.

Rather than finding myself in the dingy basement of a church at a NA or AA meeting, or on top of my surfboard, I sat in my parked car half a block down from where I used to go to score coke when my usual dealer-to-the-stars was unavailable.

I'd been here for a while and watched as car after car pulled up to get their prescribed antidote for whatever ailed them from douchebag dealer after douchebag dealer.

I thrummed my fingers on the steering wheel, needing some way to expend the anxiety coiling inside of me that was desperately looking for release. I wished I still carried around my one-day sobriety chip. After that last close call, I should have learned my lesson. If I made it to the end of this day with-out giving in to my demons, I'd never make the mistake of not having it with me again.

One thing I was realizing about addiction was that the minute you thought you'd beaten it, that's when it stuck its insidious tentacles into you, dragging you back to ground zero. It wasn't unlike a movie where the villain lay dead on the ground, only to get one last breath with which to reach for the gun lying beside him, sending one last bullet flying at his target.

I was sweating, even though the air conditioning in the car was on full blast, and I ran through the exercise in my head of all the good things I had in my life . . . the short list of people who truly cared about me, all that I would lose if I gave in to my addiction, how I'd feel about myself once I'd sobered up. Both of my parents had seen reports of what had happened on set and texted me while I'd been sitting here. I let them know I was okay but that I couldn't talk now. I was sure the tabloids had thrown around some unsubstantiated stories as soon as they caught wind of Frankie being rushed to the hospital.

Mostly I thought about the two people who I couldn't bear to let down—one here on earth, the other in heaven. If there even was a heaven, though I had to believe there was for my own sanity, since that was where Akoni deserved to be.

The shrill ring of the phone in my hand startled me from my thoughts. I didn't even remember picking it up. I glanced at it, but the number wasn't familiar to me. Could be the press. Something in me—some feeling in my gut—told me it wasn't though, so I answered the call.

"Yeah?"

"Calder? It's Frankie's manager, Brock."

Fear sent an icy surge through my veins. "What's happened to Frankie?"

"She's fine. The same. Still unconscious. I haven't been able to get hold of her mother though. I've spoken with her dad. He's coming in on a flight tomorrow."

Something wasn't right. Without any concern for the fact that I'd pushed her away and that she likely wanted nothing to do with me, I spoke. "What do you need me to do?"

"I know you two have had a falling out recently . . ." He

cleared his throat. "I was wondering if maybe you had a different number to reach Gianna, other than her cell phone?"

"I don't even have that. But I'm going to go by the house. If she's not there and I can't find her, I'll let you know."

"Thanks. Sorry to bother you. I know how close they are and Frankie would want her mom by her side."

"You did the right thing." I ended the call and tossed my phone onto the passenger seat. Without so much as a glance at the notorious street corner, I drove by what I once thought gave me the strength to deal with all my shit and headed off in the direction of a different life. One where I took ownership of my feelings, one where I knew I had value . . . a life where I put the needs of the people I loved before my own.

chapter thirty-three

Calder

I was thankful that Frankie had given me the code for the gate after we'd had our what-the-hell-is-going-on-with-us conversation. It'd made my mission a hell of a lot easier.

When I pulled up to Frankie's place, the first thing I noticed was her mom's car parked in the driveway. Thank God. There was no plan B if she wasn't here.

I approached Gianna's end of the house with trepidation. Frankie had confided to me about her mother's issues, but I'd never actually seen any of them with my own eyes—only the evidence she left behind in the form of the sheer amount of crap in her house. I didn't know what I might be walking into.

I knocked on the door and waited. No answer. I knocked again, louder this time, and waited some more. God, I hoped she was just sleeping or something.

I tried the handle. Unlocked. Pushing the door open, I made my way inside. The hallway looked the same as it had the first time I'd been here, with neat piles of boxes and magazines stacked high on either side.

"Hello?" I called out. No response. I continued forward with careful steps, making sure not to bump one of the piles that could start a domino effect down the long hallway. With each step I took, I prayed a little that I wasn't going to find her corpse or something. I'd just walked away from temptation—I was sure I couldn't handle something like that.

Reaching the end of the hallway, I stepped out into the living area, my eyes widening at the sight in front of me. Sure there had been a lot of stuff in here before—the place had been packed solid—but everything had been piled neatly and reminded me of organized chaos. Now, magazines were strewn all over the place, the neat stacks replaced with haphazard mounds. They looked like they'd been thrown or tossed across the room. And they were . . . everywhere.

"Hello," I called out again.

I heard some rustling in the far corner behind a bunch of clear plastic containers that appeared to be full of magazines and books, so I carefully made my way in that direction.

When I reached my destination, I saw Gianna sitting on the floor frenetically flipping through a magazine, her back to me. "I know it's here somewhere. It has to be here somewhere," she muttered to herself.

I placed a hand on her shoulder gently, not wanting to scare her. "Gianna, are you okay?" She ignored me, tossing the magazine behind her and almost hitting me in the head with it. Then she picked up another one lying to her right and began the process over again. I squeezed her shoulder this time, trying to draw her attention. "Gianna. Did you hear me? Are you okay?"

She turned to the side, blinked a few times and gave her head a shake, seeming to come out of the trance-like state she'd been in. When her gaze met mine, her face crumpled and she began crying.

"What are you doing here? You shouldn't be here seeing all . . ." she motioned with her hand around her, "this."

"It's okay. I would never say anything."

She placed her hands over her face and shook her head. "It's so embarrassing."

I moved in front of her and hunched down so we were eye level, then pulled her hands away from her face. "There's nothing to be embarrassed about. We all have our demons. They manifest in different ways for each of us."

"I can't control it. I try to control it, but I can't." She began crying again, tears streaming down her face, her skin red and blotchy.

"You forget who you're talking to." I let out a chuckle with no humor in it.

"You couldn't possibly understand." The look on her face gutted me. I knew that look, understood what she was feeling so well. It was self-loathing at its worst, and I knew first-hand the downward spiral it could take you on if you gave it any room to fester.

"Look at me." She continued looking anywhere but me. "Look at me," I said with more authority, and she finally did as I said. "On paper, I'm the guy that should've had the world at my feet." I paused. "In reality, I was an overindulged rich-boy junkie with an overabundance of ego."

And then without provocation, I blurted the whole thing out to her. Every single reason why she wouldn't want her daughter dating someone like me—I handed it to her on a silver fucking platter. Every deplorable thing I'd ever done, every woman I'd slept with and treated like a piece of shit the next day, every time I'd put my addiction ahead of the people in my life. All about the night of the accident. She listened patiently and soon lost the anguished expression on her face. When I had finished, I couldn't believe what she said next.

"Oh Calder, those things that happened don't make you who you are." She placed her hand on my cheek and patted it in what felt like a motherly gesture. "How you choose to live your life every day when you get up in the morning, that's what makes you the person you are. You know better now, and so you do better. That's all any of us can do."

I knew now where Frankie got her compassion from. She'd told me the same thing. I sat for a moment, considering the truth of her words. They settled into my consciousness, permeated my soul, and became a part of me. I couldn't undo the past, but I could do better moving forward . . . and that was exactly what I was going to do.

"Thank you," I whispered.

Her forehead creased. "For what?"

"For helping me recognize the truth."

She patted my face again with a small smile on her lips and dropped her hand. "Where's Frankie?" she asked, beginning to thumb through a magazine in search of something again.

All my muscles tensed. She'd been so frantic when I came in here that I wasn't sure if the news that her daughter had been in an accident would be the thing to push her over the edge. I wrestled with what to do for a moment, finally deciding to deal with one problem at a time.

"She'll be meeting me here soon." I wasn't sure if she was going to buy it, but she eventually nodded and went back to looking through the magazine. "You know, it's been my experience that when I find myself regressing to some unhealthy practices, there's usually something that set me off." I motioned to the mess surrounding us.

She let out a big sigh and dropped the magazine into her lap. "My doctor is retiring. He told me earlier today at our session. I don't know what I'm going to do without him." Tears gathered in her eyes again.

Okay. This I could deal with. "That sucks. I know how I would feel if my sponsor wasn't available to help me anymore."

"He's been so good for me. He's really helped me get some of my tendencies under control."

I wondered how good the doctor could be given the sheer amount of crap in this place, but I kept that to myself. "You're the one that's been doing the hard work though. You're the one, day after day, that puts the effort in—not him, right?"

She shrugged. "I suppose."

"This is Los Angeles. It's the capital city for narcissists everywhere. I'm sure there are more than enough good doctors to go around." I reached out and squeezed her shoulder.

"I'm so afraid." Her bottom lip trembled. "What if a new doctor isn't able to help me and I get worse?"

"What if you get even better?" I countered. "Look, Frankie loves you. You know she'll do whatever she can to protect you.

If one doctor isn't able to help you, then she's going to get a different one. She'll keep searching until she finds one that you're comfortable with."

She bit her lip, seemed to ponder it for a moment and then nodded her head. "Yes, yes. You're right. There has to be someone that can help me."

I squeezed her shoulder again and then dropped my hand to my side. "See? It's going to work out okay. Now, what are you looking for in all these magazines?"

"It's stupid." She dropped her head and looked to the floor.

"What is it? Tell me so I can help."

She raised her head and with a hopeful expression, said, "Really?"

"Really."

"Frankie gave an interview in one of these magazines when she first started getting a lot of acting jobs. They'd asked her what she hoped for the future and I wanted to pull it out so I could show it to her. She seemed upset when I saw her last so I thought maybe this would help."

I cringed inside, knowing that had been my doing. What an idiot I was. All I could do now was set everything to rights.

This must've been one of those moments Frankie had talked about where her mom would get fixated on something and couldn't stop thinking about it. "Alright, do you remember what magazine it was in?" She shook her head. "Do you remember what year it was?"

"Probably six or seven years ago."

That was something at least. I glanced around at the piles and boxes of reading material that surrounded us. "I suppose we should get started then."

chapter thirty-four

Calder

Many hours later—on the longest day *ever*—Gianna sat in my passenger seat as I parked my car in the hospital lot. Darkness had already descended on the city. She'd been upset that I hadn't told her about Frankie right away, but after assuring her of everything the doctors had said and explaining my rationale, she seemed to have cooled off some. Gianna had been angry with herself for leaving her phone on vibrate in her purse near the front door. I managed to convince her she had nothing to feel bad about and I'd heaved a sigh of relief, afraid that she'd go down a dark path if I hadn't been successful in that endeavour.

We reached Frankie's hospital room and Gianna pushed the door open slowly. A nurse was inside checking some of the equipment and writing stuff down on a chart.

"How is she?" I asked in a low voice. The nurse gave us each the once-over. "This is her mom." I motioned to Gianna standing by my side.

She seemed appeased by that. "No change. She hasn't woken up yet, but everything so far looks okay. She'll wake up when she's ready."

The knot in my stomach tightened. Until the moment Frankie opened her eyes and I knew she'd be okay, I wasn't going to be able to relax.

"Is it okay if I stay with her tonight?" Gianna asked, her voice trembling.

"Of course. But let her rest. Don't try to wake her up," the nurse replied before leaving the room.

I grabbed a couple of the chairs that were set against the wall and placed one on each side of the hospital bed.

"You don't have to stay, Calder. I can call you when she wakes up." Her face was pale and she was obviously distressed. I was staying as much for her as myself.

I shot her a look that invited no argument. "I'm not going anywhere." I took my seat on Frankie's left and reached for her hand. Lying there hooked up to a bunch of medical equipment, she still looked so breakable. But her color was better than it'd been earlier in the day so that gave me some comfort.

Frankie's mom ran her hand over her daughter's cheek. "You sleep now, sweetie." Her voice broke and she wiped a tear from under her eye. "Get better and then come back to us when you're ready."

We sat there silent for a long while, each of us immersed in our own thoughts and memories of the silent woman lying in the bed. I set my head against the side of the mattress when I felt my eyelids getting heavy. Maybe a quick snooze would do me some good. It had been a long day—and it still wasn't over yet.

"Mom? Calder?"

The sound of Frankie's raspy voice stirred me from my sleep. I opened my eyes to see her looking down at me.

"Frankie, are you okay? How are you feeling? Should I get the doctor?" I sat straight up in my chair, ignoring the stab of pain in my neck from sleeping in such a jacked position.

Gianna stirred as well and sprung up from her chair when she realized that Frankie was awake. "Sweetie. Oh, thank God. Are you okay?"

Frankie gingerly touched her hand to her forehead where she had a nasty bruise. "My head is a little sore. I'm achy all over, but besides that I'm okay, I think. How long was I out for?"

I didn't know the answer, though sunshine now poured in through the partially closed slats in the window blinds, so it was at least morning.

Gianna glanced over at the clock. "Less than a day. I was so worried, even though the nurse said everything would be fine."

Frankie fixed her gaze on me and an uncomfortable feeling stole over my skin. My elation at seeing her awake was wearing off, and I was beginning to feel like an unwelcome guest, given the situation between us before the accident.

I pushed my chair back and stood. "I'll leave you two to talk. I'm going to let the doctor know that you're awake."

Frankie just nodded. "You don't have to go, Calder—" her mom started to say.

"It's fine, really. I'll come by in a little while." I pushed my hands into my pockets to prevent myself from reaching out and caressing Frankie's cheek, then left the room.

Whatever was to happen between the two of us aside, I was happy to see Frankie on the road to recovery. I suppose in a sense we both were now.

chapter thirty-five

Frankie

A soft knock sounded on my door.

"Come in," I said as loud as I was able. My throat was still dry and sore, regardless of the amount of water I'd consumed since I'd woken up.

Calder poked his head in and a small part of me was thrilled. I tried ignoring that idiotic girly part of my brain. After all, I should still be angry with him for pushing me away, though after my near-miss, I found I didn't care that much anymore. I only wanted to be with him, but I had no idea where his head was at or why he was here.

"Can I come in?"

"Sure," I said, motioning to the chair at my bedside.

He walked over and I admired how smooth his movements were—like I always did. He took a seat and we held each other's gazes for a moment, some unknown emotion passing between us.

"I hope you—"

"My mom told me—"

We both started at the same time. He ran a hand through his long locks and gave an awkward chuckle. "You first," he said.

"My mom told me what you did for her."

He shrugged. "It wasn't a big deal." That was such an

understatement. I realized it was further proof I'd needed that he *did* care about me and had only pushed me away because of his own fears.

I reached for his hand and he let me take it. "It is to me. Thank you for treating her with such compassion." Tears formed in the corners of my eyes.

"I know what it feels like to be broken, Frankie. I would never treat her any differently than the way I did. We might not be fighting the same war, but a battle is a battle."

I pressed my lips together and nodded in an effort not to cry. "You know, she really likes you."

"I like her, too. But I have a problem."

I narrowed my eyes. "What problem?"

"I'm in love with her daughter." I sucked in a sharp breath. "I screwed up, Frankie. I let my fear take hold and I didn't treat you the way you deserve to be treated. I don't know if you can ever forgive me, but I need you to know that I do love you."

A tear escaped, rolling down my cheek. Calder pulled his hand from my grip and wiped away the salty trail.

"I love you, too. So much. But if this is going to work between us, you have to believe you're someone deserving of love." More tears escaped. "I can't freely give you my love, only to have you push it away every time you're afraid."

He hung his head for a moment then looked back up at me, his blue eyes piercing. "I realized something about myself. For the majority of my life, I felt undeserving of the attention that I got. I was put on a pedestal because of who my parents were, not because of anything I did. I didn't feel worthy. I put up a good front, but inside I hated myself and I didn't care about what I was putting my body through, or the pain I was inflicting on the people around me."

A sob escaped me as I realized how much pain Calder must have been in to feel that way. He rubbed my cheek with his thumb.

"I know now that I *can* be someone worthy of adoration and praise. Or at least I can try to be. Every day. One day at a time. With you beside me."

His words brought a joy to my soul like I'd never known. He'd finally set himself free. Calder had finally granted himself the forgiveness only he was able to give.

"Oh, Calder. I want to be on that journey with you. Every day. One day at a time."

He leaned forward and crushed his lips to mine, taking me in a possessive kiss. I winced inside, but didn't dare mention the pain—I was craving physical contact with him. I wrapped one arm around him and drove the other one into that silky mass of hair that I loved so much. When he pulled away, he brushed my hair back from my house.

"There's one thing I still need to do. It's something I should've done a long time ago."

I placed a hand on his cheek. "Of course. What is it?"

He squeezed his eyes shut for a moment. "I need to go and see Akoni's mom."

My hand fluttered to my chest. I knew what a big deal that was for him. "That's good," I whispered. "When are you going to go?"

"Whenever you're out of this place and back at home. I need to know you're okay first."

I considered for a brief moment fighting him on it and telling him to go now in case he changed his mind, but I knew if the roles were reversed I'd be doing the same. "The doctor wants me to stay for a couple of days for observation." I rolled my eyes. I knew for a fact they were being overly cautious because the accident had occurred on set, and it was likely that the insurance company was insisting on it.

"I'm glad they're taking such good care of you," he said, taking my hand. "Where did your mom go?"

"She went to get something to eat in the cafeteria. Oh, and Niles called. He wants to come by at some point."

Calder nodded. "He called me before I came in here. Shooting has been postponed until you're ready to return to set."

"I'm sure everyone loves that."

"Everyone loves that you're going to be okay, baby. That's the only thing that matters." I smiled at him.

"There's one other thing . . ." His voice sounded unsure. I didn't know what to make of it.

"Okay . . ."

"Since you're gonna be stuck here for a couple more days, I thought it might do your mom some good to come stay with me in Malibu. I can sleep on the couch and we could drive in together to see you. I don't know." He shrugged, still looking uncertain. "I know she's having a hard time coming to terms with her doctor retiring and I thought it might be better for her if she wasn't alone. And who doesn't love the beach, right?"

He smiled the smile that had charmed many a woman before me. Instead of irritating me, the thought brought me happiness—because I knew that smile was reserved for me now. And because he was the most thoughtful person I knew.

"That would be wonderful. I'm sure she'd like that."

He stood from his chair. "Terrific. I'll let you fill her in then. I'm going to head to my condo and have a quick shower and change my clothes, but I'll be back before you know it." He leaned forward and placed a chaste kiss on my lips before turning to leave the room.

"Calder?" He turned to face me, one hand on the door. "I love you. Remember that."

He exhaled a long breath. "Now that you've given me those words, I will *never* forget them. I love you, too." Smiling, he left the room.

I didn't think I'd ever tire of hearing those words from his mouth.

chapter thirty-six

Calder

A few days later, Frankie had returned home, feeling as good as she ever had. She'd ended up catching her dad before he'd gotten on a plane and told him not to come. He'd fought her on it, but finally accepted that she was fine and stayed away. Frankie thought it was better that way so her mom wouldn't have to see him.

With that all squared away, I went over to Akoni's mom's house.

I sat in my car out front of the modest bungalow. It didn't look any different than the last time I'd been here. The white stucco could still use a paint job and the garage door still sat off kilter, but Kailani's pride in her homestead shone through in the well-manicured flower garden and the trimmed grass out front. Akoni's mother had raised his brothers and sisters on her own so they'd always had to live modestly. They were basically all grown now, but since I hadn't been around, I had no idea whether any of them were still living with her or not.

Akoni and I had met on the beach. I remembered how nervous he was the first time I'd come here because it wasn't like the huge mansion that I'd grown up in. None of that had ever mattered to me though.

My palms sweat around the steering wheel as I summoned

the courage to get out of the car. Unable to put it off any longer, I climbed out and made my way up the small pathway to the house. Before I could change my mind, I knocked on the door.

My stomach rolled in my gut. The scene was so familiar to me. I had done this so many times and it almost felt as if Akoni himself would answer the door.

A minute later, footsteps sounded behind the door and I knew the person on the other side was looking through the peephole to see who it was. I shifted my weight on my feet while I waited.

The door crept open, creaking at the hinges as it did, until Kailani's stunned expression came into view. Her hand was on her chest, her eyes wide. She wore her dark hair shorter than the last time I'd seen her, but with her petite frame and golden skin, she hadn't changed much.

"Calder," she said in disbelief.

"I'm sorry to just show up like this. I should have called."

"Calder." She stood there in obvious shock until finally her face crumpled and she darted forward, pulling me into a hug, crying into my chest.

I'd braced myself in case she was going to slap me. The fact that she was embracing me—*me* of all people—lifted some of the weight that'd been dragging down my heart. I squeezed her tightly on that front stoop as tears of my own escaped the confines they'd been held in for so long. Then I sobbed like a baby. We both did until there were no more tears to fall—only words that needed to be said.

She pulled away and wiped under her eyes. "I'm sorry. I just can't believe that you're here. Come in, come in."

She stepped inside and motioned for me to follow. The familiar smell of her home cooking greeted me while memories of the moments I'd spent here during better times assaulted my mind.

"I just made some food. Would you like some?"

I shook my head. "No, thank you. I'm okay. I wanted to talk. Is it okay if we sit in the living room?"

"Of course." She walked down the hall and entered the

heart of the home, taking a seat on the couch.

I glanced around. Nothing much had changed since the last time I'd been here. I gulped as my eyes roamed over an urn on one of the end tables with a picture of Akoni beside it.

"Come, sit next to me, please." Kailani patted the seat cushion beside her, and I did as she asked.

It was the strangest thing—in some ways it felt like no time had passed at all and everything was as it had always been. But then I remembered the gaping hole in both of our lives with Akoni gone and that fantasy dissolved quickly, leaving me without the right words to say.

"How have you been?" Kailani asked with genuine concern in her voice. How was that even possible?

I cleared my throat. "It's a struggle. I've been to rehab. I'm working on my recovery every day."

She nodded. "I'm glad," she said softly and patted my knee.

"I'm sorry it's been so long since I came by. I was too ashamed to face you." She opened her mouth to speak, but I held up a hand to cut her off. "Please, let me finish. I need to get this out. It's been eating at me for too long, and you deserve to know the truth."

She pursed her lips, not looking happy about it, but allowed me to continue.

"The night of the accident . . . Akoni wasn't supposed to be driving. I'd dragged him out to a club and convinced him to let loose a bit. Then when I'd had enough of that scene and wanted to go to a house party, I pretty much told him I was leaving with or without him. I wasn't in any condition to drive, and after putting up a fight, he finally grabbed the keys from me and said he'd take me." A painful lump formed in my throat and I took a moment to swallow around it. "The truth is, it's my fault that Akoni was driving that night. I'm the reason he got behind the wheel even though he'd been drinking."

I squeezed my eyes shut for a moment before I had the courage to turn and face Kailani. I'd expected disgust, condemnation, rage—there was none.

With sorrow in her eyes, she reached for my hand and held

it tight. "You are not to blame for my son driving that night. What happened was a terrible accident. I miss Akoni every day. That will never change. But he alone made the decision to get behind the wheel, as much as it saddens me to admit that."

I shook my head. "No. If it weren't for me—"

"Enough." She waved her free hand in front of her. "He could have let you go, or called a cab, or taken the keys by force. He didn't. We both lost someone we loved that day, but instead of being able to grieve our loss together, we've been suffering apart." Frankie had told me the same thing, and at the time I hadn't been ready to accept the truth of those words—I was now.

Kailani pulled me into an embrace that was so warm, I felt like a little boy seeking comfort from my mother. Grief rose to the surface and poured out of me. Once again I sobbed in her arms, Kailani joining me, and in that release a tiny piece of my soul knitted itself back together.

She pulled away and wiped under her eyes, while I used the sleeve of my shirt to dry my own.

"I don't understand," I said. "After the accident, I sent you some checks and you sent them back. I thought you hated me . . ."

"My dear boy, I didn't send those back because I hated you. I sent them back because I don't want your money. That's not your burden to bear."

"But I want to help," I insisted.

She patted my cheek. "I lost two sons that day. I understand now why you stayed away. I knew you were suffering. I also knew you'd come back when you were ready."

"I don't know what to say . . ." I dropped my head.

"You don't need to say anything. What happened was a terrible tragedy, but you shouldn't blame yourself. I'm happy you're straightening out your life. I knew you could. So did Akoni."

I looked up at her. There was so much confidence in her tone—hell, in the expression on her face. I knew then that I would not disappoint her. She'd never regret saying those words to me . . . never regret giving me the gift of forgiveness.

"I am. And I'll continue to. I promise."

"I know you will." She smiled at me like she used to, like she always had. It was still hard to wrap my brain around.

"If you won't accept my checks, I want you to promise me you'll let me know if you need anything."

She tilted her head and with sad eyes, said, "There is one thing you can help me with. I've been waiting for you to return so it could be done."

chapter thirty-seven

Frankie

It was a little before sunset and the burning globe low in the sky cast an orange glow on the sand. The ocean was calm with only gentle waves lapping at the shore. It was perfect for what we were doing here. Today was the day that Akoni was receiving his Hawaiian sea burial.

I held Calder's hand in mine, trying to offer him what support I could, knowing today would mark a beginning *and* an end for him.

A slight breeze wafted the smell of the flowers around my neck up to my nose. We all wore leis, as was tradition. I felt honored that my presence here was welcome, given that I hadn't known Akoni when he was alive. What we were doing here today felt sacred. Since he'd gone and seen Akoni's mother, Calder had spoken more openly of his friendship with Akoni, and I was beginning to feel like I knew him in a way.

I'd met Kailani the previous Sunday when Calder had attended his first Sunday feast there since his friend's death. He'd insisted I come, and I'd been welcomed with open arms like one of the family.

Kailani walked over to us carrying the urn that held her son's ashes. "I'd like you to do the honor of spreading Akoni's ashes into the sea."

Calder's hand twitched in mine. I knew he wasn't expecting

this. He looked up at the crowd of people waiting in the sand—brothers, sisters, aunts, and uncles of Akoni's were all present. Hendrix was there too.

"Are you sure?" Calder whispered.

She nodded. "Yes. You two spent so much time together in this ocean, it's only fitting. You swim out on your surfboard and I'll pass it to you from the outrigger."

Calder's eyes appeared glossy as he nodded his head up and down. Kailani reached forward and squeezed his free hand, then returned to take her seat in the outrigger. The older family members would all head into the water in the small boat, while the rest of the burial party would paddle out on our surfboards.

One of Akoni's uncles began strumming his ukulele softly and, one by one, different people recounted memories of Akoni. I knew Calder was saving his final words to his friend for the water.

When the time came, the outrigger was pushed into the water and Akoni's uncles paddled out, while Kailani sat in the middle holding the urn.

Calder and I, along with some others, silently picked up our surfboards off the sand and paddled until we came to a stop alongside the outrigger, which was gently bobbing on top of the small waves. We all sat up and straddled our boards.

Kailani nodded at Calder and he leaned over to take the urn from her. He looked into the setting sun for a long moment and sighed, his hand on the lid.

"I miss you, buddy. Every damn day. I'm sorry you're not here. I'm sorry I let you down and that I wasn't as good a friend to you as you were to me. I'm trying though. Every day I'm trying, as much for you as for me. I love you, buddy. Aloha."

Calder removed the lid and tilted the opening of the urn toward the water.

Ashes scattered in the light breeze, landing on top of the water before being dispersed by the constant push and pull of the ocean and then finally settling down into its depths. As soon as Calder placed the lid back on the urn, a large gust of wind came out of nowhere.

I liked to think it was Akoni's spirit saying his final *aloha* to his loved ones. It was time to move beyond the pain.

epilogue

A Year And A Half Later . . .

Frankie

I gripped Calder's hand in mine as we sat side-by-side, a united team looking up to the host of the Oscars on the stage in front of us. My fiancé drew in a deep breath and I squeezed his hand, knowing how nervous he was.

They'd already presented the Best Actress category, in which I'd been nominated, before the last commercial break. I hadn't won. The disappointment I'd felt the moment my name hadn't been announced had stung, but I somehow managed to keep the it-doesn't-matter-that-the-other-person-won smile on my face. Though I found the disappointment was fleeting.

How could I possibly not be content? I was engaged to the man I loved with my whole heart, my career had skyrocketed after the release of *Collateral Damage,* my mother's secret was still her own, though she was doing much better these days. There was absolutely nothing for me to be upset about.

I'd assured Calder I was okay during the commercial break. In some ways, he seemed more upset than I had been, which was a testament to his love for me.

Truthfully, of the two of us, I wished more than anything that he would win. It would be validation, not only to himself but to the world. Calder was still sober and there were bad days, but they were fewer and further between. He was once again a working actor and, to be perfectly honest, he deserved it. His performance in *Collateral Damage* had astounded critics and moviegoers alike.

I leaned sideways so I was able to whisper in his ear. "You okay?"

He squeezed my hand and turned to look directly at me. His sky blue eyes still had the power to take my breath away.

"I have you, and that's all that really matters to me. No matter what happens—I'm okay," he whispered. He leaned in to give me a chaste kiss on the lips and my mouth warmed at the contact. He pulled away, still holding my gaze. I realized that some of my lipstick had transferred onto his lips, so I used my thumb to wipe the remnants away, my fingers splayed on his cheek.

The bristles of hair there scratched my palm. Calder wore his hair much shorter now—he'd had to cut it for a movie role—but lately he'd taken to leaving a bit of scruff on his face. I wasn't opposed. The man was so beautiful.

The sound of the orchestra brought me from my daze and I turned my attention back to the stage in front of us, where last year's Best Actress winner had just taken her place in front of the microphone.

This was it.

I said a silent prayer and listened as she announced the nominees, my hand still firmly in Calder's grip.

"And the Oscar goes to . . ."

I drew in a lungful of air and held it.

She tore into the envelope and pulled the card out, scanning the contents before looking back up to the audience again.

" . . . Calder Fox for *Collateral Damage*."

Applause erupted throughout The Dolby Theater. I sprung up out of my seat, clapping and cheering with no regard for the delicate nature of my lilac silk chiffon dress. Calder remained sitting, appearing stunned and unable to process what was happening.

I bent down and grasped his hands in my own. "You won!

You won!" I cried.

That seemed to work—his head snapped up and a wide grin replaced the blank expression on his face. He stood and kissed me fiercely for the millions of viewers to see. When he was done, he embraced me before running up on stage. As he ascended the steps, he drove one hand into his pocket and I knew it was to finger his one-day sobriety chip. He carried it everywhere with him now, even though he was doing well.

Calder strode across the stage as handsome as ever in his dark navy tuxedo and set his hands on the golden statue that was his prize. I knew better though—the real prize was that this award was the proof that he was deserving of all the praise and acclaim he received. He'd already managed to find it within himself, but the recognition from his peers would only solidify all the work he'd done—and not just on the movie.

I turned around and searched several rows back to find his manager, Chelsea, and his PR people, Landon and Skye. Landon's grin couldn't have been bigger and Skye gave me an enthusiastic thumbs-up. Chelsea was pleased but, as always, more reserved in her reaction. She was smiling and gave me a little nod to show her approval.

I sat back down in my seat and my attention returned to the stage where Calder stood, looking out over the crowd, taking in the moment. He looked so proud, and as I thought of how far he'd come, tears sprang to my eyes.

Calder cleared his throat then crouched down a bit to speak into the mic. "Thank you . . . thank you. I don't even know where to begin. First, I want to thank the Academy. I can hardly believe I'm standing here holding this. I'm overwhelmed." He paused and ran a hand through his hair.

"I need to thank the studio and especially Niles for backing me as the lead on this project after the original actor wasn't able to do it. It would've been easy at the time to write me off as some overindulged Hollywood rich kid with a drug and alcohol problem who was never going to get his shit together. But he gave me a second chance. And it was one that changed my life.

"If I hadn't gotten to do the movie, I wouldn't have worked

alongside my fiancé, Francesca Leon. Her work ethic, her talent, her beauty . . . all of it had me in awe. What I didn't know back then was that I was going to fall in love with her—and not for any of the reasons I just listed. She is the most compassionate, tender, and loving individual I've ever met. Her choosing to give her love to me has been one of the greatest gifts I've ever received."

My heart swelled in my chest, and though there were tens of thousands of people in the auditorium and millions at home watching, there were only the two of us and our shared connection as he gazed down at me from the stage. I blew him a kiss and placed my hand over my heart.

He laughed a little sheepishly and wiped his mouth with the back of his hand. "I probably have some of her lipstick on me right now. She's definitely left her mark on me." The audience laughed and he waited for them to quiet down before continuing.

"In all seriousness, I want to talk directly to anyone out there who finds themselves lost and without hope. What I know is this—if I can come back from the brink of almost destroying myself, so can you. Forgiveness is a gift you have to give yourself and that validation comes from within. That's the most important lesson I've learned through all of this. You've got to forgive yourself in order to move forward. Everyone deserves a second chance to start anew. We think it's everyone else in our lives that harbor ill will toward us, and perhaps in some cases that's true. But often the self-hatred comes from within and we just need to let it go in order to see clearly. You're worth it. It does get better. So don't stop trying until you find your second chance."

The crowd roared and rose to their feet in a thundering applause. Calder gazed out over the crowd for another moment, then smiled and nodded before making his exit off the stage.

I beamed with pride at the man who had started out as an annoyance, turned out to be an anomaly, and ended up becoming my entire life.

a note to readers

I wrote this book on the heels of *Indiscretion,* which if you've read, you know was a highly emotional book for me to write. Some books come hard, some come easy. This one began on a rough road . . . and then I really figured out who Calder was and that's when the story took on a life of its own. It probably sounds strange since I control what happens in the story, but while writing this book I wanted to get to the end of the story so I could witness Calder heal and come out the other side, stronger and whole. Whether or not you struggle with addiction yourself, I think we can all relate to struggling with *something.* That feeling of the past nipping at our heels and trying to pull us back to a place we don't want to revisit. Sometimes forgiving ourselves is infinitely harder than forgiving others— but we have to try.

XOXO,
El

Keep reading for a sample of *Indiscretion*—my steamy erotic romance that's been labeled as hot, addictive, and emotional . . .

Yuanfen (Chinese):
(n.) a relationship by fate or destiny; the binding force between two people

chapter one

CHLOE

"If you don't find a man soon, you're going to die a born-again virgin."

I directed an exasperated sigh at my best friend Jackie. "Well, it's a good thing I'm feeling adventurous then. Maybe we should find someone for me to flirt with tonight."

I set my half-empty martini down on the expensive chrome-and-glass VIP table I'd been able to secure at On The Rocks, New York City's newest high-end celebrity hangout. Tonight we were here to celebrate Jackie's upcoming nuptials. Glancing around, I took in the carrera marble floors, black fabric-draped walls, and large circular banquettes running along the perimeter of the room. I was a long way from small-town Bar Harbor, Maine.

Jackie rubbed her hands together in obvious anticipation. "Ooooh, I like the sound of this. Let's pick one. Or should we wait for the rest of the girls to stop flirting with the bartender and get back here with the drinks?" I glanced over to the bar and sure enough the rest of the bridal party was there laughing it up with one of the workers. Before I could say anything, Jackie pointed across the room.

"What about that guy over there?"

I looked across the dim bar to the wine-colored, velvet banquettes, where an attractive man sat pondering the wine list. "You know I'm not into blonds. Two blonds together, can you imagine? How would we ever figure out what body parts go where?" I batted my eyes feigning innocence.

Jackie chuckled at my lame attempt at a joke, while I continued my inspection of our fellow patrons. Not much to choose from, which was disappointing. On the one night I'd decided to let loose a little, there wasn't anyone worth letting loose with. I certainly wasn't interested in the middle-aged man with the small paunch and a wedding ring, trolling for women at the bar. Or the work-obsessed Wall Street type with the suspenders over his dress shirt who didn't seem to be letting his friends get a word in edgewise. And the artsy guy was too outside the box. His bright red jeans, painted on his ass, looked like they'd been dragged behind a bus. But this was New York City—they probably cost a small fortune.

I scrunched my face up in distaste then turned in the other direction and locked gazes with a set of piercing blue eyes. The wall sconces and the lighted glass behind the bar offered the only illumination in the room, but it didn't matter. I could see from here—this guy was smokin.' And not like a 'let's cook some marshmallows over the fire' kind of smokin.' He was three-alarm blaze, call-in-the-water-bombers smokin.'

I swallowed, my lips parting while my eyes took in his wholly male presence. He was standing beside a table, and his tailored grey suit hugged his body—a body that sure as hell had spent a lot of time at the gym. His dark hair had a slight wave to it and brushed the top of his back collar.

I held his gaze for a long moment as the rest of the people milling about the room seemed to fade away. The reality that I was blatantly staring at the stranger floated into my consciousness, and I cleared my throat as I diverted my gaze. But not before seeing his sexy, lopsided grin, complete with dimple and a perfect set of pearly whites.

Heat rose up my neck, and I traced the condensation pattern of a cup no longer there.

"Wow. He's something else."

I turned my attention back to my friend and gave her a weak smile. "He sure is."

With a suspicious smile, Jackie said, "I haven't seen this side of you in a while. I have to say, I like it."

I rolled my eyes. "I'm not that bad, am I?"

"Well, not at my bachelorette party, you're not," she said, sliding a shot in front of me. "I still can't believe you got us in this place."

It hadn't been easy. The group of us were only in town for the weekend, but luckily one of my past clients had a connection with the owner, who'd agreed to let us use the table without the usual bottle service requirement. Five hundred a bottle was too rich for my blood—and my bank account. In exchange for the table, I'd committed the ultimate sin and agreed to sell his oceanfront home at a reduced commission when the time came. Tit for tat, that was always the way. But a maid of honor couldn't put a price on keeping her nearest and dearest friend happy, now could she?

"Bottoms up," Jackie said, picking her shot up off the table.

I fidgeted in my seat, pulling down the too-short hem of my dress. How I'd let Jackie talk me into wearing this thing I'd never know. "I think I've had enough for now," I said and looked over at my friend.

"Come on," Jackie whined and placed the shot back on the table. "You've finally let loose. It's my bachelorette party . . . please?"

"Don't bat those eyes at me."

Jackie continued to give me her best version of a puppy-dog face, which in her inebriated state more closely resembled a botched Botox job.

I laughed. "You were always the noceur not me."

She rolled her eyes. "Alright word nerd, none of that tonight. I plan to have *way* too many drinks in me to try and figure out what the hell you're saying."

I shook my head and gave her a cheeky grin, knowing I'd used the word purposely just to bait her. I'd had a thing for words as long as I could remember. I loved discovering rarely used words, but my absolute favorite was finding words in other languages that had no English equivalent.

Jackie didn't share my love for all things literary. But it *was* just like my free-spirited friend to want to crank the party up a notch. We'd met twenty-eight years earlier when we were babies and both our moms had sent us to the same babysitter. I couldn't remember a time in our lives when we hadn't been there for each other.

"Fine, pass it over." I reached for the shot, sure it would be my undoing. "But I can't be held responsible for my actions." I laughed. Jackie always did have a way of talking me into things.

I sprinkled some salt on my wrist, licked it off, and tossed back the tequila. Grimacing, I grabbed a lime off the table, put it in my mouth, and sucked. The tequila burned my throat all the way down to my stomach. It was awful stuff, but a welcome distraction from the feeling of loneliness that seemed to have taken permanent residence inside me.

The idea of Jackie settling down still seemed so strange to me. "How is it that after all the sleeping around you did, you ended up being the one to find Prince Charming?" I asked.

Jackie laughed. "I keep telling you, Chloe, all work and no play won't make you happy. And it definitely won't get you laid." Her face turned serious and she bumped my shoulder with her own. "Come on, what gives? You haven't seemed yourself the past few weeks. It's almost been radio silence unless I call you. I love that you're having fun tonight, but I can tell something's been on your mind. Is it because you haven't been out with anyone in a while?"

I looked across the room and saw the rest of the girls were now sidled up to some guy at the bar who looked to be buying them a round of drinks. "God, no," I muttered. "I haven't been out with anyone because there's no one worth going out with. We can't all be as lucky as you and have Prince Charming rescue us from the side of the road when we get a flat tire."

Jackie's eyes narrowed. "And you don't stand a chance of meeting Prince Charming unless he up and falls on your windshield while you're driving around town showing houses," Jackie countered. "I think you deliberately avoid situations where you might meet him."

"I don't need to meet Prince Charming . . . I'm perfectly fine with the way my life is now." The conviction in my voice almost made me believe it myself—almost. Attempting to lighten the mood,

I added, "Maybe I'll become a nun, be celibate, and live happily ever after."

Jackie flicked her long, black hair off her shoulder and pressed her lips together, her green eyes unblinking as she stared impatiently at me. "Sounds like a lot of fun," she said dryly. "Can I make a suggestion? Try having fun for the time being. Find some hot guy, have lots of hot sex, and don't worry about whether he checks all the boxes on your extensive list of items meant to weed out any man with a pulse. Seriously, what's the worst that could happen?"

I twisted my lips to the side and pretended to think about it. "Hmm . . . I fall madly in love with said hot guy, not be able to live without him, and turn into Glenn Close's character in Fatal Attraction?" I laughed.

"Okay, smartass. Ever the optimist," Jackie quipped, sarcasm evident in her voice. "We all have needs. And you haven't gotten laid in forever. Hellooo—it's called sexual frustration."

I could always trust Jackie to put it all out there without softening the edges. "I'm not sexually frustrated. They make stuff to take care of that sort of thing," I teased.

"It's not the same and you know it. A vibrator isn't going to kiss you like it can't get enough. You can't feel the heat of its skin against you or gaze into its eyes when it's on top of you, just before it—"

I raised my hand up to stop her from continuing. "Okay, I get your point."

I had that familiar pang in my chest, a lonely ache coupled with another ache brewing further down as I imagined what it would be like to be with a man again. Having that intimacy with someone would be nice, but some things just weren't worth taking the risk for. Life had thrown a lot at me, and I'd learned that being that dependent on another person for my happiness wasn't worth the pain left behind in their absence. My sister was all I had left now.

"I understand." Jackie looked at me sadly. "After what happened with Jeff, I get it. But that was forever ago. Maybe you could keep it casual? You're gorgeous. You've never had a shortage of male attention."

I sighed. I was no fool. I knew exactly what Jackie's end game was. She hoped that if I put myself out there, I'd magically stumble into Mr. Right like she had. *Never. Going. To. Happen.* I just wasn't that girl who had everything fall into place for her. My past was proof enough.

Jackie's hand came down on top of mine. "I want you to be happy. I worry about you. What are you going to do once your sister's moved halfway across the country? I'm concerned about where that's going to leave you. Ever since Jeff, you've kept every guy at arm's length. And that was years ago. You need a man in your life."

I gulped. Jackie's concern was genuine, and none of what she'd said was news to me. I'd had those same thoughts plenty of times, but I kept pushing them away, telling myself I'd deal with them later. Well, later was fast approaching.

Hearing it from Jackie's mouth brought home the realization that I couldn't continue to put off dealing with the inevitable—my sister was leaving for college. Dread formed in the pit of my stomach as I tried to picture how I'd fill my days once she was gone. The person who had been my primary focus for the past ten years would soon no longer be a part of my daily routine. I'd taken a chance on Jeff and after how that turned out, well, I'd thought it was better to focus on raising my sister and securing my own future. My love life could wait.

"If you'd walked in on your boyfriend banging his secretary on his desk, you wouldn't be keen on dating either," I deadpanned. "But that's not it . . . I've been stressed out with work. I'm not sure I'm going to meet my sales quota by the deadline. I need that bonus," I said, massaging my temple. Impending loneliness had been the least of my concerns over the past few weeks. Ever since my Broker's offer to buy into the firm, I'd been working like mad to make every sale I could at the new condo building.

"Sales aren't going well?" Jackie asked.

"Well enough." I shrugged. "Still, I'd feel better if I'd reached my goal already, or if I was only a handful of sales away. That's the only way I'm ever going to have enough money to buy into the brokerage."

Months ago, the broker in my office approached me with the deal of a lifetime. To semi-retire, he was going to need a partner to keep the brokerage afloat on a day-to-day basis. He'd offered me first dibs on the buy-in, saying he'd always admired my 'grit and deter-mination.' I was ecstatic, of course. I needed this. I had no college education to fall back on, and years ago I'd grown tired of chasing the next deal.

God, if I could make this happen, it would change my life. It would mean that even after losing my mother so young, I'd have the stability and security I'd always sought.

"You're a great agent," Jackie assured me with an encouraging smile. "I'm sure it'll all come together."

I returned the smile though I didn't really feel it. "Thanks, but you're my best friend. You have to say that." I let out a heavy sigh, wishing I shared my friend's confidence, and pushed the feeling down. Now was not the time to reflect on life. I was here to have a good time and celebrate Jackie's happiness—to hell with my own issues. Tonight was all about my best friend, and I'd be damned if my own problems were going to bring my friend down. Jackie loved a good time, and as maid of honor it was my job to make sure I de-livered.

"Enough talk about the heavy stuff. Let's get back to finding a guy for me to flirt with tonight."

"I thought we'd already found one." She nodded mischievously toward the insanely hot guy with the blue eyes.

"Yeah, right," I scoffed. "A little out of my league, I think."

"Oh, please," Jackie frowned. "For all we know, he could be covered in back hair and have a small dick."

I burst out laughing and gave my friend a light smack across the arm. It took me a minute to catch my breath. "You're horrible." I grinned at her. "Do you know how long it's been since I flirted with someone? Maybe I should start with more of an average Joe."

I was in the mood for some innocent fun tonight. Being away from home and all the memories and responsibilities it held seemed to have had that affect. Even so, I had a feeling any conversation with the blue-eyed stranger had the potential to turn into something not entirely innocent.

"Alright then." Jackie leaned in to give me a hug as the rest of the bridal party returned from the bar and placed down a variety of drinks and shots. In the spirit of the evening, I picked up a shot of

God-knows-what neon concoction and held it in the air. The other girls followed suit.

Smiling at my friend, I shoved down the lump of nostalgia. "I'd like to propose a toast to Jackie and her upcoming nuptials. May she and Rob have a long and happy life together, full of nothing but love, trust, joy . . . and because it's Jackie, a whole lot of mind-blowing sex."

All the girls cheered and clinked the assortment of drinks and shots before tossing them back. Jackie beamed. Whether a result of alcohol, love, or the fact that I was looking to have a little fun, I couldn't be sure. I hoped it wasn't the latter or my friend would end up disappointed. Despite what I'd said, I had no intention of pursuing anything beyond a mild flirtation with anyone—blue-eyed stranger included.

Ninety minutes, one drink, and two shots later, I stood in front of the gilded bathroom mirror, mulling over my earlier conversation with Jackie.

It was hard to admit she was right, but I knew it wasn't normal for a twenty-eight-year-old single female to put as much effort into avoiding a relationship as most others put into finding one. Even so, I wasn't interested in opening up my heart to be hurt again. My father, my mother, and my ex—all gone. My sister would be added to that list soon. All for different reasons, but gone just the same.

I had no illusions of a happily-ever-after for myself, but there was no denying that a little sexual satisfaction would be a welcome addition to my life. I'd never considered casual sex before, but I hadn't thought I'd be alone at this age either.

I smoothed the material down on the front of my dress. *Focus, Chloe*. No more thoughts about sex.

But my mind kept wandering.

Maybe if the sex came with no strings attached . . . and with someone who looked like that guy I'd noticed earlier in the bar. Spending a night between the sheets with a guy like that certainly wouldn't be a hardship.

Shit, I'd lasted all of five seconds not thinking about sex. I had the mind of a thirteen-year-old boy tonight. Had to be the booze talking—I sounded nothing like myself.

Whatever. It wasn't like I had to make a decision on the spot. For tonight, I'd have fun at my bestie's bachelorette party and see how I felt in the morning—after the effects of the alcohol wore off.

My arms were heavy as I fished a small comb out of my purse and ran it through my long blonde strands. Some hairspray would be good, but there was no sign of the usual assortment of beauty products on the expansive granite counter. Too bad, especially since there hadn't been enough room to fit any in the microscopic cocktail bag I was carrying.

I returned the comb to my purse and straightened the pale yellow dress Jackie had talked me into wearing. Apparently hems that reached only mid-thigh were for streetwalkers and the trendy alike. As satisfied as I was going to get, I headed toward the bathroom door to re-join the girls. My legs felt leaden, like I'd spent hours in a hot tub, as my stilettos clicked on the marble floor.

With my hand on the door, I glanced back to make sure I hadn't left anything on the counter when I noticed . . . urinals?

What. The. Hell.

Shit. *Say it isn't so.* No, no. I did not go into the men's room. No freaking way. But with one more panicked glance, I realized I most definitely *did. Definitely blaming this one on the booze.* Either that or the artsy signage outside the door that left anyone guessing as to whether the figure resembled a man or a woman.

Turning quickly to make my escape, I whirled around and took a step forward, only to run straight into the opening bathroom door. Pain exploded in my nose and tears immediately pricked my eyes. Someone was entering the bathroom and pushing in the door.

Stunned, I took a step backward and shook my head. Warm hands settled on my upper arms and steadied me. I looked up and was speechless. The hands belonged to the man with the memorable blue eyes I'd spotted earlier. *Of course, why go for slight mortification when you could really out-do yourself?*

Sex on legs—that was my only coherent thought at that moment. And I was pretty sure from the grin on his face and the seduction in his eyes that I'd made his hit list.

chapter two

CHLOE

"I'm so sorry, are you okay?" Sex on legs said.

I didn't respond. Just stood there, taking in the fine specimen of a man—gaping at him with a dropped jaw. I'm surprised there wasn't drool making its way down my chin. Dark stubble covering chiseled features led down to an even more defined body. The black shirt under his suit jacket stretched across his muscular frame. It was open at the collar, highlighting his golden skin. I wondered if the expanse of his muscled chest had that same golden glow. The suit looked expensive, certainly custom-made. There was no way he'd pulled it off a sales rack at J.C. Penney. It fit too well. He smelled of expensive cologne mixed with expensive cognac.

I blinked a few times and came back to myself. God, how long had I been standing here, gaping at him like an idiot?

"I'm fine." It was mostly true. My nose was tender but it wasn't anything I couldn't handle. I moved to get free of his grip. It wasn't that I didn't like the feel of his large hands. I liked it *too* much. What I really wanted to do was close my eyes and memorize the sensation of his hands on my bare skin.

"I've had women fall all over me before, but this is taking it to a new level," he said with a hint of amusement.

I gave a small smirk, hoping I indicated that I didn't find his remark humorous.

He took me in slowly from head to toe. "I'm pretty sure I'm in the right place . . . but there's certainly nothing masculine about you."

I felt his gaze travel up my body. My skin heated under his close examination of what I was now certain was a dress with too little material. My face burned red hot, and I pulled at the hem of my skirt. "My mistake—obviously."

A slow grin spread across his face, showcasing a killer smile. "Well, it looks like your mistake is my good fortune. I was hoping to connect with you at some point this evening. You've saved me the discomfort of approaching a table full of women."

"You were? I mean, you saw me out there?" I motioned with my hand to the main room.

"You're a difficult woman not to notice."

"Oh." If bumping into the door with my face hadn't been sobering, this statement certainly was. My eyes widened in surprise. I wouldn't have thought a man like him would look twice at me.

He laughed, probably because I was still stupidly standing inside the men's restroom having a conversation with him. *Smooth, Chloe.*

"Give me a minute and we'll continue this conversation. Wait for me in the hall."

It didn't sound like a request. This man was used to giving orders that were obeyed. Embarrassment told me to flee far and fast, but an impulsive desire to run my hands over his body won out. There was something about him, beyond the insanely hot exterior. Like a spark seeking shelter in the rain, I felt drawn to him. I had no doubt that underneath him, that spark would ignite into a blazing inferno given the chance.

"Okay." My response tumbled out weakly. I hated myself for agreeing so easily, as he'd obviously expected me to. I probably came off like a lovesick puppy starved for attention, happy to get whatever meager scraps I could. The fact was though, I did want to talk to him. Maybe flirt a little. Perhaps steal a kiss or two. Was there really any harm in that? I was a grown woman, single, and yes, maybe a little sexually frustrated. If I wanted to talk to an attractive man, what was there to stop me? For the first time in ten years, I didn't have to consider what example I was setting for my little sister.

I stepped into the darkened hallway. Unable to stand still, I began pacing. A tall, dark-skinned man headed down the hall and went into the men's room. I leaned against the wall and took a deep breath just as Sex on legs exited. I really needed to find out his name before I accidentally verbalized my little nickname to him.

As if reading my mind, he gave me a smile full of charm and character and held out his hand to me. "I'm Max. And you are . . ." His brow lifted.

My nipples pebbled at the sound of his deep, smooth voice. I took his hand and cleared my throat. "Chloe."

His hand was large and warm. He held on to mine a little longer than necessary, brought it up to his mouth, and placed a soft kiss on my knuckles. A tingling sensation ran up my arm from our point of contact. I looked up into his eyes when he released my hand and gulped. The butterflies in my stomach were working overtime. I'd never really understood what those romance novels I read meant when they said a person could get lost in someone's eyes. But at this moment it all made perfect sense. It was like we were having a conversation without speaking.

"It's a pleasure to meet you, Chloe. Would you be comfortable heading down to one of the VIP rooms to talk? It'd be quieter. Private."

Private. Oh, God. Should I?

He seemed harmless enough, but I was more concerned with myself at the moment. So what if I wanted to claw his clothes right off of him? I wasn't an animal. Surely, I could control myself.

"Um, sure." I shrugged feigning nonchalance. "Just let me go and tell my friends where I am. It's your turn to wait in the hall. I'll be right back."

He laughed, and I pushed off the wall. It took me a moment to fully get my balance. I headed toward the bar area. My limbs felt wooden and my movements stilted under his watchful eye.

When I reached the main room, my pace quickened until I stopped short of the table and motioned Jackie over. She got up, which took some doing. I grabbed her arm to steady her wobbly stance and turned my head to the side when I got a whiff of her vodka-infused breath.

"What's up?" she asked and cocked her head to the side, narrowing her eyes. "Where have you been?"

I pressed a hand to my racing heart. "You're never going to believe who I just met. That guy we were talking about earlier, the one across the room."

Jackie's eyes widened. "That hot piece of eye candy in the suit?"

"Yeah. He's asked me to go with him to one of the private rooms in the back so we can talk, but . . . I don't know."

She craned her neck back, looking at me like I was crazy. "Oh, come on. Are you serious? The hottest guy in this place wants to chat you up and you're thinking of turning him down?"

"What if that's not all he wants to do?" I asked with a meaningful look.

"Let's hope it's not. Did you see that guy?" She wagged her eyebrows up and down. I couldn't help the small smile that escaped my lips.

"I don't know anything about him. He could be a serial killer for all I know."

Jackie had a give-me-a-break look plastered on her face.

"We're here for your bachelorette party," I pointed out. "Not for me to pick up some random guy. It's your day."

Not having it, Jackie grabbed both of my shoulders and gave me a small shake. "Have you been tuning me out all night? Nothing would make me happier than seeing you pick up that beautiful piece of man candy tonight. Think of it as an early wedding gift to yours truly." She winked.

I laughed. "You don't mind?"

"Go!" She shooed me away. "Seriously. Have fun for once. You're allowed. Your sister will be leaving for school soon to start her own life, and besides—she isn't here anyway. You don't have to spend every waking moment taking care of everyone else. You didn't have a choice before, but you do now. Have fun. No one here is going to judge you." Her face was serious and her words heartfelt.

Suddenly, I found myself wanting that freedom that Jackie had been trying to shove on me all night. I felt almost . . . giddy. I hugged my best friend, and Jackie said in my ear, "Keep your phone on you. Don't you dare leave this place with him, and if you're not back in an hour, I'm coming after your ass."

I laughed at her comment and nodded before heading back to where I'd left Max. His gaze never wavered as I made my way closer to him.

"Everything okay?" he asked.

"I reassured my friends that you didn't seem like the serial killer type, but if I'm not back in an hour they'll send out the search party."

"Let's not waste any time then. I have a feeling an hour won't nearly be long enough."

Need shot through me fast and fierce, concentrating in my core, and images of the two of us in all sorts of sexual positions came to mind. I wasn't even sure they were all anatomically possible. It was all I could do not to fan myself.

He led me down the darkened hallway away from the main room, his hand on my lower back. It was an intimate gesture, and I revelled in the feeling.

With giddy anticipation that I hadn't experienced in a lifetime, it occurred to me that I'd never done anything like this before—go off to a private room with a complete stranger. That sounded more like Jackie than the responsible and driven woman I'd had to be these past ten years. But I *was* in the mood for some fun, flirting, and maybe a make-out session.

What's the worst that could happen?

acknowledgements

I need to begin by thanking Regina Wamba from Mae I Design for another amazing cover! And it wouldn't be what it is without the perfect photo that photographer Sara Eirew captured during the custom photo shoot.

Angela Smith, Developmental Editor—another one under our belt! I can hardly believe it. You are the consummate cheerleader and I'm proud to call you a friend. It's a comforting feeling knowing that you're in my corner.

Sheri Thomas, Line Editor—my hard to please, meticulous friend. ;) It was a pleasure working with you again and there is no question that you make my work better. You take that rough diamond and make it shine! Thank you for committing so much time and effort into my manuscript and treating it as if it were your own.

To the ladies at Perfectly Publishable—you always take my last-minute requests in stride and go above and beyond what I expect in a formatter. Thank you for your professional approach as it makes for one less thing for me to worry about!

Thanks to all my early readers: my sister-wife Roxie Madar, Becca Liberty (who laid claim to Calder a LONG time ago) and Shawna Donner-Gavas (my reading buddy since we were teens). A special thanks to my later readers (who I won't name specifically in order to protect their privacy) for your valuable input on the addiction aspect of the story. I appreciate the time you all took to read the manuscript and pass along your thoughts to me.

The rap that Frankie does in the beach house originally

appeared exclusively on Shh Mom's Reading Book Blog. I want to thank both Neveah Lee and Michelle Lynn, as well as the blog, for allowing it to appear here. If you want to get to know rapper Trace better (which I highly recommend), you can find his story in Michelle & Nevaeh's book *Collaboration*.

I've managed to surround myself with a bunch of women in the industry, whether bloggers or other authors, who choose to lift each other up, rather than try to tear one another down. Let me tell you—it is a wonderful thing to behold. Celebrating their successes has been just as exciting as celebrating my own. I'm truly blessed to have stumbled upon such a wonderful group of strong, creative, business-minded women who freely share of themselves, their time, and their enthusiasm. #IndieChicksRock #FYW

I have a few mottos that I try to live by in regards to my writing . . . work hard, stay humble . . . comparison is the thief of joy . . . gratitude makes what you have enough. When I published my first book, my goal was to earn back the money it cost me to produce the book in a year. What happened with that book far exceeded any goal I had set for myself. No, I can't lay claim to being a USA Today or New York Times Best Seller. It doesn't matter to me. The gift that all the readers have given me is its own reward. To see the eagerness and enthusiasm you have for my work is what keeps me going late at night.

I dedicated this book to the readers because, more than a year later, I'm amazed that you've still stuck with me. Not only that, you recruited some friends to join you! LOL As I write this, I am solely an indie author. I do my best to get my books out there without being all, "Look at me, look at me!" and that would be IMPOSSIBLE to do without the help of all you amazing readers. Leaving reviews, telling your friends about my books, tagging me in posts when blogs ask who your favorite authors are . . . every little bit helps and I am truly grateful and humbled by all that you do to help get my name out there. I wish I could do more or say more to you so you really understood how it feels, but my sincerest thank you will have to suffice.

To all the blogs—some of which have been there from the first book—you all work so tirelessly, and all for the love of the written word. I've been a reader my whole life, and before I ever wrote something that I wanted to share with the world, I read your blog posts and found myself a home with other people that felt like I did about books. You all work so hard and get too little recognition. As an author and a reader, thank you.

As always, I'd be remiss if I didn't thank my husband for putting up with me while I pieced this novel together. This man has always supported my dreams and always believes I'm capable of far more than I could ever hope to dream of. Love you, babe.

stay informed

I'd live for you to join myself and other readers in the Gabbing With Grace Group on Facebook, where I give advance sneak peeks, do ARC giveaways, and generally just have some fun! *http://bit.ly/WN9BNz*

You can also sign up for my newsletter to get the inside scoop and access to exclusive giveaways: *http://on.fb.me/1ak-9g5J* I'M RELEASING A FREE BOOK THROUGH MY NEWSLETTER IN 2015—AVAILABLE TO SUBSCRIBERS ONLY!

Want to know when my next book comes out?
***** If you're U.S. based and you want to receive a text message as soon as my next book goes live **text ROMANCE to 313131** *****

about the author

One of the best ways to support an author is by leaving a review! If you enjoyed this story, I'd appreciate it if you'd consider leaving an honest review, whether short or long, on the retailer's site where you purchased the book. Reviews on retailers' sites really are one of the best ways to help indie authors find their readership. Alternatively, if you prefer to leave your reviews on Goodreads, you can visit here: *http://bit.ly/1gLAiUT*

Elisabeth has a soft spot for happily-ever-afters and a hot spot for alpha males. If she's not curled up somewhere with a romance novel in one hand and chocolate in the other, you can probably find her typing madly on her keyboard, creating her next story. She currently lives outside Toronto, Canada with her husband, two small children, and a killer cat.

Questions? Comments?
I love to hear from readers! Feel free to connect with me via e-mail at *authorelisabethgrace@gmail.com* at any one of the social media platforms listed below. I love talking books— even if they aren't my own! Please drop me a line!

Website: *http://elisabeth-grace.com/*
Facebook
Twitter

other books by elisabeth grace . . .

The Limelight Series—New Adult Romance
Rumor Has It (Limelight #1)
Picture Perfect (Limelight #2)
Collateral Damage (Limelight #3)

Erotic Romance
Indiscretion: Vol 1–4
Indecision—Coming May 2015

Standalone Novels
Moment Of Impact—Release Date TBD

www.ingramcontent.com/pod-product-compliance
Lightning Source LLC
Chambersburg PA
CBHW021952170626
46808CB00001B/128